Edel Coffey is an Irish journalist and broadcaster. She has worked as a presenter and reporter with RTÉ Radio, editor of the *Irish Independent* Weekend Magazine, books editor of the *Irish Independent* and books editor of *The Gloss Magazine.* She is a regular contributor to *The Irish Times* and RTÉ Radio One. Her debut novel, *Breaking Point*, was a No.1 Irish bestseller, was shortlisted for Best Debut and won Best Crime Novel of the Year at the An Post Irish Book Awards. Her second novel, *In Her Place*, was also a No.1 Irish bestseller and was shortlisted for the RTÉ Radio 1 Listeners' Choice Award. *In Glass Houses* is her third novel. Coffey lives in Galway with her husband and children.

Also by Edel Coffey

Breaking Point
In Her Place

IN GLASS HOUSES

EDEL COFFEY

SPHERE

SPHERE

First published in Great Britain in 2026 by Sphere

1 3 5 7 9 10 8 6 4 2

Copyright © Edel Coffey 2026

The moral right of the author has been asserted.

*All characters and events in this publication, other than those
clearly in the public domain, are fictitious and any resemblance
to real persons, living or dead, is purely coincidental.*

A CIP catalogue record for this book
is available from the British Library.

Hardback ISBN 978-1-4087-2248-0
Trade paperback ISBN 978-14087-2249-7

Typeset in Sabon by M Rules
Printed and bound in Great Britain by
Clays Ltd, Elcograf S.p.A.

Papers used by Sphere are from well-managed forests
and other responsible sources.

Sphere
An imprint of
Little, Brown Book Group
Carmelite House
50 Victoria Embankment
London EC4Y 0DZ

The authorised representative
in the EEA is
Hachette Ireland
8 Castlecourt Centre
Dublin 15, D15 XTP3, Ireland
(email: info@hbgi.ie)

An Hachette UK Company
www.hachette.co.uk

www.littlebrown.co.uk

For Henry, Arthur, Edith and Frieda ...
and for David, always.

Prologue

THE CITY

Nothing attracts a crowd like a crowd

New Yorkers don't look up. We see more in one day than most people will see in a lifetime. If you want to make us look, you have to do something special. Today, however, we stopped and stared like tourists.

The sky pool was pretty special, even when there wasn't a body floating in it. Eleven metres of shimmering perspex slung across the sky between the building's East and West towers. Some days the people floating in the pool looked like exotic fish in a giant aquarium. On other days, they looked eerily like corpses, floating motionless mid-air. Even more so today, if you considered the long blonde hair rippling like seaweed and the cloudburst of red turning the water a rusty-reddish brown.

The crowd was growing now, heads craned back, eyes squinted and shielded with hands. Is it an art installation, someone asked. Whatever it was, one of us decided it was time to let the authorities adjudicate, because from all the way down here, it looked like nothing more than a dead body.

PART ONE

1

EDDIE

*A washed-up journalist catches
the scent of an old story*

The minute I opened the envelope, I knew something was about to happen. Call it journalistic intuition, call it foresight, but the very nanosecond I opened that invitation and saw the Bryant Fox Developments logo, I knew we were going back to the Juliet murder. And God forgive me if I didn't feel a thrill of excitement pulsing through me at the thoughts of it.

You are cordially invited to celebrate the grand
opening of the Sky Building and Sky Pool

53 West 53rd Street, NY10019

Where living feels like flying

My editor – Trudeau, I called him – walked in. I decided to give him a couple of minutes to settle into his office before accosting him. I called him Trudeau because he looked like that perfectly dressed, plasticly handsome Canadian politician. Gussied up in a navy suit every day, not a hint of facial hair, as if he had been shaved by a Turkish barber in the elevator on the way up, a haircut so neat it suggested ... well, psychopathy. He was young and slick and of the city – too young if you asked me; what thirty-eight-year-old knew how to run a newspaper?

I RSVPed to the email invitation for the Sky Building party and asked the press officer to send back a guest list, the basic tool of the social diarist's arsenal. I watched Trudeau deliberately unpack his phone, his pen, his laptop, from his slim briefcase, and place them at right angles to each other on his desk. He never forgot he was in a glass office, under scrutiny, never lost concentration and distractedly picked his nose. There was a time when workers had doors or dividers, some semblance of privacy, but now it felt like anything behind a closed door was untrustworthy, hiding something. We had to be on display at all times, from our social media accounts to our workplaces to the glass houses we increasingly chose to live in. My email pinged. My stomach flipped even before the information had travelled along my optic nerve to my brain. The names on the guest list were names that

I recognised. Names from long ago, from old police reports and investigations, interviews and late-night articles. We were going back. Everything was lining up. I took two sharp, deep breaths then walked across the newsroom.

Trudeau sat in his office like a sleek puma, beautiful but useless behind his desk, waiting for someone to bring him a piece of meat. Well, here it is, I thought, with a glorious offering hanging from my jaws, literally *begging* to be eaten.

I stepped into his office and was hit with the over-powering scent of his cologne, suffusing the room like a noxious gas. I could taste his cleanliness in my mouth. I coughed.

'Uh, got a minute?'

He looked up, wrinkled his nose as if I was the one who stank and then waved me in. Trudeau was the kind of guy who was confused by women he was not sexually attracted to, discombobulated by messy fe-males like me, who wore their hair natural, wiry and black with the kind of grey usually seen around the eyes of sad old dogs. What were women like us even for? He never knew how to relax in my presence.

'I have a social invite here from the property devel-oper Bryant Fox which might be of interest for the supplements. He's got that new development, beside MoMA on West 53rd? They're having a grand opening a couple of weeks from now ... May I?' I gestured at the chair on the other side of his desk and he hesitated, clearly preferring that the worn seat of my jeans would not come into contact with the pristine cream leather of his Eames chair (such an obvious choice), but he eventually nodded for me to sit down. 'You remember his daughter was murdered, twenty years ago this summer? Juliet Fox? I thought perhaps we might do an anniversary piece ... Fox has already described the building as his monument to his daughter and a lot of the people from that era will be at this party ...'

Trudeau swivelled his eyes around before saying, 'I remember. My eldest brother was in college with Juliet at the time. My parents were actually friends of theirs. Juliet was a brilliant tennis player, a real beauty too ... all of us little kids were in love with her ...' he drifted off.

Jesus Christ, this guy.

I tried not to let my thoughts bother my facial expression, and kept a firm grip on my eyes' desire to roll dramatically. 'Right,' I said. 'Well, I covered the story at the time, still have all my contacts, and notes. It might be worth revisiting in the light of the new building. Fox might talk to us for a human interest piece; we could talk to Juliet's friends from the time, where they are now, how the murder changed their lives ...'

'Mmm,' Trudeau sat back in his chair. He looked surprised. 'I like it, Eddie,' he said. 'Go ahead with it. We'll run a piece in the weekend magazine, the week of her anniversary, but keep me in the loop OK? This is a sensitive story. I'd hate to upset the family.'

Of course you would. Wouldn't want things to get awkward at the tennis club.

I suppressed an urge to smile but Trudeau seemed to sense my satisfaction as he said, 'But I still want your regular duties covered. I want those social pages to sing!'

Even his smug power trip couldn't dampen my genuine delight to be working on something of substance for the first time in years.

'You got it, boss,' I said through a grin. He looked perturbed by my unusually good mood and deferential reference to his position. I felt alive again. I returned to my desk with a spring in my step, or what might be called a spring if my sciatica wasn't bugging me so much. I took a celebratory bite out of my cold bagel and a blob of cream cheese flopped onto my jeans. I smeared it away carelessly, as I pored over the guest list again. I could feel it. We were going back. Back to the Juliet murder, back to the story that stole my career and ruined my life.

2

CLEO

A defence lawyer is haunted by a past mistake

You really could see everything from up here. Beyond the bucolic green haven of Central Park, the Empire State Building glittered downtown in the morning sunshine. It was still impressive, despite all the young pretenders that had sprung up on these streets.

The Sky Building, my new home, was one such young pretender. I grabbed my briefcase and left the mezzanine. As I walked down the angled mirrored staircase, done in the style of Coco Chanel's Paris atelier, I looked back at my many reflections, all slightly different. In the kitchen I waited for my coffee to brew. It was another beautiful morning. My phone buzzed. I flipped it over on the marble-topped island. My assistant, sending my updated closing arguments for today's case. They were unnecessary, of course. I turned the phone back to face-down position. I had been defending the wealthy for so long now I had a sixth sense for whether we had won. And I always won. If you're accused of murder any-where between midtown and Harlem, I'm your woman. Innocent or not, I'll get you off. Of course, I preferred it if you were innocent, but my job wasn't to figure that out. My job was to defend you so that you appeared in-nocent, or at least not guilty, which weren't always the same thing, especially in New York. It turned out that I had a natural talent for sowing doubt in minds, for finding holes in arguments, and raising unanswerable questions in cases. I could squeeze a whole murder case through a legal loophole the size of the eye of a needle. Something gifted to me by a childhood spent watching wealthy people using their money and influence to get exactly what they wanted. I suppose you could say it was a privileged upbringing.

The wealthy didn't like it when the law held them to account. I knew that first-hand. It scared them, made them feel ordinary, helpless. I'd gotten used to that small, brittle feeling that enters a room when the wealthy first realise they can't buy their way out of a situation. And when you have them so vulnerable and desperate, they will pay any price for you to get them out of that room. I learned that long before I became a defence lawyer. And it's how I made my living now. Naturally, I made a killing.

By the time I set up my own firm, I had made a name for myself as a kind of legal wunderkind. To be fair, I had pulled off some unlikely coups – an NBA player charged with murder, a bigamist accused of killing wife number one, a drug addict rock star accused of attempted murder, all exonerated as a result of me being extremely diligent with the details. Everything was in the details. I was meticulous and it paid off. My price increased alongside my reputation until I was the most expensive defence lawyer above Washington Square. And that was because of my 100 per cent hit rate. Well, almost 100 per cent. More accurate to say 99.9 per cent hit rate, if you counted that one error ...

Don't.

I pull my thoughts back.

Stop.

I drum my finely manicured fingertips on the marble, trying to ground myself. I look at the shiny, pointed almond tips. A beige colour, perfectly appropriate for every shade of murder. I try to recall the useless phrases my therapist told me to repeat when I found myself travelling down old re-traumatising pathways.

You are here now.

You are safe.

I repeat them and, even if I don't believe them, they at least divert my attention and temporarily short-circuit the spiral.

I do what I can to assuage my conscience. I help the

underprivileged, *pro bono*, in my free time, even though I don't have any free time. I've set up a department in my firm that specifically helps defend minorities and disadvantaged communities. So why does it make no difference? Why do I feel like a billionaire planting trees to offset my carbon footprint while I jet around the world? The truth is I could free a hundred innocent men, defend them all until the day I die, and it still wouldn't erase the spot made by that single error of judgment. I tell myself it wasn't my fault. There was nothing else I could have done.

Sometimes the only person you can save is yourself.

That's another one of my therapist's dumb lines. He's got lots of them, an endless supply it seems.

Innocent people get convicted all the time.

Juries are unpredictable.

It's not your fault.

I jump as a bright light flashes outside the window. The reflection of an airplane wing? The glossy feather of a falling bird? But all is still outside. I've tried to balance my guilt by building a shrine to perfection, a mausoleum to entomb my mistake, an attempt to silence it. But like a tell-tale heart, the beating only gets louder the deeper I bury it. I grind myself to exhaustion every day just so I don't have to feel its pulse. I've relinquished my desires, a personal life, and still when I climb into bed and slip between the cool silken sheets, my anxious mind begins its familiar trek to that distant outpost of throbbing guilt. It's worse on days like today, when my path doubles back on itself, and pulls me into the past.

The view from the Sky Building had been one of the major selling points of this development but every time I look out my window I seem to lock eyes with some resident or other. In this building of glass, a house of mirrors, where reflections are everywhere, it's hard to tell what's real and what's just a phantom image. The sky pool is eerily still, empty and rippling in the morning sunlight. Another flash of light catches my eye and I jump again. I see a man in the apartment across the way. The light is reflecting off his glasses as he looks directly at me.

And suddenly the view is one I don't like.

3

EDDIE

A journalist recollects in agitation

The weeks before the grand opening of the Sky Building seemed to drag by. There wasn't a minute when I wasn't thinking about it. At last, the day arrived. My desk was a hive of industry. My sleeves were up. I was even more dehydrated than usual as I made a list of people I wanted to interview. I had dug out my old boxes of files and clippings from the Juliet case. I hadn't been this motivated by a story, well, since *this* story, twenty years earlier. I thought that this was the story that would make my career. I was going to single-handedly take down the DA, and the Bentwell Brothers law firm, and clear that poor scholarship kid's name in the process. The only person I took down was myself. I mean, when I say it out loud now, I really was naive.

But I knew the kid had not been guilty. He was good to his bones, well raised, full of humility, hard-working and helpful, grafting his way through a degree and about to change his life, and his destiny, against all the odds when: wham! He slams into the brick wall of privilege and goes down for someone else's crime. When I tried to expose it, I was balled up like a piece of yesterday's newspaper and slammed into the same brick wall. That's how it works. The Bentwells protected their own. Turns out the police protected their own too and powerful people have powerful friends in powerful places like the mayor's office, which appoints the police commissioner, who appoints the first deputy and so on and so forth, and down the tentacles of influence reach, into the furthest depths of the police department. But life is long and boy had I bided my time, waiting patiently in the long grass for a moment like this to come around again. If any story was personal, this one was.

Every nerve ending in my body was alive. You see, I couldn't help it. It was just my nature. I was an investigative journalist, not only by training, but perhaps more importantly by instinct. Unfortunately, like most journalists pushing fifty, particularly the ones who had managed to hold on to full-time newspaper positions in the digital age, I had become more of an administrative and managerial taskmaster than the investigative hack I was in my bones. The jobs I did now were ones that used to be done by long-obsolete positions like sub-editors, graphic designers and copy editors. Those jobs went the way of the dinosaurs when spell check was invented. If I didn't want to join them in obsolescence, I had to shut up and put up. Which is what I did, most of the time. And so my crime correspondent's finely honed mind went to seed whilst working on the letters pages, the TV listings and the puzzles section. (And I can tell you, I'd take my chances with a gangland family any day over the wrath of the daily bridge players.) The worst job of all, however, was the social diary. But needs must and beggars can't be choosers. I was lucky to have an iron-clad contract drawn up before the internet tore down my industry, which meant it would cost the paper more to get rid of me than to keep me on as an administrative drudge who happened to know where all the bodies were buried.

Besides, I could put up with a menial, demeaning job if it meant I got to come into the office every day. You see, what nobody tells you when you're starting out is this – being a journalist makes you unfit for pretty much any other job. It breaks your brain so that it's only happy when it's fed a constant diet of unpredictability, overstimulation, multitasking, impossible deadlines, horror, stress, fear and a dash of gentle bullying. I know, it's an acquired taste, but I loved it and found I couldn't live without it. So what if I had been neutered? I still got to have conversations with smart people about politics, news, security, state secrets, celebrity affairs, and I got to vicariously feel that charge every time a big story broke, got to feel a part of something, even if I wasn't really part of anything in that way any more. It allowed me to tell myself that my life still had some meaning, that the damage wrought by the Juliet murder had been worth it, somehow.

I had tried to give normal life a go once, a few years before the Juliet case. Cassie, my ex-wife, begged me to get out. She wanted us to have what she called a 'normal' life, one filled with evenings watching television, weekends sharing long home-made lunches with friends, summer holidays where nobody checked their emails and maybe, if we were lucky, children, and soccer runs and PTAs and everything that involved. She had grown tired of me surreptitiously taking calls at dinner parties, filing pieces in bed at midnight and cancelling social events at the last minute so I could work on some breaking news story or other. So I took a year-long sabbatical and found a 'normal job' in the corporate communications office of a big accountancy firm. I really did try to give normal life a go, but I could never get far enough away from the newsroom's gravitational pull. I lasted eight months, which was as long as I could stick it before it made me want to kill myself more than making my wife unhappy did. So I left the corporate world, and soon after Cassie left me; journalism and I have been together ever since.

Cassie moved to Cleveland and now she has three kids with a school teacher, exactly the kind of life she always wanted. And I'm happy for her, happy that she found what she wanted. *But what did I want?* Truth was I had no idea.

Sometimes I wonder what might have happened if I had managed to stick it out. Would my life have fallen apart so spectacularly? Would I be living in Cleveland with high blood pressure and a few kids? Would it have worked? If I'm honest, the thing that made Cassie leave me is the only thing I love: work. And I'm grateful that I still have it because when days are long and nights are lonely, journalism is the thing that never stops. It keeps me from dwelling on all the ways my life went wrong – Cassie, the Juliet case, my career and the Bentwells' part in all of it.

4

VIVIAN

A lonely widower catches a break

The morning sunlight shuttered through the revolving door of the lobby entrance. I liked mornings best. Mornings were busy with residents coming and going. I loved the bustle, the company, the little chats I had with different people. Some were friendlier than others.

'Good morning, Mrs Black,' I said, as Samsara Black walked briskly past me, her high heels clicking like a dressage pony. She worked at a slick PR company – they were handling the building's launch party – and she was married to William Black. She didn't look at me but said good morning in the same way she might say it to a homeless person – crisply polite but holding herself apart, demarcating the difference between us.

Unlike Dave, who was one of my favourite residents. He looked right at me when he spoke to me, asked me how I was, and he meant it. I could tell. He remembered things I told him, about myself, my family. Sometimes he asked follow-up questions from previous conversations we had had. He was one of the cost-rental lottery winners, which is probably why he was so friendly. But I hadn't seen him yet this morning.

I cried when I got this job. I had been unemployed for a few years by that point and felt like I was at rock bottom. I retired officially at seventy-four, after years of working as a private doorman. But I had to keep working because my pension was too small. It's harder to find a job in your seventies than you might think, so I knocked a decade off my age and nobody was any the wiser. Young people had no way of telling the difference between sixty-four and seventy-four; to them I was just old. I got a job as a hotel doorman but the shifts were outdoors and the freezing-cold winters exacerbated my arthritis. I loved that job. It brought so much meaning to my life after the previous decades of nursing my wife Dodi through her cancer, then grieving her. When she eventually died, I needed to get out of our apartment. I couldn't be there alone all day long, the place where we had spent so many years together. Without her, the place felt hollow, I couldn't find any rest or relaxation there. It felt like walking around inside her corpse. Morbid. Wrong.

21

So I worked double shifts and split shifts at the hotel and walked the streets until I was exhausted enough to enter the apartment without thinking too much about Dodi's absence. The job meant I wasn't alone. I got to talk to people, imagine their lives, distract myself from my own life. And I liked helping them find their way around the city, giving them the best tips for where they were going, helping them enjoy what was often a once-in-a-lifetime trip. It made me feel useful again.

I scraped through the first winter, my joints stiffening with each passing day, but by the second winter it was obvious to everybody, including me, that this wasn't going to work. And so when the hotel manager had called me in for a 'chat' I understood where they were coming from. They were fair, sent me off with six weeks' pay and a glowing letter of recommendation, but after that it had been hard to find any work. Nobody wanted to hire an old man. My demographic sat just one notch below the most unwanted employee category of all – women of child-bearing age. People looked at me as if I was a halfwit, even though I had more capability, experience and common sense than most twenty-five-year-olds. But it didn't matter. Nobody wanted to hire someone who wasn't 'internet native'. I knew how to use a smartphone. I was on Facebook – I don't know why I was on it but I was on it! – but it wasn't enough.

As the months passed I thought I might go under. The lack of family crowded in on me as I saw men my age looked after by their adult children or helping out with their grandchildren. I wanted what they had so badly. Lucy would be thirty-eight now if she was alive, probably married with a couple of kids too. I started to go back to morning Mass in St Paul The Apostle on West 59th Street. The priest suggested I get busy, volunteer, and so I started offering my time at the local library, took up free tai chi in the park, joined a bereaved husbands' social group on Meet-up, which I dreaded but which actually turned out to be quite friendly. And then one day I was parked outside a women's shelter and noticed the young woman with a single refuse sack of belongings walk into the place. Something about her reminded me of a young girl I used to know ... I got out of the car right there and then, and walked into the shelter behind that girl. I offered myself as a volunteer and the tired woman behind the counter said: 'When can you start?' I was already police vetted because of my job as a doorman, so the answer was right away. It was actually thanks to the shelter that I ended up getting the job at the Sky Building. I had seen an A4 sheet pinned to the notice-board advertising jobs.

Do you have what it takes to work at the height of sophisticated living?

Of course I didn't, but as I scanned the positions listed – cleaners, janitors, parking attendant, concierge – I realised I didn't have to. I could do any of these jobs. I took out my cheap phone and took a photo of the contact details. It made an embarrassingly loud camera shutter sound that made everyone in the shelter look up at me accusingly. I apologised and pocketed the phone. I found the application later on a thing called LinkedIn and, with some difficulty, applied for the job. I didn't have much hope but my desperation overcame my lack of confidence. Working with people less fortunate than me in the shelter had given me perspective. I wasn't expecting much but I knew I wanted to be useful again. I was shocked when the recruiting agent told me I was one of their top candidates.

'You're exactly what we're looking for. No ties, no dependants, mature, available and one hundred per cent reliable,' she said.

'Well, that's me down to a tee,' I said. I understood it was just corporate speak for 'we want you to work twenty-four/seven' but I didn't care because the truth was twenty-four/seven suited me just fine. In fact, that's exactly what I was looking for from the job. When I found out the building was owned by Fox Developers it felt like fate. But I wasn't willing to leave anything to chance. I got on the phone to a mutual friend who owed me.

5

EDDIE

Some days are just special

It didn't bother me that Trudeau liked to shit on me with his endless menial tasks. Frustrated by his lack of empowerment to fire me (we still had a union at this paper), he threw every shitty job my way instead. One of the first things he had done when he got the editor's chair was to try to fire me. But he hadn't checked my contract. That was awkward for him because he knew I knew that he wanted me gone, that he didn't rate me. I suspect he saw me – female, close to fifty, tipping into the higher end of the BMI scale – and made some lazy assumptions. It was awkward for him too because he was ordinarily so suffocatingly politically correct. He was *flawless*. Maybe I was just jealous because I was not flawless. In fact, if there was a physical representation that constituted the opposite of Trudeau, it was me, but I don't really care for hysterical hygiene. Maybe it's because I grew up in an apartment that had a tub in the kitchen with a slab of plywood on top that doubled up as our kitchen table, so I never got the ingrained habit of daily showering. I pulled myself together every morning, I was presentable, but no matter what I did I always looked a little rumpled, a little worn. Cass used to ask me, 'how do you do that to clothes?', mystified by my ability to make even a sharp new suit look untidy, but I guess it was just my special gift. My body spilled further and further over its outline as the years went by, a melting church candle slowly collapsing on itself. I did my best to contain myself but it was never enough. My doctor told me there was nothing medically wrong with me but that women's bodies changed as they got older, the menopause made it harder, and had I tried losing weight? Thanks, genius. That was $450 I'd never see again. I'm aware of my appearance. I am not decorous in the traditional female way but forgive me if I don't think that is the point of being alive. I am at peace with my humanness, with the fact that no matter how much we wash and groom ourselves, we're all still going to end up in the same place – the graveyard.

I think Trudeau's main issue with me, though, is I have a tough time keeping my opinion to myself. And I never learn. He once overheard me loudly ribbing him.

I was just kidding around but did I mention Trudeau didn't have much of a sense of humour? He gave me a lecture on the importance of fostering a professional environment of 'respect and dignity for all'. He wasn't too worried about *my* personal respect and dignity when he tried to fire me, and then assigned me to the social diary, but I suppose that's what we call a double standard. What did I need dignity for anyway? I had long since traded my dignity for a salary.

The social diary was a comical position for someone like me to hold. I am social death. People at parties give me a wide berth. I am universally shunned by the young, the hip, the cool, the beautiful. Or I *was* ... until I started writing the diary and then suddenly I was plagued by young influencers looking for a bump in followers. It was disconcerting for all involved but we tolerated each other in the purely transactional way whales and barnacles do. They gave me copy, I gave them exposure. Most days were a different version of the same old story – the opening of a new hip restaurant/bar/nightclub/spa – but some days, like today, were special.

The mind of an old hack was a dredging machine and certain names pulled different levers, dragging ghosts from different corners of the past. In the case of Bryant Fox it was a literal ghost: his daughter Juliet, who had been murdered in the back alley of their mansion on the Upper West Side, twenty years ago, after a student party to celebrate the end of summer.

The police had moved quickly – too quickly if you asked me (which nobody did) – but the pressure had been on to solve the case because of who Juliet was. Haste makes waste, that's what my mother used to say when she was sober enough to impart such nuggets of wisdom. Well, I apply that philosophy to most things, including police investigations. The kid the cops fitted up was just some poor scholarship boy who was foolish enough to think he could date Juliet Fox without any repercussions. But every rich kid from a twelve-block radius had been at Juliet's party that night and one of them had killed Juliet, which meant one of them had spent the last twenty years sitting on their secret. They must all think they are safe now. Twenty years was a comfortable buffer zone between a crime and a guilty conscience. A delicious thought warmed my mind – they had no idea I was coming for them. And this time I had absolutely nothing to lose.

The truth ran to its own timeline. It didn't care about the passing of time or deadlines or convenience. The truth would come out when it was ready, like a sac full of pus ready to explode. And I could feel it gathering pressure. If there was one thing I had learned for sure in more than three decades of journalism it was this: the truth always finds its way out.

I put my files back in order. I couldn't sit still. I was too agitated, so I decided to take a walk to the Sky Building, clear my head in the process and see what I could find out in advance of the grand opening party. No time like the present, I thought. Besides, I always did better in person. It was easy to hang up a phone on an anonymous voice, and I had the kind of smart-ass tone that rubbed people the wrong way. It was not so easy to slam a door shut in another human being's face. And I had an honest face, the kind that people trusted. I didn't look like a slick, ambitious journalist who would gut you for a story and ruin your life. But no doubt about it, that's what I was.

6

VIVIAN

A stranger arrives

Don't get me wrong, living and working in the Sky Building wasn't easy. Because the building was new and architecturally designed to be beautiful from the outside as well as the inside, a lot of rules were written into the 'residents' charter', such as, no drying your laundry on the balcony, and no pets allowed apart from pre-approved (meaning pedigree) small-dog and cat breeds. No shoes indoors, as they made noise but also posed a risk to the beautiful hardwood floors. All recycling must be done through the central garbage disposal system in the basement. Then there was the no-window-coverings rule – no curtains, roman blinds, French shutters, Venetian blinds or any other covering apart from the pre-approved sheer blind. *Windows must be kept uncovered in keeping with the architect's vision for the building and to perpetuate the Sylvan effect of all residents living in harmony.* Would a prison have as many rules?

I was pulled from my reverie by the woman walking into the lobby. The light shuttered through the revolving doors and I was momentarily blinded until she was almost at the desk. She looked very familiar.

7

EDDIE

A journalist makes an unexpected discovery

I had to concede the Sky Building was impressive, gleaming and glamorous in the morning sunlight. I passed the building on my way to the office every morning – part of my attempt to get 10,000 steps a day – but I had never been inside. There were mirrors and glass everywhere, giving the illusion of infinity.

To be perfectly truthful, the sky pool creeped me out. They called it a sky pool because it bridged the east and west towers before they merged into one giant tower a few storeys up. It was a spectacular feat of architectural engineering genius. The perspex had been flown in from Japan in one giant piece. How much did that cost? And did we not have slabs of perspex here in the US of A? The pool stretched from a duplex 'pool penthouse' on one side to a luxury triplex with a rooftop garden terrace on the other. Swimming in it was like flying, the developers said, just floating in the sky, looking down on the world from amongst the clouds. They said it was like heaven, as if any of them was going to heaven. Although they probably knew what it was like to look down on people from a great height. They were good at that.

I was in two minds about these modern buildings that were sprouting up all over New York with greater frequency. Something about them seemed to push further and further away from humanity. They were built for rich people for a start and they seemed to be about cutting people off from one another, rather than becoming part of a community. And the interiors were so luxurious the people never wanted to leave. I would never have that problem in my apartment. I couldn't care less about interiors and carpets and thousand-dollar taps and underfloor heating. The ways in which people fooled themselves into believing they were not going to die were of no interest to me. I lived in the same grubby apartment where my mother had died. I had moved back in there after Cassie had left me, having sublet the place all through our marriage, because, well, everyone knows you don't let go of a rent-controlled apartment in Manhattan. Lucky for me I didn't because I had nowhere else to go after the break-up and I certainly couldn't afford rent at market rates.

There's something about returning to your old childhood home, though, that makes you feel like an acute failure, back to the bed your childhood body slept in, remembering your hopes and dreams for the future, looking at the same view your innocent eyes enjoyed, and everything seeming shrunken because, of course, you are so much bigger now. It was a far cry from the Sky Building, that was for sure, but I was glad of it just the same. At least it felt honest.

I pushed the rotary door into the lobby and it made an expensive whooshing sound. I was met by a fully uniformed concierge, complete with hat. I was eager to get access so I smiled a big, friendly smile and threw out my hand. 'How'ya doing? Eddie Wright, *New York Post*.' The man's body language recoiled immediately. 'I'm doing a feature on the opening of the building and I'm hoping to talk to a few people who live and work here, get an impression of the place, what it's like to live here, to float in that giant bathtub of water dangling up there in the sky.' I laughed and gave him my best *rich people, huh?* face. He smiled back but stayed professional. It was going to take more than that. 'We're also going to do a feature for the magazine on Bryant Fox's contribution to Manhattan's new skyline of instant architectural classics.' OK, so that was a lie but I needed to soften this guy up. I didn't tell him I was really here to revisit Juliet's murder and hopefully solve it. That's just how journalism works sometimes. You can't just come out and say what you're really up to. You follow your gut and make the path that is most likely to get you into the next room. I wanted to talk to the people who were involved in the police investigation, her friends, her then boyfriend, or boyfriends if you believe what people said, and see how their consciences had settled over the course of twenty years.

But this guy wasn't budging.

'I spoke to Grace? In Bryant Fox's marketing department? She said she'd hook me up with a tour of the communal areas and one of the vacant apartments? She didn't email you?' I said, tapping my finger on the marble ledge that housed his screen. 'Check it on your computer there ...' I was getting tired of begging for access.

He looked at his computer, deliberately tapped a few keys with unnecessary force, as if he was using an old manual printing press rather than the latest state-of-the-art desktop. It made me like him just a little bit. The Gen Zs in our office gave me a lot of shit for thumping out my copy with two fingers, but when you're a doorman you don't have a lot of cause for polishing your typing skills.

'Oh, OK, sure,' he said, surprised that I hadn't been spinning him a yarn. 'I see Grace's email here. Sorry about that ... As you can imagine, we get a lot of people coming in here with all sorts of stories, influencers, that kind of thing, looking to get access to the pool ... You can't be too careful. I can give you a tour, but not until after ten a.m. if that's OK. There's a bit of a rush between now and then with post, and couriers. I'll send a circular to our residents and see if anyone is willing to talk to you.'

The elevator pinged and a ripped guy stepped out.

'Morning, Viv,' he said with a terse nod.

'Morning, Mr Hart, you have a good day now.'

I locked eyes with him.

I know you.

I saw him clock me too and he looked away quicker than he should have. He was gone through the glass door but I *saw* him. I never forget a face. The elevator bell went again and a young woman, who couldn't have been more than twenty, emerged from the elevator with a little girl. I watched the concierge's face transform. 'How are my two princesses today?'

What do you have to do to earn that sort of greeting, I wondered.

8

CLEO

A lawyer's interest is piqued

'Knock, knock.'
Oh, for god's sake, just knock, I thought, as I looked up and saw a young associate at my door.

'Sorry to disturb you, Cleo. Do you have a minute?'

Of course I don't have a minute but I'm supposed to be an approachable mentor for younger female associates so I closed the manilla folder in front of me and pushed it aside. 'Of course, come in.'

'I'm wondering if you would take a look at this brief I've been passed? It's from a woman who wants to make a historic sexual assault charge and I'm a bit nervous about taking it any further.'

Everyone her age was nervous. They all needed so

37

much hand-holding. I took the folder from her and scanned the contents. 'What's your reservation?'

'Well, I'm a bit concerned because a) it was over twenty years ago, b) she is on her own, as in she doesn't have a group of other women claiming he did the same to them, so at the moment it's an isolated incident he said-she said, and c) it's against a very powerful man.'

I flicked through the sheaf of typed pages of the woman's affidavit until I found the named defendant. I inhaled sharply. Thoughts tumbled and ruptured, carefully compartmentalised feelings strained at their boundaries.

'Bentwell . . .' I said, the name a bitter taste on my tongue.

'So, you see my reservation . . .' the associate said. I had to be fair to her. She was right to be hesitant when it came to Bentwell.

'Does she have any evidence, anything circumstantial, proof? How did it happen . . . ?' I asked.

'She was a young realtor,' the associate said, taking the file back from me and flipping through it. 'She was working at a firm that handled properties for the Bryant Fox group. She went on a walkthrough of one of the group's buildings, under the impression that there would be more than one person at the viewing, but instead it was just Bentwell and her. She says he raped her in the primary suite.'

I could believe it. 'Why didn't she say anything at the time? Why *now*?' I asked.

'Well, she says she went to the hospital that day, did a sexual assault kit at the time, filed a report with the police. She had every intention of taking a case. But then Fox's daughter was killed, and she knew he'd feel responsible for sending her out to a viewing on her own. So she put it aside. She felt bad for him, didn't want to add to his troubles. But I'm not worried about that. There is no statute of limitations on rape in New York City. The police will have the rape kit. Or should do . . .'

I didn't correct her. Didn't tell her what she should know – what I already knew – that some police departments in states all over the country trashed rape kits without even testing the DNA. So chances were there might not be any evidence of the crime. The associate was flipping through the file again. 'She says she has lived with the effects for over twenty years, including the shame. She's been in therapy ever since, her marriage has fallen apart . . . and she says it all comes back to the trauma of this assault. She wants him to pay for ruining her life. She says she doesn't care if she wins the case or not, she just wants to look him in the eye in an open court. She wants to shame him. And she knows that even an unproven accusation will hurt him. But my concern is it might hurt her more.'

My heartbeat was slowing down enough for me to

think a little. 'Or it might hurt *us*. If there is a record of the original police complaint and the SAU report and kit it might be worth taking, but we don't want to go up against the Bentwells without a solid case. The best chance you have is to find more women. You know how to do that?' I asked her, standing up so I could herd her towards the door, signalling that our mentoring session was over for today. 'Track down women who worked with Bentwell, particularly around that time. Then look at the ones who moved on quickly from Bentwell's firm, that's a telltale sign. Get one of the investigators to come up with some lists for you. If you can find these women and get them to support your client, you've got a shot. Stick to the two years before and after your client's incident, then broaden your net outwards if you need to. It's unlikely luring and raping an estate agent was a first crime. There will have been lesser assaults, a trajectory, escalating behaviour. Find women who he creeped on, took for drinks, roughed up, anything that we can build into habitual predatory behaviour.'

'So you think go ahead with it? Even though it's Bentwell?'

'If you can find the other women,' I said. 'But you will. I'm sure of it.'

'I hope you're right,' the associate said, before leaving. 'I'm hoping to have a long career in this town.'

'Trust me,' I said. 'I'm always right.'

I closed the door, leaned against it and exhaled shakily.

I was right. Bentwell was a sexual predator. And I had it on excellent authority.

9

EDDIE

I've never been too good with names, but I remember faces

The girls smiled at Vivian and he pulled a lollipop from his desk, handed it over to the child.

'Vivian, her teeth will fall out,' the young woman protested.

'She's four, she's got a spare set,' the old man said. That made me laugh. Old school. Children deserved sweets and not desiccated rolled-up fruit.

'Off to school?' I asked.

She looked at me oddly, then said, 'Camp. It's August. School's out for summer,' she smiled.

'Ah, easy to tell I don't have kids,' I said.

'You all set for the launch party tonight?' Vivian asked.

The woman's face changed, looked uncertain. 'Oh, I don't know if we'll go. I have a lot of work to get through,' she said, 'and Flo gets tired.'

The little girl kicked up, 'I want to go to the party, mama.'

Vivian smiled at her. 'It would be a good way to get to know the neighbours,' he said. 'Everyone's invited, and some of them are very nice. Cleo, the lady in the pool penthouse? She is very down to earth. And Dave, the other cost-rental tenant, he is a lovely man, couldn't be more helpful. It's good to have someone to call on in an emergency, Marley ...'

'Well, that's what you're for,' she teased him ... She looked at me as if seeing me for the first time.

'If I could choose my family, Vivian would be number one on my list. We go back a long way, don't we, Viv?' she told me.

The doorman couldn't hide his pleasure. This girl was the apple of his eye. I was intrigued.

'All right then, I'll go, but only so Marley can try the pool. I just wish they were a little friendlier ... you know.' She looked at me again. 'How do you find living here?'

'Oh, I don't live here,' I said. 'I'm Eddie Wright, I'm doing a piece for the *New York Post* on the grand opening and hoping to talk to residents actually, about what it's like to live in a place like this. You might consider talking to me for the piece.' My card was in her hand before she knew what was happening.

'Marley's one of the lottery winners on the cost-rental scheme,' Vivian said.

Jackpot.

'So how do you two know each other? You said you go back?'

A cloud scudded across Vivian's face, but the girl was all openness. 'Vivian was volunteering at a women's shelter. I was living there at the time. He was one of the few men that was welcome in that place. Everyone loved Vivian. When I saw him here at the Sky Building it was like a sign. It felt like I belonged here, even though I clearly don't – am I right?' she laughed, looking across at him. 'Not like the other residents do.'

'Sure you belong here, you've every right to be here,' I told her.

She made a face. 'Most of the others already know each other, they all went to the same schools or holidayed with each other's families, or shared an architect or an interior designer. And they've had housewarmings or drinks or dinners and the parties at the sky pool, which we can't attend ...'

'Why not?' I asked.

'Those of us on the cost-rental scheme have no access to the sky pool or the other facilities. I suppose you could say we're on the basic package, and the owner-occupiers get the premium package.' She smiled sadly.

'Huh,' I said. 'Why does that not surprise me ...?
Say, it would be great to talk to you about that, living
here, trying to fit in ... do you think you might be free
in the next day or two for my article? I'll be at the party
tonight too ...'

'Sure,' she said. 'I'm not doing anything before the
party tonight, if you want to come a little early?'

'Absolutely,' I said.

Vivian broke in. 'Why don't you use my apartment?
Things will be quiet there before people start to arrive
for the party and I can keep an eye on the front desk
from the CCTV ... sound good?'

I realised Vivian wanted to keep an eye on proceed-
ings. He was protective of this girl, didn't want her
saying the wrong thing or maybe didn't want me manipulating her naïveté in any way.

'*Mom!*' The kid's patience had run out.

Marley smiled and said, 'See you later,' as she backed
out the door.

'So there are a few cost-rental units in the building?'
I asked. 'Nice.'

Vivian looked at me, as if he was trying to decide
whether to trust me or not. Maybe not that. He knew
he couldn't trust me. I'm a journalist. But whether he
trusted me as a person.

'It's part of the planning laws now,' he said.

'Yeah, but I didn't think anybody actually abided
by planning laws, least of all big-shot developers.' He

said nothing and I looked up and whistled at the huge atrium. You could see the edge of the sky pool. 'You know, I grew up a few blocks west of here, on Ninth Avenue, in a one-bed with my ma and we had a bathtub in the kitchen that doubled up as our dining table.' I laughed. 'It was a *long* way from this.'

Vivian laughed suddenly too.

'No kidding,' he said. 'I didn't think there were any of those units left.'

'I'm older than I look,' I said, preening for him. That made him laugh a bit more too. OK, I think I finally had the measure of this guy. 'I still live in the same apartment. Bathtub is still there in the kitchen. I live alone, so not really any need to put in a fancy bathroom suite or fitted cabinets. It's good to know how little you need to survive; it makes you stronger, more independent. Makes you realise you can survive most things.'

He smiled at me, and it was a warm and genuine smile. Not quite the smile he had for the little girl but definitely a barriers-down smile. He nodded his head. 'You're not wrong.'

'Great neighbours too,' I said. 'Although they're mostly dead or gone, moved on to the suburbs. 'What about you? Will you talk to me for this piece? What's it like to be the gatekeeper of a place like this?'

The smile tightened. 'Much as I would like to I can't do that. Discretion is a huge part of this job. What I can tell you is that I'm really grateful to have this job and I really want to keep it.'

My mind kept drifting to the guy's face . . . I couldn't remember where I knew him from.

'Who was that guy?' I asked, as casually as I could. 'The guy who just got out of the lift . . . I feel like I know him from somewhere.'

'Dave? He's one of the other cost-rental residents. Nice guy. Quiet. Keeps to himself. Always either working, or working out.' Mr Hart. Dave Hart. Oh my god.

'Viv, I just remembered something so I gotta run but I'll come back later for that tour,' I said, and hot-footed it out the door as fast as I could. I needed to find Dave.

10

EDDIE

Catching a big fish

I spotted him heading downtown. There were women laughing and pushing strollers, people rushing to work, tourists gaping, and a new bane – social media influencers talking into their extended arms. Christ, it was like an assault course just trying to get down the sidewalk.

I hadn't seen that face in twenty years. But it was him.

I just needed to speak to him. My piece would be next level if I got to talk to the guy convicted of killing Juliet . . .

I crossed the street as fast as I could. A car blasted its horn, its fender grazing my thigh. I gained on him so I could get a proper look at his face. It was him, I was sure of it.

I risked calling him. 'Dave!'

He slowed momentarily, as if he had snagged on something, before picking up pace again.

I tried again, and this time I was almost level with him. 'Hey, Dave.'

He gave me a sideways look but didn't break his stride. 'Sorry, wrong guy.'

'Wait,' I said. He stopped then and the sound of his body pulling up short on the pavement made my insides curl up. This guy could pummel me to mincemeat in seconds if he wanted to, but I trusted my instincts that if he wasn't the kind of guy to kill a woman, he probably wasn't the kind of guy to hit one either.

'OK, *who* are you?' He looked very pissed off.

'You don't remember me? Eddie Wright? The journalist? I wrote about your trial. I spoke to you, after the trial. I thought you were innocent.'

'Listen, I'm just trying to move on with my life, keep a low profile. I don't need journalists digging up the past. That's the last thing I need. Juliet's dead. I served my time. End of story. Nothing you or anyone else can do is going to change any of that.'

'I respect that. I don't want to make things worse ...' I risked it. 'Don't you want to clear your name, though? We live in a democracy. If we don't believe people can be rehabilitated we have no democracy.'

'That's a nice line but I know journalists, you'll say anything to get what you want,' he said.

He wasn't wrong. 'Fair, but have I not always been

on your side? Just hear me out? I'm doing a piece on Juliet Fox's anniversary ...'

He cut me off, started to walk away. 'No way. Absolutely not. Just no ...'

'Wait!' I was skipping now to keep up with him. I wasn't used to skipping or any other kind of bouncing, jogging, running motion, and the grim humidity of the August morning rose up from the pavement and pressed down from the reflections of the buildings and had me sweating in seconds. Dave on the other hand was powder-dry. He stopped again and visibly tried to collect all of his patience.

'I know you're innocent,' I said. 'I knew it then and I know it now.'

He said nothing, which I took as my cue to make my case. 'Here's what I think. I think you were just a kid, and I think you were stitched up by some very powerful people who had a lot of resources and even more to lose. If you had done it, don't you think they would have stuck murder on you? Even the police couldn't do that, which tells me there was no evidence to suggest that you did it. What I'm hoping is if we refresh some guilty memories, people might start to talk ... It's been twenty years. You'd be amazed what time does to a guilty conscience.'

He stared at me. I have yet to meet a pregnant pause that I will not, well, further impregnate with my verbal diarrhoea.

'You'll have full copy approval. If you don't like it,

I don't run it. Just talk to me. Tell me your side of the story from where you're at now, twenty years on ...' Finally I ran out of words. Finally he spoke.

'You still believe somebody else did it?'

I relaxed. He was on the hook. Now I just needed to gently reel. No. Sudden. Moves.

'It's obvious. The most they could put you down for was manslaughter and that was all circumstantial. Why was that, huh? That rich kid literally had an argument with her at the party in front of everyone, but he said he was at home tucked up with a friend of the family when the murder happened so sure, here's your get out of jail free card?' I remembered every detail of this case, could recall all the information with perfect clarity, the facts coming to me without my having to pause for thought. Each day of that case seemed to be connected to a corresponding point on the downfall of my work and personal life. I could plot it out like a graph. 'And the CCTV that mysteriously stopped working at the time of the murder? And the unidentified DNA taken from the scene of that crime that they never managed to match? It's kind of ridiculous. Come on, there were so many huge holes in the case. It should have been enough for a Not Guilty verdict.'

Dave was silent. 'You think?'

'I think.'

He looked back up towards the Sky Building and let out a huge sigh. His body language was totally different now. 'I've tried to move on but I feel like I'm living a half-life. It's like a cancer that I have to cut out before I can heal ... I'm free now, I can get on with my life but somehow I can't seem to. I just can't let it go.'

'Of course you can't.' I looked at him with what I hoped was a cross between sympathy and righteous rage on his behalf. I needed to strike just the right tone if he was going to trust me again. He wiped his jaw with his hand and it made a scraping noise even though he was closely shaved. 'All right,' he said, 'I'll talk to you. But under the conditions you said. If I don't like it, we drop it, the whole piece, no questions asked, OK?'

'Deal,' I said, sticking out my hand. I realised it was sweating. We shook.

'I promise, you can trust me,' I said.

He shook his head, like he was already regretting it. 'So,' he said, 'when do you wanna do this?'

When you've hooked a fish, you don't leave him on your rod to think about all the ways he might wriggle off. You reel him in.

'I'm free now if you are.'

'Good for you. Some of us have to work for a living.'

'What about the party tonight? Before? After?'

'No, not tonight. Tomorrow morning,' he said. 'Early.'

'I'll be at your building at eight a.m.,' I said.

'Wait, how strict is the dress code at this party to-night?' I asked. I didn't own a dress, but I did own a tuxedo jacket that I usually wore with a white shirt and jeans. It took me most places.

'Oh, these people love a dress code,' he said. 'If it says black tie, they mean black tie *plus*. This is cocktail so you've got some wiggle room. I'm wearing a suit. I only have one.' He paused. 'It's the same one I wore to Juliet's funeral. And my court case. I guess that's probably appropriate given the full-circle moment.'

I said nothing. It felt less appropriate and more like a bad omen to me, but I kept my mouth shut.

11

CLEO

Asking for a friend

I ran as fast as my Jimmy Choos would take me. I was late for lunch. With Bentwell. We disliked and respected each other in equal measure, but we were professionally bound since I had interned for his law firm in my final year. He offered one prestigious internship to law students every year. Everyone wanted it, but I got it. And he was one of the most powerful players in Manhattan law, connected all the way from DAs and judges right down to court clerks, so I liked to keep him on the right side. We met up a few times a year to discuss legal cases, new developments and, of course, gossip. What I had heard in my office this morning, however, would not be shared.

'I'm dealing with a tricky paternity case,' he said,

tearing some bread from a roll in the basket and washing it down with a pricey glass of red. He was good to himself. I sipped my sparkling water.

'A guy who has been paying off young women for decades has just been contacted by a woman who thinks she is his offspring.' He paused to let the horror of his words land.

'Awks,' I said, as my salad arrived, dressing on the side.

'So, he's thinking of offering to pay her off in the way that he's paid off all the illegitimate offspring of the women he has slept with over the years ... but get this, she doesn't want money. She wants to meet!' He dissolved into cackles. 'Can you believe it?'

'So what does he want you to do?'

'He's thinking of taking out a barring order against her, for harassment and invasion of privacy. She may be his child but he didn't agree to her birth and he doesn't want anything to do with her. He's happy to pay her off but he's not happy to have a relationship.'

'Woah, that brings commitment-phobe to a whole new level,' I said.

'Well, what would you do,' he asked.

'I'd give her what she's asking for. She's not asking for a relationship. She's asking to meet. He can make his situation clear. She'll have done enough research to realise that the odds are he won't want a relationship, and she'll likely accept that. But offering to pay her off, well, it's a bit insulting, isn't it? It suggests that she's after money rather than a true connection with her father. I'd tell him to tread lightly. If he meets her he might avoid having a relationship *and* paying her any money.'

'Hmm, good point,' Bentwell said.

'But if he goes in with the money first he risks alienating her, pissing her off and who knows where that will end up?'

'Very true. What about you? Anything interesting?'

I wiped my mouth with my napkin and picked up my espresso, which the waiter had brought. I shook my head. 'Nothing of note. Some inheritance battles, a possible #MeToo class action ...'

'It's amazing what's classed as sexual assault these days,' he said. 'When did propositioning become harassment?'

He mopped his saucy pasta with some more bread, and then ordered a brandy. His stomach strained against his pristine white shirt. 'Whatever happened to all's fair in love and war?'

'Oh, I think a lot of people still play by those rules ... I don't know how you can concentrate after all that food and wine. I'd be asleep by three p.m.'

'Superior breeding,' he said with an insufferable grin. How I would enjoy wiping it off his face.

12

EDDIE

A girl pulls a loose thread

I arrived at Vivian's apartment an hour before the party started. There was a hired event security team in place for tonight's party and they were already directing eager guests towards the pool. Vivian's place was directly off the lobby, the only residence on the ground floor. It was kitted out with a bank of CCTV screens just inside his door – not very homely, but pretty cool all the same. The wall of screens showed the main entrance, the lobby, the delivery entrance at the back of the building, the east tower exits, the basement car parking area, and some of the sky pool and terrace. I could see catering staff milling around the pool already, event planners and some early guests mingling.

Vivian made us coffee, and set Flo up with a cartoon

while I chatted to Marley. There was something tremulous and quivering beneath all that positivity. She was just a vulnerable kid.

'So what's it like living in your *dream home*?' I said, giving the term some heavy irony. I had decided all three of us were confidantes now, us against the kind of people who normally lived in a building like this.

'Well, it's amazing,' she said. 'I just have a sense of a complete weight being taken off my shoulders. It's not so much the luxury but the security. For the first time in my life, I have a long-term lease, stabilised rent and a sense that I can put down roots, make a home for me and my daughter. We even have an option to begin a rent-purchase programme in three years' time, which means I am on a path to home ownership, which is beyond my wildest dreams. There are rules, of course, lots of them, but this is the kind of deal people would step over their own mother for so we try to stay in line.'

'What about management fees? How do you afford them on a place like this?'

'We're exempt, another reason I try not to complain about anything at the resident meetings. If it means Flo and I get to live somewhere like this, I am not going to rock the boat. Flo has never even had a playdate because our home was so embarrassing. I didn't have anyone over either. The moms at Flo's school kind of froze me out. I didn't want to be their friend anyway – they were all old, in their forties, and they thought I was the au pair so they totally blanked me ... I don't have to worry about any of that any more now that we have our own home. Sorry,' she said. 'I'm a bit nervous.'

'We're just having a conversation here, OK?' I said. 'Anything you say is just deep background, which means I can't use it and can't quote you on it, OK? And then later, I'll go over the quotes I'd like to use and you and Vivian can tell me if you're happy or if you want to change anything. Does that sound OK?'

She relaxed visibly and broke into a smile.

'We're not doing an exposé here, all right?' Not on Marley anyway, I thought. 'And look, Vivian is here. He won't let you say anything you shouldn't, right Viv?'

Vivian smiled as he brought the coffees over. 'No chance!'

'OK, so what is your favourite part of living here?'

'The view. Hands down. I can see everything from my apartment – downtown, the skyline I used to dream about as a kid. But it's not just the city views. I can see up towards the sky pool, I can see the swimmers and people drinking on the patio. I can even see inside a few of the apartments,' she said. 'You should see some of these places ...' Her eyes took on a faraway look. I tried not to talk. I found it was better to just stay silent, let them say what they had to say. 'I think that's actually the biggest perk of living here, just getting to watch everyone else. Their lives seem so glamorous.

Their homes. Their clothes ... I like it best in the blue hour. As soon as the evening starts to fade into twilight and the lights of the various apartments flicker on, I can see everything. It's like watching a TV.'

I walked over to the balcony and looked out over the edge of the rail. It was still bright but there were lights on in some of the apartments. We were on the ground floor, which meant Marley could probably see even more from her apartment on the third floor. I could see Dave, topless, lifting weights in his spartan room. I looked up towards the pool and could see the caterers prepping the party. I could see the third floor of the triplex too. A willowy, blonde woman (was there any other kind in this building?) was gesticulating wildly in her underwear. The apartments looked like dolls' houses, and the people inside were the picture-perfect dolls living in them. Across the way a woman was taking off a sharp suit. Disrobing quickly and function-ally, I blushed and looked away. Even from here I could see she was strikingly beautiful. Movie-star beautiful. I let my eye rove over the building. Some people were making dinner, others staring at laptops and phones, some doing homework, some sharing a glass of wine, some already having arguments. How terrible to buy a home like this only to have arguments in it. I turned back towards Marley and Vivian.

Marley looked at me. 'Nice, isn't it? For so long I have been allowed to look, but not touch, this kind of life. I have always had my face pressed up against the glass. Even with my family. There was always something barring the way between me and them. But now I am almost one of them. Living in Manhattan with my little girl, invited to the grand opening of the most exclusive building in town, which will be full of residents, glamorous guests, influencers ... What do you think their lives are really like?'

'Oh, I'd say they're not as lovely as you think,' I said. In fact, I think they're downright rotten.

13

CLEO

A wealthy heiress reveals a secret

I stepped out onto the sky pool terrace. It wasn't quite six o'clock yet but it was already packed with influencers wanting to get a perfect shot for their socials. I didn't want to get caught up in this mess. I scanned the terrace and my eyes caught Samsara Black. She made a beeline for me – oh *God, why?*

Samsara was Bentwell's daughter. She was married to William Black, who worked for her father at Bentwell's legal firm. Samsara was smart but she didn't like hard work, so she played at having a job in a PR firm, which was mostly kept afloat by her father's wealthy contacts. They treated it like a charitable donation to Bentwell.

'Cleo,' she purred. 'You look lovely as always.' She looked me up and down in a way that suggested the opposite of the words she had just spoken. I was wearing a fine felted cashmere dress, light enough for the weather but structured enough to give it a certain formality. Not enough lace and plunging necklines for Samsara's style, which was more West Coast than Upper West Side. She leaned in and confidently kissed the air on either side of my head. It always made me laugh when she did this. Even though we had had mutual acquaintances in college, she still had to be re-introduced to me several times over the years before she finally managed to deem me important enough to remember. It was probably around the time I overtook her father as the number one attorney in Manhattan and was named one of *Time* Magazine's most influential people of the year.

'How's the new place going for you,' I asked, master of small talk me.

She grimaced. 'I was perfectly happy in our town-house in Lincoln Square, but it was my dad's idea. And once he and William get together on a plan I have no chance. Dad said *this* would be better suited to us now that Josh would be going to college. We needed to future-proof, he said. Funny, I don't see him future-proofing. He has a great nose for property though, I'll give him that. He said he wanted me and William and Josh to be closer to him and Mom, now that they are getting older. It's like he's never heard of a taxi. The mountain must come to Mohammad. But that's fathers, am I right? They still think they have a right to run our lives. It's like he thinks I'm fourteen, not forty-one. It's not a bad complaint, I suppose. Most people would kill for a dad like mine.'

'Mmm,' I said but couldn't agree, considering what I had read in affidavits that morning. 'Nice turnout,' I added, hoping to change the subject. 'Bryant will be pleased with you.' I lifted a glass of champagne from a passing tray. I hadn't intended on drinking but being trapped in Samsara's web of relentless small talk meant that was no longer an option.

'I'm not so sure,' she said. 'The company is rather ... *mixed*,' she stage-whispered.

I gulped some more champagne. Samsara had always been an insufferable snob.

She tilted her head across the courtyard, unsubtly using it to point at a guy.

'I did a double take when I saw him first too,' she said, misinterpreting my frown. 'What's someone like *him* doing in our building. Josh tells me I'm classist and elitist ... as if that were a bad thing!' She laughed. 'But you can't be too careful these days, I say. Better safe than sorry. Although I have to admit it is getting harder and harder to tell who really *belongs* anywhere these days. You know the billionaire who bought the top three floors? He looks like the delivery guy who leaves my packages from Vestiaire with Vivian. The first time I saw him in the lobby I gave Vivian the nod to call security ... I mean, can you imagine, Cleo?'

Jesus, I was going to have to cut her off. She was the kind of person I feared in a witness box, just blathering on and on, the ones who might say *anything*. I started thinking about the sexual assault brief the young legal associate had brought to me that day, while Samsara prattled on.

'... and then the penny dropped. He was one of the cost-rental residents, the housing lottery scheme. The city has gone mad, if you ask me. It's OK for Bryant. He's living in his billionaire bubble, he doesn't have to slum it like the rest of us who have to live alongside his planning trade-offs. I'll keep the peace for tonight but it sticks in my craw how people like you and me and our families work and pay for everything we have, while people like that get to live here scot-free.'

I laughed. Samsara had never paid for a single thing in her entire life.

'I had lunch with your dad today, Samsara,' I said. 'He told me he bought this place for you and William as a gift. Really nice gesture,' I said, lifting my glass to her and excusing myself. I looked again at the guy she had pointed out. He was standing uncomfortably alone on the other side of the terrace. I made my way towards him. I was the best criminal defence lawyer in Manhattan. Of course, I recognised him.

14

EDDIE

Members only

We had finished our coffee and it was getting close to party time. I needed to wrap things up. 'So can you tell me a little bit about yourself, and how you ended up applying for the cost-rental lottery?'

'Talk about a hard question,' Marley said and laughed.

'I thought that was the easy question,' I said.

'Not when it comes to my life . . .' she said, and proceeded to fill me in on how her adoptive parents had kicked her out when she got pregnant at sixteen.

'Jesus, I thought that kind of behaviour went out in the nineteen fifties . . .'

She grimaced a smile. 'That's how I ended up in the women's shelter with Flo, and how we met Vivian. They taught me the true meaning of family.'

'Are your birth parents ...?' I asked. 'Are you in touch with them at all?'

'I've tried but I have no idea who they are. I asked the church that organised my adoption but they told me they cannot share any records, that everything had been done under the strictest of confidence. I presume that's a story to cover the fact that they probably paid vulnerable young women like my birth mother to sell their babies to "decent families". I've done a DNA test and put it up on the genealogy sites in the hope of getting a match with someone but that's a needle in a haystack at the moment. However, I'm not giving up just yet.'

'Good for you. What about downsides to living here? Is it as good as us mere earthlings think it is? There's gotta be something that doesn't work?'

'The only downside is the sky pool and personally I don't mind not having access to it – to tell you the truth it gives me the heebie-jeebies. I still can't get my head around how it stays up, all that water. Besides, we all have our own little plunge pools on our individual balconies, which is plenty for me. Our own little slice of heaven. But it's tough on Flo. Flo doesn't really understand why she can't use it. That's really the only reason I'm going to the party tonight, so she can try it.'

This was low even by Fox's standards, keeping the lower classes out of his slick Manhattan sky pool.

Suddenly, Marley looked panic-stricken '... but wait,

you won't write that, will you? I don't want to get evicted. Please just say how much I love it here and how life-changing it is for me and my daughter because it is! It really, really is life-changing! It's a huge opportunity for us to move up in our lives.'

I smiled. I knew that fear. 'Don't worry hon, this is a feature piece. It's about good luck, happiness, turning things around, it's supposed to be feel-good. I'm not going to write anything that would jeopardise your security. I'm on your side.' I had learned over the years that it didn't pay to burn anyone for the sake of a story – politicians, lawyers and property developers excepted of course – but ordinary decent folk were strictly off limits. And this kid had already been through so much. I was not about to make her collateral damage just so I could take a shot at Bryant Fox.

'I really hope getting this apartment is just the first step in your luck changing,' I said.

'Oh, I know it is,' she said with all of the certainty of faith of a twenty year old.

I thought back to how I had dealt with my own personal tragedies.

'You know, I was on my own too when I was your age. My father died young and my mother took it hard, got hooked on booze, couldn't cope. She died when I was still just a teenager. I had to look after myself. I found it really hard and I didn't have a kid to look after. I managed to hold on to our rent-controlled apartment, got a job at a local newspaper and thankfully social services were so backlogged that I had aged out by the time they got around to doing a welfare check on me.'

I could feel Vivian listening intently, even though he was staring at the CCTV screens.

'But you wanna hear something strange? Even though I had nobody, I learned to trust life. I had no safety net, no family, and yet there was something that made me feel calm, like, what was the worst that could happen? It had already happened in my opinion so I sort of ended up believing that the universe would look after me, and in its own way it kind of always has.'

Her face lit up. 'Yes! I totally believe the universe is working for my highest power too!'

'Wait, what? What the hell does that mean?'

She laughed. 'Manifesting! It's how I got this place ... Two beds, two baths, two reception rooms, a kitchen, storage, walk-in wardrobes, utility, parking and storage, more beautiful than anything I could ever have imagined for myself. This was the stroke of luck we needed to stand on our own two feet. We can finally put down roots. I have a path to buying ... all I have to do is stay here, keep my head down, and not get into trouble. I just know our luck has turned. Next up, I'm going to find my birth parents. This is New York City, after all. Miracles really do happen here.'

I started packing up my stuff. 'I'm sure you're right.' I smiled at her weakly. I really did hope she was right.

I had seen these stories so many times before. Some people just didn't want to be found.

'To think I might actually one day own a place in this building,' she sighed as she stood up. 'We might not belong yet – but one day we will and then nobody will be able to stop us using the sky pool. One thing I know for sure is the only way they'll get me out of here is feet first.'

'Let's hope it doesn't come to that,' I said with a laugh. But it rang hollow.

15

VIVIAN

A doorman shows a journalist the lie of the land

I waved Marley and Flo off and watched the journalist pack up her things. She had been kind to Marley and what she had said about her own difficult childhood made me view her in a new light. But I also knew that journalists would say anything to get what they wanted so I took it all with a pinch of salt. But she seemed sincere. And I wanted to believe that she had Marley's best interests at heart, but I thought I'd better spell it out, just in case.

'Hey, Eddie, you are going to write something positive about Marley, right? She's had it really tough and she's taking a risk talking to you for your piece.'

'What do you think I am, a *monster*?' she asked.

'That kid is a shining light of goodness. I'm not going to do anything to mess with that.'

I smiled and walked her past the bank of screens towards the door. I could see the people gathering on the pool terrace. It was going to be a busy party.

'This is all very high-tech,' Eddie said, stopping and staring at the various angles. 'I can barely work my smartphone. I'm constantly getting ribbed about it by the Gen Z dicks in my office,' she said. I got the impression she enjoyed letting them think she was a dumb Gen X-er before surprising them all with her knowledge.

'Well, it's very simple, really,' I said. 'Believe me, if I can use it, anyone can. Everything is so intuitive now. Look, it's as easy as a computer game. This wheel here selects which zone you want to see. This one controls the live feed. You can use touch-screen controls to scroll back and forward in the live feed. And then if you want to go back you just select the date and time of the file you want to access and you can call it up and scroll through, just like on a phone. Select, copy, cut, zoom, whatever you like ...'

'Impressive,' she said. 'I still think I'd probably delete everything if I touched it.'

'Well don't do that,' I warned her. 'I'd like to keep this job.'

She laughed and walked to the door. 'Hey, thanks for letting me use your apartment. I think Marley was much more relaxed having you there. You're really like a father to her, aren't you?'

I felt myself getting emotional, and cleared my throat. 'I try to be. She doesn't really have anyone else.'

I put my hand on the door handle and opened the door for her. 'OK, I'll take you up to the terrace now – ready to party?'

16

EDDIE

A night to remember

Vivian punched in the elevator code for the pool and I instantly memorised it. I didn't even mean to. It was just something I did automatically. I knew the access codes to half the doors, safes, alarms and buildings on the Upper West Side at this stage. An occupational hazard. It surprised me how simple the code to the pool terrace was. You could almost guess it after two or three goes. It should have been longer, harder, more complex, more random. There should be an elevator key for the people who lived here, or even just for Vivian, considering this elevator gave you access to some of the wealthiest homes and people in the city, but that would involve trusting someone like Vivian. These people never trusted anyone but their own. They say money can't buy you love but the thing money really can't buy you is common sense as far as I could see.

Still, I was curious to see the place.

'Have you been up here much, to the pool I mean?' I asked Vivian as the elevator rose silently.

'A couple of times. I've never actually been *in* it but I've been up and down to deliver parcels to the residents. It's not really my thing. A bit flashy. I swim in the pool on the ground floor. It's twenty-five metres long and eight lanes. A much better pool but hardly anyone uses it. Have you been up here yet,' Vivian asked.

I laughed out a dry chuckle that surprised even me with how bitter it sounded. 'I have not. I know I'm only here tonight because it suits the developers to have me here. I'm useful, for now.'

Vivian smiled.

When the elevator doors parted I was met with a vast view of the cityscape, twinkling over the sky pool. I caught my breath. Much as I hated to admit it, it really was something. Two servers held silver platters of drinks towards me as I stepped out of the elevator. I took a bottle of beer and allowed the magic of this city to take me over, just for a minute.

Vivian stayed inside the elevator. 'Enjoy your evening, Ms Wright,' he said, as the elevator doors whispered shut.

I looked around and it was like a fairy tale. Across

the sky pool I could see into apartments as people got on with their evenings. I forced myself to look away. I scanned the terrace instead and saw so many people from the past, from Juliet's past, that it made my head swim as if I was underwater. I stepped forward and it felt like stepping off a cliff.

17

VIVIAN

A reunion of sorts

'Big man!' The unmistakably irritating voice of Bryant Fox greeted me as I stepped off the elevator in the lobby. I tried to remind myself that he too had suffered the loss of a child when I felt myself being ungenerous. It's not that he was particularly terrible, it's just that he was fake. He didn't want to accept that there was such a huge gulf between him and the rest of humanity. He wanted to feel like an ordinary person. But the fact was, he wasn't and would never be.

'Hello, Mr Fox. All set for the party?' I kept things formal with Fox. Getting on familiar terms with someone like that was a fool's errand. He led you to believe you were friends, equals, until push came to shove and you were landed on your ass in the cold. I didn't need to be taught that lesson twice.

Fox came from generations of wealth. His great-grandparents established some of the first banks in New York but his mother had married in, and he used her upper-middle-class origins as the daughter of an accountant to sustain his man-of-the-people act.

'Everything's just great, Viv,' Bryant said, leaning over and giving me a firm, warm handshake, as if he were a presidential hopeful garnering votes.

'Do come upstairs for a drink too, won't you, Viv,' he added. 'Let your hair down a bit.'

'Very kind of you, Mr Fox,' I said, both of us knowing there was no way I would be having a drink at the party.

He flashed his brilliant smile, tastefully done, but still fake. 'And don't forget your budgie smugglers! It's a pool party after all.'

Christ, he was unbearable. Niceties out of the way, he leaned over the console desk and said in a conspiratorial tone, 'Listen, there'll be media, socialites, influencers, journalists all coming tonight, as well as the cost-rental residents,' he said meaningfully, 'so I'm relying on you to be my eyes and ears, OK? It wouldn't look good if the cost-rentals weren't ...' he searched for the right word, '*integrated*. Samsara is doing the PR and I told her to make sure that they are welcomed as much as possible by other residents but she had a lot of complaints at the residents' meeting last month. I mean, it's not like any of us wants them here but it is what it is. I'm just not sure she's entirely committed to putting on a united front tonight. If they're left standing apart or looking like they don't know anyone, well, it might look a bit, you know, *segregated*,' he whispered, dramatically. 'Do you know what I mean?'

I smiled stiffly and nodded, 'Of course, Mr Fox, no problem. I'll keep an eye on everything.'

I still couldn't quite get over how rich people acted as if being in a lower-income class made you a lower form of life. It was wealthy people who were the exception. They called them the one per cent for a reason – they were an extreme minority – and yet they acted like ordinary people were the aberrations. I had grown up in a utilitarian apartment but it was in Manhattan. The city was ours as much as theirs. Central Park was my playground, the library and galleries and museums were my university. Those were the days when ordinary hard-working people could still afford to live side by side with the wealthy in this city. It was a tapestry. Now we were being pushed out further or clinging desperately to the few tiny primitive rent-controlled apartments left in the city before they eventually found their way into the hands of vulture funds or foreign princesses who wanted to study in New York City for a few months. The city was losing its people, and if it wasn't careful it would lose its character too, just like had happened in London and countless other once-great cities around the world.

It must really be killing Fox to have Marley and Dave in his building, bringing down the tone as he saw it. But Fox was ultimately a businessman first and foremost. He knew he wasn't going to get planning without the cost-rental units but he also knew they didn't have to be of the same luxurious standard as the rest of the units. And it's also how he came up with the idea to block access to the 'premium facilities'. It said nothing in the planning laws about giving social housing tenants full privileges. So he had given them the bare minimum only. *Why should they get to use the pool?* Fox had casually said to me one day before the building opened. *They don't pay for it the way the rest of the residents do. They shouldn't even be here. And I don't hear them complaining. No, and that's because they know they're lucky to be here in the first place.* This attitude was why he was a good businessman, if not quite a good human being. Developers had become celebrities in New York during the noughties property boom. Bryant had teetered on the edge of infamous when the crash came, but it would take more than a global property crash to bring down someone like him. He didn't care about *people*. He cared about profit. He cared about things. Something that might have played into how and why his daughter ended up dead twenty years ago.

As if he hadn't been clear enough he said, 'The

planners are totally detached from reality. It's like they don't even get it; the reason people want to live in luxury developments like the Sky Building is precisely so they *don't* have to interact with people like, well, you know who I'm talking about. They shouldn't have to feel guilty about their lives, about their money … They don't want to be confronted at the pool or in the elevator. There has to be some reprieve. This kind of integration is frightening for them.'

That made me sad to think that New Yorkers could be so removed from their fellow men. That used to be one of the best parts of New York, all walks of life mingled, you could pass a movie star on the street one minute, a naked preacher the next. But now it was about sealing ourselves off from each other. Fox and his type had more to fear from their Ponzi-scheme investment banker neighbours than from people like Marley and Dave, but there was no explaining that to him.

'Why is it frightening … ? We used to all live side by side in this city.'

Fox looked at me as if he were seeing me for the first time and he said, 'Well, between you and me I think they don't like to be reminded that they could be poor too, that all this could one day go away. Not me, though. Tonight, everybody is my neighbour.' Fox didn't want bad publicity. That's why he was organising this grand opening party. A headache for me but necessary to show the various residents all mixing, all around the sky pool – everyone equal, everybody integrated in the class utopia of the Sky Building, in honour of Fox's daughter Juliet. I tried not to think of her and the thing I had kept hidden in the dark recess of my mind for twenty years, the thing that got me this job, the thing that could undo everything everybody thought they knew about the Juliet murder.

18

EDDIE

A journalist gets to know the neighbours

These apartments were not really apartments at all. They were enormous, totally different to Vivian's modest apartment, the servants' quarters I now realised. I spotted Dave standing on his own and made my way over to him. 'How's it going? You scrub up well,' I said.

'You didn't dress up?' he asked, slightly baffled.

'This is my best tux jacket . . .' I said, mock offended, then explained. 'Press privilege – the same rules don't apply to me as apply to you. Kinda like this place.'

Dave sipped a bottle of lite beer. 'You know, it's funny, but the one place this development reminds me most of is . . . prison.'

I scoffed. 'Really?'

'I'm not saying that my time inside was luxurious or anything, it's more like the way everything is the same, each apartment, the endless rules, the lack of privacy, the motion-sensor lights that blind you in the corridors, the CCTV observation, the unshakable feeling that you are about to be punished for a transgression you didn't know existed . . .'

I laughed. 'Well, when you put it like that I can see how it would.'

I looked across the courtyard at the triple-height apartment that led out onto the pool terrace, at the men talking animatedly inside. It looked like the lawyer Bentwell and his son-in-law William Black. 'What I don't get is why does it not bother these people to be constantly on display?' I pointed towards Bentwell and Black with my beer bottle. 'Take these two guys. It all looks a bit heated, doesn't it? Maybe they're used to people looking at them, maybe they like it, but me, I prefer a little privacy.'

'Maybe they just don't have anything to hide,' Dave said.

I gave him the kind of look that the comment de- served. 'Please, you're telling me the head of one of the biggest law firms in New York has nothing to hide? Besides, this is Manhattan. Everybody has a secret.'

'Oh yeah, and what's yours?' I ignored him.

I spotted Samsara Black across the way. I remem- bered her well from the Juliet case. She didn't look too different. Slightly more surprised, slightly more frozen, but recognisably herself. I looked around for Cleo but couldn't see her. I rarely saw Cleo these days. I was careful to avoid her where possible but I had seen her name on the guest list for tonight. We'd had a fling a few years back but it had ended. Amicably, but still, I always felt a little awkward as she had wanted to take things further and I just wasn't able to, so I always felt a bit embarrassed.

My eyes moved over the other guests at the party, making a mental list of the socialites I'd need to get a comment from. 'The women here are so perfect,' I said. 'It's eerie.'

'I can't tell them apart,' Dave said. 'They all look the same to me. Like skeletons with fake shiny skin stretched over the bones. They always look like they've been boiled or burned.'

'It's hard to believe women like that are even human. They look like exotic fruits, but don't be fooled, Dave. They all have hard stones at their centres, instead of hearts.'

He laughed.

'I read this thing once about food "styling", how it is someone's actual job to make food look delicious for photoshoots by spraying it with all sorts of glue and hairspray and lacquer and gunge so that it *looks* enticing and mouth-watering but is actually disgustingly inedible. I have this idea that that's what it takes to make women like these appear so perfect. What does she look like when you crack her open?'

I was a little creeped out by this and turned to show him my bemused face but he was staring across at Samsara. 'The woman over there, from the triplex, she's a bit like that, I think. Looks utterly perfect but it feels a little uncanny.'

'Maybe it's just as banal an explanation as wealth,' I suggested. 'Wealth has so many tells, from the basics of manicured fingernails and soft skin, to the bigger reveals of your zip code and how you travel. I see it all the time at parties like this. There are so many ways we can't escape how money betrays us, even when we're trying to hide.' People say wealth whispers but sometimes it sounds like a scream.

I made my way through the party, stopping here and there to take a comment from a prominent broadcaster, a well-known philanthropist. I felt that old impatience rising up in me, the one that made me want to drop everything and focus on the Juliet story. But I had learned over the years that my impatience got me into trouble. *Easy*, I told myself. I grabbed a fistful of canapés from a passing tray and shoved them into my mouth. I dropped one on my blouse. *Hell!* I smeared it away with a napkin. It left an unsightly stain but I wasn't here to win a beauty contest.

I needed to calm down, appear normal. I was too

amped up. I spotted the PR and grabbed her. Was it just me or did every young professional woman look like a TV anchor now? Immaculate hair and full make-up, primary-coloured dress and heels, groomed to perfection. This was an everyday standard now: ridiculous. What happened to having a shower, putting on a white shirt and blazer and being ready? These women were wasting their lives in front of a mirror.

'Hey Grace,' I hissed. 'I think I have spoken to everyone I need for my piece. I just need a word with Bryant and I'll be done.'

Grace tried to rearrange her expression from disgust to professional. It was a common reaction to me. 'Just give me a minute,' she said. 'I'll be right back.'

We saw each other at the same moment. She looked as drop-dead gorgeous as ever. A tiny black woollen dress with a plunging neckline, vertiginous hemline and long sleeves to keep it demure. Her blonde hair was loose around her shoulders. She looked both effortless and immaculate. How had I ever said no to this woman? As she closed the distance between us, I found myself wondering if she still smelled the same, that gentle perfume, mild enough not to be distracting, distinct enough to make a statement. Hair, face, clothes, silky blonde hair, she looked like a contemporary Grace Kelly.

'Cleo!' the PR drawled. 'Let me introduce you to Eddie Wright from the *Post*. She's doing a story on the launch ... I'll be right back with Bryant.'

'How do you do?' she said, as if it was her first time meeting me.

I wiped my hand on my jeans and played along, taking Cleo's delicate extended hand in mine. It felt good to touch her again, even just in this way. I caught the faintest hint of her perfume, and tumbled down an olfactory rabbit hole. It was sparkling, like diamonds if they had a smell. Clean and cool and sensual and expensive all at once. Dangerous and sharp too, I remembered. Just like Cleo. Things hadn't worked out with us before. She wanted more than I could offer her at the time but I had always felt as if she too had held back a little of herself. Maybe we had both moved on. It seemed all of the ghosts from my past were coming out to play tonight.

19

CLEO

An old flame

I had always liked Eddie. She was the exception to my general rule of disliking journalists, and ex-lovers. Partly because she was a straight shooter, and partly because she was the only person I've ever wanted a relationship with. It was me who had said I hadn't wanted a relationship at first. They were always my terms for getting involved with someone, and I had never been compelled to change them. But with her, I had changed my mind. And I had messed things up. I came on too strong and she got cold feet. And that was the end of that. We stayed friendly, though. I always had a use for a friendly journalist. And she was a great journalist, even if she had been in the sin bin for the last twenty years. The thing about her was she never interpreted, always simply reported, but she knew *what* to report, *which* facts would allow people to interpret for themselves. I braced myself. Even though she was not glamorous or beautiful strictly speaking, and she was a lot older than me, something about her made my heart skip a beat. I tried to quell that old feeling again.

When the PR left us, I dropped the pretence and smiled warmly.

'You look well,' Eddie said.

'Thank you,' I said. 'I wish I could say the same for you.'

She got the joke. 'Us lowly journalists can barely afford to dress ourselves, never mind in the latest fashions like you wealthy lawyers. How've you been? It's been a while . . .'

'You know, keeping busy . . .'

She held my gaze. There was still something there. What was it about her? I could never put my finger on it but it was always there, whatever it was.

'So, seeing anybody?' I asked.

'Nah, I don't have time,' Eddie said.

'Me neither,' I said, meaningfully. It somehow felt important to let Eddie know that I was still single after all these years. I wanted to leave a door open. Despite her clothes, and her face, which looked a little like an undercooked scone, I still felt an irresistible pull towards her. Out of everybody in this room, she was the one I wanted to talk to.

I saw Bentwell moving in the throng. She clocked him too. 'That guy is such a dick. They destroyed an innocent man's life by putting him away for Juliet's murder.'

I gave a sympathetic tilt of my head but that was the extent of my ability to offer opinions on anyone in the legal community, especially to Eddie, who was, after all, still a journalist.

'So, you're writing an article on the opening?'

'Yes, but a bigger piece too, on Juliet's murder, and the possibility of it being unsolved. There are some very interesting people in this building this evening, people who go back a *long* way – Samsara, William Black . . . They were all close to Juliet, all at the same party the night she died. You probably knew them too, right?'

I shook my head. 'I was a few years younger than that crowd, but I knew who they were. And everybody knew Juliet. Why do you think the murder merits revisiting?'

'William Black's alibi. It was dodgy. We never even got to know who the alibi was because whoever they were, they were a minor at the time so their name was never public. But there were witnesses who saw William leave the party an hour later than he claimed to have done. And Dave *saw* William in the alley,' Eddie said, her voice vehement with passion.

'Even if that's true,' I said. 'I'm not sure what can be done about it now. The guy who did the crime only served a few years, no real harm done. It's all too far in the past, I would have thought. They obviously never found any conclusive evidence that could convict someone else.'

'*Exactly,*' Eddie said, 'and equally nothing conclusive enough to put a kid away for murder.' She moved in close to me and I caught my breath. I could feel her body heat, and the strangely erotic smell of her cooled and reactivated sweat. 'Can you keep a secret?'

'I've built a multi-million-dollar business on my ability to do just that,' I said.

'Well,' Eddie said, 'the guy who went to prison for Juliet's murder? He's here, at this party. He *lives* in this building … Another coincidence or someone's guilty conscience pulling strings to pay recompense for him taking the fall for them?'

'Do the other residents know?' I asked.

'Do you think he'd still be living here if they did?' Eddie said. 'You don't seem surprised, though, Cleo … you already knew?'

I shrugged. 'I don't forget legal cases. I can't afford to.'

Eddie slugged some more beer and watched the other guests.

'I don't see what the residents could do anyway,' I said. 'It's not illegal for him to be here, to live here … and surely he needs a second chance more than most. You're not going to write about it, are you?'

'So your neighbours can get all hysterical and form a

witch-hunt committee to evict him from the building? I don't think so. You people have put him through enough. I won't be blowing his cover. I want to help him. I know he didn't kill Juliet.'

She finished the rest of her drink with a loud, satisfied smack of her lips. 'What about you? Got any hot tips to share with an old friend before I go do my job?'

'Hmmm. Like I said, my business depends on me keeping everybody's secrets ...'

But there were a few secrets that I would like to share with Eddie.

A squeal of feedback announced Bryant Fox over the PA system.

'I'd like to thank everyone for being here tonight and if I could ask you to charge your glasses, please, I'd like to share some important news. Tonight doesn't only mark the beginning of a new relationship with the housing authority – what I hope will be a very long relationship – it also marks the official opening of the Sky Building, which I hope will be a model for how we as people from all corners of our community can live together as neighbours and friends, without any of the divisions that have historically kept us apart. By offering different integrated levels of housing for people from all backgrounds and financial brackets, we hope to build an authentic community of New Yorkers in a model that will be replicated by other developers in the future. Don't call me a communist—' he smirked to a smattering of laughter '—but I like to think of this housing model as meeting everybody where they're at – if you're a single mom starting out in life or a financier on Wall Street, there is a home for you in the Sky Building.'

I felt the urge to roll my eyes but clamped down on my eyeballs as best I could. 'Home is a place where we should feel safe, and my promise to every single resident in this visionary development is that everyone is safe here, living as equals ...'

'Equal, just not equal access to facilities,' Eddie muttered under her breath.

'... side by side, as neighbours, as the kind of community we have forgotten how to be in this great city, the kind of community who knows each other, helps each other, socialises with each other. So please raise your glasses for a toast— to friends and neighbours!'

Fox waited for the applause to subside before he started talking again.

'We are launching a new charity tonight aimed at helping young people in disadvantaged areas to get on the housing ladder, to buy their first property. I'm setting up an investment account with five hundred dollars for every child born in a five-mile radius, which will be available to them when they turn twenty-one to use exclusively against a mortgage. These are high-yield accounts. These funds can only be used in conjunction with a house purchase, so no parent can access the money and spend it on a seventy-five-inch television. I'm calling it the Juliet Fund, in honour of my late daughter, and I hope it will turn things around for the community who trusted me to build my projects in their neighbourhoods, who didn't object to the planners, who trusted in my vision of community. Now please,' he said over the applause, 'try the sky pool ... it feels like flying! And at the very least let's all have a boogie and enjoy the rest of the evening.' A DJ appeared from somewhere and started blaring noughties classics, the kind that nobody could resist dancing to, whether ironically or in earnest. Bryant did the latter but it was so bad it looked like the former.

'Jesus Christ,' Eddie said. 'My eyes!'

I had to laugh. 'You're not sold on the man of the people act?' I asked her.

'I am not. His business practices tell a different story. You can be sure nobody's going to see a single penny of that mortgage fund. You know the terms and conditions say that if you don't use it in one year of the fund maturing it reverts to Fox Developments. What twenty-one-year-old kid is going to have their shit together to avail of that? That's a tax break if ever I saw one. You don't seem to be drinking the social utopia Kool-Aid either, though,' she said.

'The community he's talking about building is the kind of community he consistently tears down to make

95

way for his buildings. But something tells me you're already digging into that, amongst other things?'

'You still know me too well,' Eddie said, and she clinked my glass.

'Not as well as I once did . . . not as well as I'd like to again.' I thought I had come on too strong but she held my gaze, her eyes swimming with emotion.

'That is one of the first things I have heard all night that I can honestly drink to.'

20

CLEO

Making a splash

Our moment was interrupted by Grace the PR, who had Bryant Fox with her, as promised.

'Cleo, looking beautiful,' Fox said, slithering towards me. He made to plant a kiss on my cheek but I blocked him, pivoting and raising my glass high between us, as if to toast him. These guys never got bored of trying to press some area of their bodies against mine, but I had decades of practice defending a wide exclusion zone around my body.

'Mr Fox, congratulations. You must be very proud tonight,' I said.

'Thank you, Cleo. It's been a long road but I knew we'd get here and now it's already being called the jewel in the crown of the city's skyline. Did you see the piece in the *New York Times* at the weekend? I am so pleased with how it's all turned out, especially considering the buildings that are starting to lean downtown. Fine for Pisa, not for Manhattan. How about you? How are you settling in?'

'Oh well, it's an adjustment,' I said. 'Living in a shared building like this is new to me but the commute from my brownstone in Brooklyn was actually killing me and there is something about living in a building like this with a doorman, proper security, that makes it feel so much safer, you know, particularly as a woman.'

A shadow crossed his face. I felt momentarily guilty when I realised he must be thinking about Juliet. But the shadow passed like a scudding cloud and he said, 'I find it hard to believe that New York's finest legal defender isn't safe wherever she goes.'

I smiled. 'Not everyone is happy when the accused are proven innocent . . .'

'. . . or when the guilty walk free,' he added, wolfishly.

Eddie interrupted, 'Mr Fox? I'm Eddie Wright, with *The Post*, you know, the other paper? Can I get a few words for the diary?' She didn't wait for him to answer but launched instead into a question. 'You are one of the first developers to adopt the new planning laws requiring a percentage of all housing to be siloed for social housing. How do the owners feel about the mixed nature of the tenancies, blending rent-control tenants with, well, wealthy owner-occupiers? Any issues?'

She really was no small talk.

'My own mother didn't come from money ...' *never missed an opportunity* '... so I think it can only be a good thing for the city to break down the divisions of wealth and class,' he said. 'It's what's wrong with this city. I've yet to meet the cost-rental tenants but I am hoping to do so over the coming weeks and months, and I hope they can feel at home here in the Sky Building.'

Just then someone screamed '*Cannonbaaaaaalllll!!*' and we were showered in a spray of pool water.

'Flo!' a young woman shouted as she dashed towards the sky pool and Eddie took off after her.

21

EDDIE

A girl makes an enemy

Marley looked terror-stricken, like she might be thrown out any minute. She started to tremble. I went to her. She was balancing a canapé, a glass of champagne, a tiny handbag, her phone and a wallet. 'Here, can I hold something for you?' I asked.

'Oh, thank you,' she said, handing over her phone and wallet. I shoved them in my satchel and stepped between her and the guy who was glowering at her. William Black.

'Hey,' I said to her, 'hey, it's OK. Look at me. Nothing's wrong. Nothing's going to happen.'

She was on the verge of tears. William Black was standing with his arms out, horrified at the few flecks of water that marked his shirt.

'Idiot,' he muttered loudly as Marley pulled Flo and her unicorn floaty from the pool. 'You should control your daughter,' he said loudly and directly to Marley.

'I'm so sorry. It won't happen again,' she said, her voice small and quiet.

'This is why these people don't have access to the pool,' he said to the few people gathered around him. 'They can't be trusted not to act like savages.'

'Hey, there's no need for that,' I said. 'She's just a kid having fun. Weren't you ever a kid?'

'Who asked you?' William said.

'I don't need to be asked when I see someone being rude. I'm here to report on the beautiful social utopia of the Sky Building for the *New York Post* so I'm just taking notes ... and I have to say, it's not looking so idyllic from this vantage point. Nothing like Bryant Fox just described ...'

A skeletal blonde presence oozed up beside me. 'Hi, I'm Samsara Black ... What seems to be the problem here?'

'This rug rat has gone feral in the pool and destroyed my custom Valentino ...'

I couldn't help but stifle a giggle. 'It's a white cotton shirt, for Chrissakes. It's not like she spilled a glass of red wine on him.'

'William darling, why don't you go change ...'

But I wasn't happy to let him go. I wanted to humiliate him the way he had just humiliated Marley and Flo. 'Hey,' I said, 'don't I recognise you?'

'I can't imagine from where,' he said.

'No, I do,' I said, making my voice louder for every-one to hear. 'Weren't you a suspect in the murder of Juliet Fox? It is you, isn't it? I knew it, I never forget a face ...' I'll admit I was deliberately being a dick now but I wanted to provoke him.

'You're mistaken,' he said. 'Juliet was a dear family friend. Now if you don't mind, I'm soaking wet.'

I was goading him now. 'Oh, I wouldn't call that soaking wet,' I said, standing firm in his path.

'Jesus, I'm surrounded by morons ...' he said, pinching the bridge of his nose, as if it was a patience-secreting gland.

He went to side-step me but misplaced his pointed leather shoe. It seemed to happen in slow motion, as these things so often do. A small crowd had gathered around my raised voice and they let out a pantomime gasp as William lost his footing. He did that thing people do where they try valiantly to stop themselves from falling, a bit like Roadrunner spinning his legs in thin air even though he has overshot the edge of the cliff. It was painful, pathetic and embarrassing to watch. And it seemed to take forever.

I stepped forward to grab his elbow or arm or any-thing I could to try and save him. The last thing anyone needed was for him to go down and crack his head on the terrazzo tile and sue me for his injuries. But instead of breaking his fall, he grabbed onto me as if his life depended on it and dragged us both into the sky pool. We fell through the water holding onto each other, eyes locked. I could see the city beneath us, an unsettling feeling as I floated above lines of traffic inching up and down the avenue. I rolled over and saw the distorted figures of the people at the edge of the pool.

I broke the surface and dragged myself out of the water. William came up gasping and spluttering as if he had fallen into a vast ocean and not a 1.4m deep swimming pool. He coughed and choked and gasped. I crouched down and pulled him out.

I laughed. 'OK, *now* you're soaking wet,' I said, in an attempt to break the tension and make light of his previous behaviour. 'It wouldn't be a pool party if we didn't get wet, right?' Why was it always women trying to smooth these things over? But I needn't have bothered. He couldn't see the funny side.

He ignored me and turned to Samsara. 'I want that girl and her kid out of here by the end of the month.'

22

EDDIE

An empty space at the centre of everything

The city skyline was lighting up as twilight fell. I stood dripping on the terrace beside Samsara. I never understood how these people lived the way they did – get married, consolidate familial wealth, propagate, preferably a male heir, and above all don't get divorced. Put up a good front. Never show what's going on behind the scenes. William and Samsara looked like they hated each other. I presumed they would live separate lives as soon as their kid was in college. I watched him with his mother now. He was complaining about how embarrassing his father was, while Samsara was acting as if nothing had happened. These people were all about saving face. Bad behaviour was the norm. Nobody batted an eyelid. Maybe because nothing ever

104

went wrong that couldn't be made right by their parents, or cousins, or old boys' network or, failing that, cold hard cash.

I squelched closer to them and heard him say, 'No, Mom, it's mortifying. I'm going to work on my biology project.'

It was time for me to call it a night too. Maybe it was the twentieth anniversary that was getting to me. It didn't feel like so many years had passed. Two decades of *my life*, never coming back. Twenty years I had been thinking about this story, trying to solve this mystery, ignoring the people who loved me, pushing them away until they eventually gave up and left. And what did I have to show for it? The story was still a mystery. And I was still alone.

Remembering that summer, the party, the murder, the tabloids, the court case, the anniversaries, how the police closed ranks and how the Bentwells suffocated Dave's defence into submission. I pushed the elevator button and waited. Everything was getting stirred up again and I could feel my head spinning with the effort of wrestling the facts into their place. Something just wouldn't fit, like a jigsaw piece that looked right but somehow wasn't. The whole picture was skewed. If I could just unlock the one wrong piece everything would fall into place.

The doors opened and I stepped in, like an underwater creature. I wondered could I handle going back to this story. But what more could it take from me? I had already lost everything. I would find it this time. This time I would discover the truth. This time I would end it.

23

VIVIAN

There's no place like home

I stood at my console desk in the lobby. Most of the guests have left. Anyone remaining was either a resident or being rounded up by party security. My formal uniform's tassels made me look like something out of a period drama. Thankfully, this was for formal occasions only, but I didn't mind it so much. It reminded me of the old days.

In this part of town, luxury used to mean the giant old townhouses that still had servants' quarters and coach houses out the back that were now renovated into party rooms or gyms or office spaces. But buildings like the Sky Building were introducing a new template for luxury.

When I first started working as a doorman, people

wanted their homes to look like homes, places to display their family heirlooms, places that had evidence of
generations of breeding. Now rich people wanted their
houses to look like blank canvases, hotels, business
centres, spaces to pass through, which upon consid-
eration was probably exactly what they were. I could
understand the desire to have a restful space, something
that allowed you to zone out, particularly if you worked
in something stressful like wealth management, but I
couldn't understand the need to eradicate all evidence
of a personal life. I never knew there were so many
shades of beige until I started working here. Still, in a
way, I was grateful for the blandness. My blank room
was a welcome respite after the constant memories that
assailed me in my old studio apartment. Everywhere I
looked had been a painful reminder of Dodi. I had let
it go to wrack and ruin, paralysed by the depression
that seemed to emanate from photo frames, the New
York Marathon medals that Dodi had collected over the
years (she always walked the marathon but raised thou-
sands for children's charities, as if by doing so she could
reduce the pain of having lost our precious daughter).

I knew Dodi had her own pain as a mother, but I
had been devastated by Lucy's death too. As the years
passed I had yearned for another child but we were too
old, and then the pain started afresh when our peers
started having grandchildren and I realised that was
something I would never experience either. That's why

I had become so attached to Marley and Flo. Some of the most enjoyable months of my life had been spent working with the girls and women in that shelter. It was a balm on the raw spot that had been left by Lucy, like I was connecting with the experience of being a father again. I had learned so much over the past few years about home, and family, and how very little we need to be happy in this world. Those women taught me that. All you needed were a few simple things. The first thing you need is safety. If there is danger, there can be no peace. Some of them preferred to be homeless than to live in a house with a violent or dangerous man. The second thing you need is kindness. If there is no kindness there is no love. And without love there is no home. I thought maybe I should check on Marley before I turned in for the night. William Black had gone pretty hard on her earlier on.

'Vivian, come in . . . is everything OK?'

'I just wanted to check in, make sure you're OK after what happened at the pool.'

'Oh, yeah. It gave me a bit of a fright but I don't think he can do anything about it. I spoke to a lawyer who was there, and he said I had done nothing wrong, that I was an invited guest and that guy was just blowing off steam.'

'Who was that?' I asked.

'Bentwell was his name, probably around the same age as you,' she said.

'That's Samsara's dad, William's father-in-law. I guess there's not much love lost there.'

'Oh my god, I'm glad I didn't badmouth him,' she giggled nervously. 'I just really don't want anything to endanger our lease here. When I came home here tonight it made me realise I have nobody. If I had a mom I would have called her, told her about everything and she could have told me things would work out. I really want to find my birth mom.'

A light went on across the courtyard and we both looked at the glamorous woman pouring herself a glass of wine.

'Who's that?' Marley asked. 'I saw her at the party.'

'That is Cleo Fry,' I told her. 'Hotshot defence lawyer. Totally independent. Single. No kids. Rich as Croesus. Bought that apartment in cold hard cash, paid for it herself. Unlike Samsara,' I said, smiling. I knew Marley liked the gossip about the rich residents. It was like a soap opera to her and I knew I could trust her.

'A lawyer? She looks like a movie star ... Imagine being a hotshot lawyer. I'm going to be like her one day. I might be working and studying for another ten years until I get there but I will get there.' A silence passed between us. 'What do you think it's like to grow up like that, Vivian, to know exactly who you are and where you come from and who you belong to and where you're going and, if you should falter, who will catch you. What must it feel like to be so tightly enclosed inside a family, to know that no matter how badly you mess up, there will always be support, a job, a monthly allowance to hold you up while you find your way back. Every day I walk a high wire through this world without a safety net. One false move would see me and Flo spinning through space.'

'Are you sure you want to continue down this road of looking for your birth mother, Marley? It might bring up all sorts of unexpected things . . .'

'Like what?' she asked.

'I don't know, people who don't want to be found? People who might not be good for you, who might unsettle your life . . . I have a friend who discovered in his eighties that he has a sixty-year-old daughter. Can you imagine that? Apparently she was the product of a brief fling one summer the year before he got married. He never knew about her. I think there are probably a lot of people like that out there, walking around, related to people and they don't even know it. So just be careful what you wish for.'

A silence floated between us before she asked, 'Do you ever wonder whether you might have a child like that, Vivian, the product of a night of passion . . .' She laughed, but I didn't.

'Well, like you, Marley, I never really knew my family. My parents died young and us kids were separated and put into care. We stayed in touch but we were never a proper family again. My wife, Dodi, who I told

111

you about before, well, she became my family. We had a daughter too but she died when she was just thirteen.'

Marley gasped. 'Oh, Vivian, I had no idea.'

'She would be thirty-eight now. I'm afraid to say we never really got over it. It's not something you get over.'

'I can imagine what an amazing dad you were. You've been like a father to me and Flo.'

Flo was softly singing to herself in her bedroom.

'Come on, why don't you do a test, it's so easy. See if we can find any distant relatives.'

'Oh, I don't think so,' I said. 'I'm too old for surprises. Try not to worry too much,' I told her. 'You'll get there. Your luck is already on the up.'

'You're right,' she said. 'Thanks, Vivian.'

I stood to leave. 'Text me if you need anything.'

Marley's eyes went wide and she gasped, 'my phone! I gave it to Eddie to hold and forgot to get it back ... Don't worry, I can use my iPad to WhatsApp you if I need anything. I'll get my phone back tomorrow.'

'Alright, but lock this door behind me, OK?'

'Vivian, nothing bad could ever happen in a place like this.'

Experience told me otherwise.

24

EDDIE

A safe haven

I walked west towards Ninth Avenue with a few odd looks from passers-by. I ignored them. If a soaking-wet woman was the strangest thing they had seen on the streets of New York City they didn't belong here. I needed to order my thoughts. I liked walking, not for the exercise but for what it did for my head. Not everything had to be about losing weight. I never worried about being attacked. That was one of the benefits about being a woman of a certain age. And I was of this city. My fellow natives recognised me and kept their powder dry for softer options.

When I got home I stripped off my cold wet clothes and looked around my flat. It was a depressing vista, particularly following the evening's location. I clicked the gas on my stove and put the kettle on the ring, let it work on boiling. My bones felt weary, my skin sat heavy on me. I pulled the table top off the tub and let the shower head run until it steamed. I stood under the stream until the kettle started to whistle.

I sat in a towel, warming up with my tea. I looked at the window ledge which was piled with detritus: business cards, lidless pens, scraps of paper with numbers scribbled on them, elastic bands, spare buttons. Would it matter if I swept those things off the windowsill and directly into the bin? Was I really ever going to follow up on any of those items? When was the last time I had sewn a button onto anything? Did I even possess a needle and thread? Some clean, rumpled laundry sat piled on the end of the couch. The flat was clean but it was a mess and I didn't seem to have the wherewithal to update it or even manage it. It was as if an invisible gravity took hold of me as soon as I crossed the threshold, weighing me down so that I became helpless in the face of my hovel. I could have transformed this place, decorated it, paid someone to decorate it, but I was paralysed the minute I entered its atmosphere. A shrink might say I couldn't move on from my past until I got closure on the unresolved mystery of Juliet's murder. And maybe that was it. Part of me felt that if I could just find the missing piece in the Juliet murder, maybe my life would fall back into place too. My eyes flitted over the dishevelled room. A cheap bedside locker that my mother had bought, mismatched furniture, a light with peeling paint that heated up and smelled if you left the bulb burning for too long. What would Cleo Fry think of this place, I wondered, and the thought made me laugh. To think I might now be living in the Sky Building with Cleo if I hadn't messed that up too. But I had never known what was good for me. I put my mug in the sink and dragged myself and my laptop bag towards the bed, where I would write up the bones of my column, then set my alarm for 5 a.m., when I could read over the piece with fresh, or less exhausted, eyes and tidy it up before sending it for publication at 6 a.m. I opened my satchel and saw inside Marley's phone and wallet. *Shit.* Bed would have to wait.

25

CLEO

Marley's family tree

I kicked off my shoes the second I got into my apartment. I poured a glass of wine and sipped. Peace at last. I looked across the courtyard. I could see him moving around his apartment. He never seemed to relax. He didn't look ready for bed. There was no difference in how he held himself outside and inside of his apartment. I had seen him in the lobby, and he was as stiff there as he was now at home. The other residents picked their noses, scratched their butts and picked toenails as if we weren't all living in a glass building watching each other, but *he* never seemed to let his guard slip. I knew he had been in the army. Vivian told me that. Perhaps that communal regimented lifestyle had led to this impressive self-control.

I watched him work out. I wondered: is this how women feel when they're attracted to men? I rarely saw a man that struck me as attractive. Men were most often an irritation, with their unsubtle and unsolicited hands underneath my elbow, on my shoulder, small-of-my-back, all the usual spots, all the usual lines crossed. They made me want to punch walls.

I rarely thought of my body's physical needs. Most days I was consumed by one of two things – my cases or my guilt. Most days I treated my body the same way a carer treats a patient, something to be washed and dressed and fed to prepare for another day in the world. I rarely *inhabited* my body, my *physicality*. Mostly I just felt like a brain in a jar. But it was short-lived. My peace was short-lived. My phone buzzed. What fresh hell ...

A WhatsApp message from a number I didn't recognise.

> Hi Cleo, My name is Marley. I live downstairs. I got your number from the building WhatsApp group, I hope you don't mind. I was hoping we could talk? Do you have a minute?

The girl whose kid splashed William, she was called Marley.

I shrugged. No rest for the wicked, I suppose.

I texted back:

Sure, how about tomorrow evening after work?

Her reply came back almost instantaneously.

Please, It's important. I need to talk to you.
Tonight. I'm in apartment 3B. Can you come now?

Would this day never end? I sighed.

I'll be right down.

26

CLEO

A hotshot lawyer still has to take out the trash

My feet were killing me after an evening standing in heels and a formal dress so I dressed quickly in sweat pants and a tee, and slipped on my clogs. I grabbed the garbage and recycling from the kitchen. Might as well kill two birds with one stone, I thought, as I made my way to the elevator. I walked to the central garbage chute for my floor. *Out of order.* 'What kind of luxury building is this supposed to be?' I wondered aloud. I walked to the elevator bank and hit the button for the basement. The elevator stopped and the doors parted to reveal ... him.

A stranger is just a friend you haven't met yet.

His face broke into a friendly smile. Fear started beating through my veins. I could feel its pulse in my fingertips, hear it forcing blood through my ears like a rushing river. He must have been 6′4″, but he looked bigger because his body was enormous too from the daily pushing and pulling of the machine that took up his living room. The vast expanse of chest and biceps strained against t-shirt sleeves, pecs and delts bursting forth. I reminded myself he was just a stranger; if I didn't know who he was, I would not be scared of stepping into an elevator with him.

'Are they for the trash?' he asked, pointing at my bags.

At last I found my voice. 'Oh, yes, the garbage chute is broken – already! – I guess luxury condos still have the same old problems as ordinary buildings.'

'May I?' He took the bags out of my hands before I had a chance to answer. 'Cleo, right,' he said as we rode the elevator down to the basement. 'You're in the pool penthouse?'

I looked at him. *Say something.*

'Sorry,' he said, 'that sounds creepy … I'm Dave. I live across the way, sort of, well, diagonally across the way. The east tower.'

'Nice to meet you, Dave.' I extended my hand. I was grateful it was cool and dry, if not perfectly still. He took it, and an actual electric shock passed between our fingers. He laughed, 'Sorry, it's the bags.'

It wasn't the bags. It was the adrenaline pumping around my body.

'Cleo's a nice name,' he said. 'Unusual ... I knew a Cleo once – a long time ago. I've always thought it was a pretty name.'

Every hair on my neck stood on end. I was aware of everything: my hair, his eyes, my body, his hands, my breath still heaving to escape from my chest. An uncomfortable silence descended.

I smiled.

'So how long have you lived here?' he asked.

'Oh, just a month,' I said, attempting a smile as we arrived at the little walled-off area that enclosed several industrial-sized dumpsters, separated into category. He lifted the lid of the large black bin and dropped my trash in, as if it weighed nothing.

We walked back to the elevator bank in awkward silence.

'So,' he said.

He stepped closer to me. I held my breath. He leaned over and I braced myself but he just said, 'excuse me' and with a bemused expression leaned in to press the elevator call button.

The elevator arrived and we stepped inside. The silence grew like a bubble inside the elevator car. He looked at me, expectantly.

What now?

'Fifth floor?' he asked with a smile.

Idiot.

'Oh, no, third. I need to make a stop first.'

121

'So ... did you enjoy the party? How about that pool?' he asked as the lift rose.

I smiled. 'I haven't tried the pool yet.' I shrugged. 'Work.'

'How about you, did you enjoy it?'

'I did. I don't really know anyone in the building yet so it was a good opportunity for me to ... get to know the neighbours. The people who live here are not exactly within my social circle, if you know what I mean.'

'Oh yeah?' I asked.

'I grew up a little north of here,' he said. 'Harlem.'

'Oh!'

'It was a wonderful community. Everyone knew everybody back then. And we looked out for each other too. It would be nice to foster some of that attitude here, although I don't know if people are like that anywhere any more. People seem to prefer their privacy, their own bubble, insulated lives. Although there's not much privacy here.' He laughed, referring to the glass elevator and the fact that most of the building seemed to be glass.

I smiled. 'It's true. I already feel like I know everyone too intimately, even people I haven't met. And worse, they know me!'

He laughed. 'I know what you mean. No secrets here.'

Had he watched me the way I had watched him? Had he seen me watching him? I had been careful, or so I had thought.

'Still,' he said. 'You can't be too careful these days ...'

The elevator bell dinged on the third floor and he smiled and said, 'After you.'

We walked down the corridor together until he got to his apartment. 'Well, this is me. Nice to meet you, neighbour. See you around.'

As he began to close his door, I finally found my voice and I called out ...

'Dave?'

He pulled the door back. 'You're right, you know. People don't look out for each other enough any more. We should know our neighbours. Why don't you drop by my place for a beer tomorrow evening if you're free? Let me thank you for taking out my trash?'

I couldn't believe I was saying it. Nor could I believe it when a smile broke out over his face that felt so powerful I thought I should shield myself from it.

'Really? I'd love that, yeah.'

'Great,' I said. 'Say eight o'clock?'

'Perfect.'

27

VIVIAN

A private afterparty

I straightened the phone and looked around the lobby, doing my final checks. The place was immaculate. It gave me a sense of pride. It was such a relief to finally stop worrying about where I would die. I wasn't sure when I would die – I knew I didn't have very long – but at least I had certainty about *where* I would take my last breath. As the final partygoers left, along with the security detail, I switched the console phone over to night mode. I closed my apartment door behind me and woke up the bank of security screens that sat inside the communications centre in the lobby of my apartment. I was expected to 'casually' monitor these when I was at home. Nothing legally binding, but just if I happened to notice anything untoward or suspicious outside of office hours, I should log it or alert the necessary authorities.

My concierge quarters were small and spartan but comfortable. I imagined it as a Japanese Zen monk's cell. Blond wooden floors, underfloor heating that kept the apartment at an ambient temperature – never too hot or too cold – air exchange that meant it was never stuffy. It had all sorts of design features that took me weeks to figure out. The best part was there were no memories. It allowed me to think, to imagine all the ways I might settle the score before time ran out.

The job was easy. I accepted packages from delivery drivers all day and dealt with email requests from the residents, asking me everything from how to unblock a toilet to whether I could bring them an avocado. No job was too big, no detail too small. I never ceased to marvel at these people, how they had been formed, what the factors were that went into making them think that it was OK to delegate the task of seeking out a single piece of fruit to a doorman. I wondered how happy they actually were, but when I turned my key in the door of Apt A at 7 p.m. every evening, I knew I would seek out the most perfectly ripe avocados all day long if I needed to, for the reward of living in this building. I got to wake up every day, have a hot shower, shave, comb what was left of my hair, put on a clean shirt and tie and walk out the door with purpose in my step. Not many people my age got to do that. People spoke to me, looked to me, *needed me*. If I needed them too, they didn't need to know that. They kept me busy; kept me focused, kept my mind from wandering too far down the dark road of the past and thinking too much about the dark road of my future plans.

I walked over to the little island in the ivory and beige kitchen; Nantucket, the agency had told me when I was moving in, as if I should know what that meant. I put some rye bread in the toaster and when it popped I smeared it with a layer of peanut butter, and sliced a banana on top. Fibre. Important now. I pulled a beer from the fridge, lite to keep my cardiologist happy, and I sat down on the corner couch with the chaise extension, from where I could see the CCTV screens and people coming and going. It's amazing how easily they forgot they were being watched. Smile, I thought. I looked at Marley's floor from time to time and saw people coming and going there too. Dave, who lived on that floor, and Cleo – what was she doing there? Then later a man in a baseball cap. He looked familiar. And the journalist, Eddie? Oh yeah, she must be returning Marley's phone. An hour or more passed in this way until I cleared away the bottle and my plate, made the apartment tidy again. I was weary and my bed was calling to me so I lay down and listened to the humming of the CCTV and what I thought was the safe silence of the building.

28

CLEO

A familiar name echoes down the years

A child's toys were scattered across a little cotton rug. 'Cleo, thank you so much for coming. Would you like some tea? I'm making some for myself.'

'Sure,' I said. She brought two peppermint teas over to the coffee table and sat beside me on the couch.

'I like what you've done with your place, it looks great.'

'Thank you. I'm really enjoying being able to decorate. The last five years have been so stressful I haven't had time to stop and think about luxuries like happiness.' She filled me in on her story, her adoptive parents rejecting her, living at the shelter and losing her peers. 'I think my friends felt so guilty about the gulf in our circumstances that they didn't know how to talk to me any more. It frightened them to think something like that could happen to them. Up until then our lives had been sedate, comfortable, protected. They're all in college now, studying for degrees that will lead to careers and marriages. I hate that I'm not there too but I know I'll get there now in my own way, now that I don't have to worry about a place to live. It might take me twice as long to get there but I'll get there,' she said.

'I have no doubt of that,' I added and smiled.

'I want Flo to have a better life than I had. My dreams for her are so big. Anything is possible when I think of her. When Flo first came along, my ambitions for myself were so small. All I could think about then was getting a little security, somewhere we could stay for more than two months at a time, where we would not have to share kitchens, bathrooms, cupboards and fridges. A real home. And now we live in a place like *this*. It's proof that you should never lose hope. I'm studying law part-time ... we will eventually have a good life. Things can only get better for us. Flo is so happy here. I really had to struggle to keep her but I'm so glad I did. I just don't understand how my own mother could have given me up.'

'People's circumstances can be very challenging around babies,' I said. 'I've seen a lot of cases over the years. Sometimes the mothers think they're doing the best thing for their babies. They really love them so much.'

128

'I understand that,' she said. 'It's what I wanted to talk to you about.'

'Of course,' I said. 'How can I help?'

'I did a search for my mom or any genetic relatives on 23andMe and I got several matches, but for the strongest match, there was no name, just the contact details of a lawyer.'

'OK, well, how can I help you?'

'Well, the lawyer listed as her contact is . . . Bentwell and Sons. Vivian said you used to work there. I know he's Samsara's dad but after what happened tonight at the pool I really don't ever want to cross paths with them again. But I thought maybe you might be able to find out how I can get in touch with her. I can't afford a lawyer but I really, really need to find my mother.'

'Can I see what it says?' I asked. She tapped rapidly at her iPad and opened her results, passing the tablet to me.'

'Rachel Little . . .' The name came out calm and strong but it rang in my head like a siren. It was nearly twenty years since I had spoken that name. 'I'll need to go back and check my files but it doesn't ring a bell.' I tried to keep my hand from shaking as I passed the iPad back to her. 'Any of the scores of lawyers working at Bentwells at the time could have been her lawyer.'

'Can you check? I was thinking maybe you could call them and just find out. They'd be much more likely to give the information to you than to someone like me. This is the first solid connection I've found to my mother. I can't let it go. All I ever wanted was a place to belong – a family, security, a home. Now we are halfway there. We have a home, and security. Maybe one day soon we will have a family too. A mother for me, and a grandmother for Flo.'

I smiled. 'Try not to get your hopes up, Marley. This can be a long and painful process. Or a short and brutal one too. I've seen it all before.' And not everyone wants to be found.

29

EDDIE

A devil in disguise

I cursed my way back through the streets. I always had to help; always had to be the one who did the good deed. This is what I got for it. Trudging back across town when I should be in bed. I got to the Sky Building and the concierge desk was empty. I hit the elevator button and entered the same code I had seen Vivian entering earlier. It worked and I headed to the third floor.

As I turned off the corridor towards Marley's apartment, I was in another world so I hardly noticed when I ran straight into a person coming around the corner. 'I beg your pardon,' he said, stepping aside for me.

'No problem,' I said as I stared after his retreating

back. He was wearing a black baseball cap and a
bomber-style jacket and jeans. Everything about him
was designed to be anonymous. He was either a billionaire. A movie star. Or a murderer.

30

VIVIAN

A very bad morning

The moment I opened the door to Marley's apartment I could see that she was dead. It was Marley's daughter Flo who raised the alarm. She arrived down to reception by herself at 5 a.m. I heard some clattering around outside and came out of my apartment to investigate, which is when I saw her.

'Hey sweetheart, where's your mommy.'

'She's swimming in the pool on our balcony but the door is locked so I can't get out to her.'

My body went cold. I didn't want to scare Flo so I pulled out a lolly and said, 'Can you do me a favour? Can you guard my security cameras while I go check on the pool door for your mommy?' She was delighted to sit on the big chair, watching the CCTV in my apartment. 'Just don't press that big button, OK, hon?'

I knocked on Dave's door as I passed and got him to come with me. I could see Marley was dead but I forced myself to walk across the kitchen to the balcony door, which was locked. I felt like I was seeing my daughter again in that moment. Marley's body lay still and quiet in the pool, something evoking holiness, or perhaps just those holy artworks conveying drowned women in classical art. I used my master key to unlock the balcony door and I pulled her small body out of the glass mini-plunge-pool. I knew she was gone but I attempted CPR all the same, while the emergency responder stayed on the line with Dave.

31

CLEO

An unexpected death

Being part of the 5 a.m. club was rough but I made it to the gym. I found if I just put one foot in front of the other and focused on that I eventually got where I needed to be. Thirty minutes later, I was done and I emerged from the gym into the lobby to discover Dave, Flo, Vivian and a clutch of cops and paramedics.

One appeared to be holding a spreadsheet with every resident's name on it. He was ticking off people and nobody was allowed to leave. I walked to the cop that appeared to be in charge.

'Cleo Fry. I'm sorry, officer, but I need to get to work. I have a hearing in the southern district and Judge James does not look kindly on tardiness. Can I leave my card with you and have permission to leave the building?'

'I'm afraid I can't do that; there's been a death in the building and we need to speak to everyone who lives here.'

'A death? Oh my god, what happened? Who's dead?'

'I can't reveal any details but a young woman was found dead in her plunge pool this morning, so we're looking into the circumstances.'

'Who?' I asked again.

'We need to inform her next of kin first . . .'

I looked over at Vivian who was sitting at his desk, clearly shattered. 'Vivian?'

'Marley,' he said. 'It's Marley,' and he collapsed into shuddering tears. 'They think she killed herself.'

I was genuinely shocked. I had seen her less than eight hours ago. She had not seemed in any way depressed. 'But I just saw her. I spoke to her last night, in her apartment, after the party. She was fine! This doesn't make any sense.'

'Wait, miss, you were with her after the party? We're going to need to speak to you as a matter of urgency. You might have been the last person to see her alive.'

I texted Eddie. I figured she'd appreciate the heads-up before she filed her piece.

Something's going on here. Marley dead. Found in her pool. Get over here now if you want the story.

I felt a pang of guilt. Could I have helped her more? No. I had promised to help her however I could, I had promised her as much if not more than I promised my paying clients. What can you do? You can't help all the people, all the time.

I wasn't allowed to leave until the young officer interviewed me briefly. 'I'll be at my offices all afternoon if you need anything further.'

I went back to my apartment, showered quickly and grabbed my stuff. On my way out, I spoke to Vivian again.

'I can't believe it, Vivian. I know that she was agitated about finding her birth mother, but she seemed excited, not suicidal. Did she seem depressed to you?'

'Absolutely not. Cleo! She didn't kill herself! She would *never* leave Flo.'

'Something really doesn't feel right,' I said. I had a terrible feeling, like I was standing at the edge of a vortex and could do nothing to stop myself getting sucked in. I hesitated before I said:

'There was a man, last night. He was loitering on Marley's floor, after I had left her and was going back to my apartment. I don't know who it was but the police should speak to him. I don't think Marley killed herself either.'

And just like that, I was in the middle of it. Again.

32

EDDIE

Hope is a scarce commodity

I was at the Sky Building just after 6 a.m. Vivian and Dave were there, both very shaken. I spoke to the police, got what information was available then wrote up a report for online. By that time it was 7.30. I went a few doors up and got coffee and donuts for the cops and for Vivian. He hadn't eaten a thing. Dave and I had an interview scheduled and I didn't want to let it go.

'Hey,' I said, 'I'm going to walk around to Connelly's to get some breakfast. You want to come with me?'

'Sure,' he said. 'Just let me speak to Vivian.'

I waited outside and allowed my mind to run backwards to Dave's trial. I still remembered it so well. In the days leading up to it, you could see that Dave still believed that the truth would save him, that everything would be fine if he just told the truth. He was still a kid in that way. He had been brought up with good, honest principles – work hard, help others, tell the truth – so of course he believed the truth would see him right. But those principles were all very well until they came up against the might of the Foxes, the Bentwells, the Blacks. My eye was drawn to something on the corner. The detective who had been inside earlier was now in what looked like an intense conversation with a well-dressed guy. The cop looked chastised. I looked closer at the other man and recognised him as Bentwell. What the hell was he doing here? Probably laying down the law as Fox's lawyer.

'Ready to go,' Dave said, and I jumped out of my skin.

'Sorry, I didn't get much sleep last night. Let's go,' I said.

We walked to the run-down Irish bar around the corner from the Sky Building in heavy silence. We were both shocked about Marley's death.

'She was so young, and all alone. I should have looked out for her more. How could this have happened?'

'I don't think there's anything you or anyone else could have done, Dave ...'

'I suppose I just felt connected to her because we both came in on the cost-rental programme ... We were an endangered species. When I found out I had gotten the apartment, it felt like the universe was saying sorry to me. When I think of the bribery, gifts, threats, black-mail that would have gone on in an attempt to secure one of those apartments I know my karma performed some death-defying acts to get me here.'

'Oh yeah?' I asked.

'When's the last time you had to find an apartment?'

'Touché,' I said. 'I've only ever lived in my mom's rent-controlled studio. It's a shithole but it's cheap and I'm on my own so it's fine.'

'Well, you're lucky. It's a bloodbath out there. You can't get a rent-controlled apartment for love nor money. People aren't dying fast enough and when they do some niece or nephew who lives in Virginia sticks it up on Airbnb and uses it as a side-hustle so it never re-enters the rental market. The government is wondering why the housing crisis is so bad. But they turn a blind eye because it increases tourism and spending while it completely destroys the city. I almost didn't apply for the scheme but my former parole officer encouraged me to go for it. I had come to a point in my life where I decided I was going to stop letting my conviction direct the course of my life. I legally changed my name and decided to stop owning up to my criminal record. I figured if a broken legal system can rob me of my liberty, I can fight fire with fire and rob my liberty back. So yeah, I left the small detail of my criminal record off my housing appli-cation. There should be a statute of limitations on how long you can be followed by a criminal record anyway.'

'Fair enough,' I said, and pushed the door into Connelly's and directed us to a two-seater towards the back. It was private. It was weird to be sitting opposite him here again, so many years later, interviewing him in the same desperate attempt to find the missing clues that would prove his innocence. I started pulling out notebooks, bits of paper, a phone, my chewed-up pen and I laid them all out on the table in front of me, like components of a bomb-making kit.

'These are just for me,' I said, 'just so I can keep track of things. Don't let it put you off. Nothing will be published without your say-so. I just find it's easier, to write things down, keeps my thoughts in order.'

A waitress came by and poured us two coffees. I ordered two fried eggs and toast. I was getting hungry again. Dave stuck with coffee.

'Do you remember the last time we spoke like this?' he asked.

I did remember. It was a couple of years after he had been convicted, a year after Cassie had left me, and after my career had imploded. I was still obsessed with the story, still digging, still determined to find answers, convinced that if I could just solve the murder, I could solve my life too. I really believed the truth was there waiting to be found and I just hadn't turned over the right clue. But I know now that somebody was making a concerted effort to hide the truth.

After the last time I spoke to Dave, he had taken

me off his visitor's list. He couldn't afford to hope that I would put the pieces of the story together; the emotional cost to him was too great. I wrote to him a couple of times after that, transferred some money to his account which I figured he could use, but soon enough I felt like it was wrong to ignore his request. He had been through enough, I figured, so I stopped and let him get on with serving his sentence.

'I think we were both probably different people then,' I said.

The first time we met I was still married to Cassie, and I was a shit-hot, award-winning news reporter who was driven by the truth and could do no wrong. My life was on track back then. Living in a home made beautiful by Cassie, talking about having a kid. I ran at the Juliet case with all the hubris of a journalist who had solved a crime once. I could do it again, right? How difficult could it be?

Dave had been a bright scholarship kid with his whole life ahead of him.

We both learned the hard way that the truth sometimes wasn't enough.

'We've both been kicked around a bit since then,' he laughed.

I snorted. 'Understatement of the year.'

'You know your articles were the only thing that gave me hope back then,' he said. 'I always thought you would find a way to save me. But eventually keeping hope just felt like self-harm. I needed to survive in there and the best way was to resign myself to my sentence and grind it out.'

I thought I might cry. 'I really thought I would prove your innocence too. I did everything I could.'

He inhaled deeply and said, 'Yeah, I heard about what happened to you. That was rough.'

I shook my head. I couldn't go there. 'When Bentwell took the case against the paper and me personally on behalf of the Black family, I was lucky to survive. They had to pay a lot of money. I wish they hadn't settled but it was a financial decision. They would have had to pay more if they had gone to court and fought it. So they paid up and I got punished.'

'It's been so long since Juliet died, and yet it feels like it never went away.'

'Well, that's probably because it's unresolved for you.'

'Yeah,' he said. 'That conviction controlled the direction my life took. I was going to be an architectural engineer. I had dreams of designing buildings like the Sky Building.'

'Well, that's kind of what I want to talk to you about,' I said, trying to steer us onto the interview track. 'I want to know what the Juliet case did to you and your life. I want to know how you feel about it twenty years on. I want to know how you move on from something like that ...'

'Anything else?' he asked.

'Well, yeah,' I shrugged. 'I still want to know who actually killed her. I want to know who is walking around, out there, free and easy, *right now*, probably not even thinking about her except from time to time, when a siren punctures a dream or when they read a novel whose storyline veers too close for comfort. I want to know what kind of person kills a young woman then lets someone else take the rap.'

'The truth catches up with us all eventually,' he said.

'I'm banking on it.'

'OK, so where do you want to start?' he asked.

'The best place,' I said. 'The beginning.'

33

CLEO

A pattern emerges

I had to be called from my reverie several times by Judge James at that morning's hearing. In the end I apologised and told her I had got some upsetting personal news. The hearing finally came to an end and I was free to go back to my office and sift through everything that had happened since I visited Marley.

Who would want to hurt Marley? Who would orphan a four-year-old child? What could anyone possibly gain from it?

I went to my associate's office.

'Knock, knock,' I said. I had to get my kicks somehow.

'Cleo, come in!'

'I thought I'd check in, see how you're doing on that case we spoke about?'

'Well, I've looked into Bentwell employees in the year we're talking about and get this, thirteen women started working for the company and left that year. That's a high turnover, even for a firm as big as Bentwells.'

'Bingo . . . Do you have contacts for the women?' She smiled.

'Working on the list now, and planning on calling them today.'

'Let me help.'

34

EDDIE

A man tells his story from the beginning

I lifted the coffee pot and filled Dave's cup. 'Just start from the beginning.'

'The beginning?'

'Yeah, like how did you and Juliet actually meet?'

'We met in art history class, which I was sitting in on, just because I liked it. I couldn't believe I was able to access any class I wanted to. I was taking a double degree in engineering and architecture but I wanted to take full advantage of the scholarship, fill in any gaps left by my patchy public school education ... Juliet came into class late one day and slipped in beside me because it was the first empty seat available. I lent her a pen and we were friends from that moment on.

'She smelled incredible. Chocolate, coconuts, black

cherries, pepper, amber, vanilla. I didn't take in much art history that day.' He laughed. 'I could barely concentrate ... She was alarmingly beautiful. Not just pretty, but model-beautiful. People stared.

'When class ended she passed the pen back to me and said, "My saviour." I told her to keep it. We discovered we were both studying engineering, which surprised me. Not many girls studied it back then but it made sense when I found out who her dad was. She wanted to go into the family business, become a property developer too. We started to hang out and when she invited me back to her family home, a beautiful brownstone, well, you know it, she told me I was the first guy she ever had to make the first move on.' He laughed. 'I was terrified. I didn't want to assume anything. They were the kind of family that could get me kicked out of college if I misjudged the situation. But we were inseparable from that day on.'

'Were you in love with her?' I asked him.

'I was crazy about her ...'

Crazy enough to kill, I wondered?

'Before college I had known one kind of girl but NYU was like unlocking a whole new level – smart, promiscuous, sophisticated, worldly, travelled, and rich. I had never seen that kind of wealth, that kind of class. The most contact I had had with people like that before had been cutting their grass on weekend or summer jobs, catching a glimpse of them sunbathing on loungers by private pools while I went up and down their enormous lawns with the noisy petrol lawn mower, the tiny blades of grass sticking to my damp sweaty skin like hairs after the barber's. Or bussing tables at the restaurant in Saks. Juliet and her gang walked around like they owned the place. Between them they probably did. But she always spoke to me like we were equals, even though we both knew I was not. But she didn't care. I hadn't known that she had been dating William. I wasn't in their circle.'

I nodded, wrote the words WILLIAM BLACK on my notepad and circled them roughly with my pen.

'She told me that she had just come out of a long re-lationship and we needed to keep things low-key for a while ... she didn't want to make things awkward for anyone. But that turned out to be a lie. She had planned to break up with William, but just never got around to it. Probably just didn't want to engage with the messy task of dumping someone and so she didn't bother.

'William was there that night in the alley, when Juliet died. He was blind drunk. My question is this – if he was innocent, why would he lie about being there?

'I don't know, Dave, but that's what I plan to find out,' I said. 'You know William Black married Samsara Bentwell ...'

'I do,' he said. 'I was a perfect scapegoat. In their eyes, I had been cheating with Juliet, I was jealous of William, and angry that she wouldn't leave him for me. That was considered motive for murder. But what it really felt like was a punishment.'

'A punishment?' I asked, looking up from my notes. 'What do you mean by that?'

'For daring to encroach on their world, *on their women*. I was a poor kid from the wrong place, dating way out of my league. Who did I think I was? It was a way of putting me back in my box, a warning to others like me to stick to our side of town, our kind of people.

'Do you think you might have ended up together?' I asked. It would make a nice line for the article ... An *Upper West Side Romeo and Juliet* ... 'No, we would have broken up within a year. Deep down I have always known that.'

'Can we go back to the party?' I asked. 'What happened that night?'

'I shouldn't even have been there that night,' Dave said, blowing on his coffee. 'But Juliet had invited me and she wasn't the kind of girl you said no to. And it felt significant. Until that point, we had only met in private, in my rooms or at her house, the library, canteen or at class. This was the first time Juliet had asked me to any kind of social event with her friends. I thought it might be the beginning of our relationship moving to the next level. Of course, I think I knew deep down that wasn't what this night was about.'

I could sympathise. We had all been there at one time or another, degraded ourselves, allowed someone to do something in the hope that this time it would be different.

Dave continued: 'I always got the feeling that Juliet's friends knew something I didn't. It turns out they did. Juliet hadn't broken up with William like she said. And she hadn't brought me there to take our relationship to the next level. She had brought me there as a way of breaking up with William; she was using me to let him know she had moved on. I was just a pawn.'

'Tell me about the fight at the party that night.'

'When William showed up, we were playing frisbee by the pond. Juliet had flung the frisbee high up onto some hedging, I had climbed up onto the rocks and rooted around in the bushes, ignoring the thorns that tore at my hands and forearms, stinging me and drawing blood. This was what the cops later described as "defensive wounds" ... It was from retrieving Juliet's frisbee.' He rubbed his face. 'William was really drunk when he showed up. Juliet told him he was drunk and to leave her alone. He started in on me then, asking who I was, where I was from, all that. Juliet told him I was her friend. God, I still feel how much that hurt.' He smiled. 'Young love is so brutal, isn't it?!'

I could imagine what it felt like, being put in your place like that when you were madly in love.

'He started calling her names, and told me they had been dating for two years ... He was understandably upset. *I* was upset. She had treated us both badly. She

151

had told me they had broken up months ago but she had neglected to tell William. She said she was trying to be kind, hoping he would get the message. Of course, it all blew up then, turned nasty. He was calling her all sorts of names and I told him to leave it, to go home, walk it off. He was screaming and everyone was looking but because of who he was nobody stepped in. Juliet was furious. He was saying a lot of awful stuff about how she had slept with lots of men. Everybody could hear. I was telling him to stop but he ignored me completely. It wasn't until Samsara's dad appeared and gave him a real talking to that he shut up.

'I was left standing by the lake as Bentwell took Juliet away. I was actually really shocked by the things William had said about Juliet. It was all so nasty. Juliet didn't look shocked, though; she just looked angry, which made me think it was all true. Samsara's dad took her off to the other side of the lake.

'William started shouting insults again and I couldn't listen to him any more so I walked up to him, he took a wild swing at me, which I ducked, and then I shoved him with the full force of my strength into the lake, roaring and splashing like a harpooned seal.' He laughed but it was a fleeting moment.

'The things I saw later that night, the things I learned, the *behaviours* of these people, it blew my mind ... they're all rotten.'

'Like what,' I asked.

'Doesn't matter now,' he said. 'I just mean they were so *alien* in everything they did. Do you know I've never been able to have a relationship since, never been able to build something with a woman, maybe because they all pull back when they hear I was convicted of killing a woman ... or maybe because whatever happened that summer messed up how I feel about myself.'

'How did the party end?' I asked. I wanted him to tell me the full story, start to finish.

'I walked Juliet home later on, left her a few feet from her house, she was absolutely fine ... and that would have been fine had I not realised I had her phone in my pocket, so I turned around and headed back to her place. When I got to the alley behind their houses I saw William, passed out, and then someone in a hooded sweatshirt ran by me, nearly knocked me over. That's when I discovered Juliet's body. And, well, you know the rest.' His face was a blank mask, as if he was keeping any emotion at bay.

'You were a great suspect,' I said, as I got us some coffee refills. 'Ticked all the boxes.'

He smiled. 'Even though there was no motive, we all know nine times out of ten it's the boyfriend. It didn't matter that there were technically two boyfriends in this case, nor that one had more motive to kill Juliet than the other. It was never going to be William Black. When it came down to it, Juliet's dad was a huge deal and the city needed a conviction quickly. I was a slam-dunk, not to mention disposable, and I had poor representation. Even though I was a good kid, had never been in trouble, never bothered their system, never troubled their records, once the Bentwells law firm got involved I was finished.'

'What about CCTV?' I asked. 'I know it was a long time ago but it was a wealthy neighbourhood. There must have been some camera security systems in place?'

'The only building that had CCTV covering the location was – guess who? The Bentwells – and their CCTV had been knocked out for the time in question. A power cut or a surge or something like that.'

'I remember that. Strange coincidence, right?' I didn't believe in coincidences. 'Were there any other suspects?'

'There had been other people in contact with Juliet on the night of her death but everyone had been ruled out, either by the police, their class, their family connections or their wealthy lawyers who had slammed down the portcullis and would bring it up for nothing less than a warrant. I on the other hand had nobody to defend me. I was the odd one out here, the person who didn't belong. I was the one who could be relinquished, a convenient sacrifice that everyone could forget about, guilt-free. I knew then which way the wind was blowing.' He blew the top of his coffee again. 'The legal aid advised me to plead out on an involuntary manslaughter charge rather than take my chances with a jury and a murder charge. Innocent or not, he could see I was going down for Juliet's death one way or another and he didn't want to risk me getting twenty-five to life in front of a jury. This way I was out in three, I enlisted in the army with a waiver at the age of twenty-five, which gave me a path to finishing my education, healthcare and getting a livelihood. Not the life I had planned, but a life all the same. It's just the anger that tears me up now. My prison term was a short stint in the grand scheme of things but I can't let it go. I *need* to clear my name. That conviction follows me everywhere. I can't have relationships because of it, I can't get the jobs I want, I'm only in the Sky Building because I didn't own up to my criminal record. If anyone finds out, they'll try to get me out.'

'I understand that. I'd feel the same way,' I said.

'Before that night, my life had been on a golden trajectory. I was getting *out*!' He laughed bitterly. 'Out of the cycle of poverty and depression, and moving up in the world. I was at an Ivy League college, on a full scholarship, I would earn my degree, my post-grad, my PhD, and I would change my destiny. But that had all fallen away overnight. College, career dreams, everything had gone after that night. I had trusted in honesty and truth and I had been shafted by a system that ran on lies and deceit, and dollars. Once I went to prison, my dreams seemed pathetically quaint, childish even. Once I discovered how brittle dreams actually were, and how brutal reality was, I stopped dreaming. I don't think I know how to dream any more.'

'Come on,' I said. 'Everybody's got a dream.'

He shook his head. 'No, think about it. What are dreams built of? Hope. What's hope built of? The belief that things will get better. If you don't have hope, you can't have a dream.'

'Jesus.' I had heard some depressing stuff but this was bleak. 'But what about winning the cost-rental lottery, getting to live in a place like the Sky Building? Surely that must give you some hope?'

'The only time I will have hope again, is when my name is cleared and I know there is some justice in this world,' he said. '*That* will restore my hope.'

'I'm sorry, man,' I said. 'It's so rough. I still don't understand how they could have gotten away with a guilty plea when there was the question of the person in the alley, and the fact that you saw William in the alley, not to mention the fact that there was an unidentified DNA profile found at the scene.'

Dave shrugged. 'They liked how the case sat together with me as the killer. And as for the DNA, William had spat at her at the party – can you believe that? – and Juliet had struck him so his DNA under her nails was explained. Everyone had seen it happen too. Witnesses, the all-important witnesses from good respectable families.'

'And the unidentified DNA profile?'

'The police just said it was a big party, it could have been on her from there.'

He looked at me now as if he had been somewhere else, a different place, a different time.

'The thing that always bothered me, apart from all of that,' he said, 'was William's alibi. We never knew who the alibi was because apparently they were a minor. They were only ever identified at the trial by a letter, which again seemed terribly convenient.

'I had trusted that the police would find the mystery person in the hoodie, that they would see William's alibi for what it was – a confection – and they would keep searching for justice. But that wasn't how it worked. I found out later that one of the reasons the Bentwells won so many cases was because they had the power to destroy any lawyer's career. Their influence reached far and wide. Most defence lawyers were too intimidated by the Bentwells to go up against them; some of them even had ambitions to work for them one day and so they didn't want to scupper their chances by beating them in court. The Bentwells were so powerful in New York they could spike a lawyer's career if they went against them too hard. And they were vindictive.'

'I'm so sorry, Dave, it's awful. Thank you for trusting me with your story,' I said.

'It actually feels good to talk about it, to get it off my chest. I know I can never accept what happened. I am having dreams about Juliet again, like I did at the beginning, seeing the hooded figure flashing past me like a fox. There's always been a schism in my life, that sliding doors moment where I went to jail and everyone else just went back to living their lives. Juliet's name fell from the headlines and everyone went back to normal, put it all behind them, chalked it up to an awful tragedy, and they certainly forgot about me. That's why I joined the army. It was the only thing I was fit for after prison, another life of institutionalised regimens and male-based interactions. It was just easier that way. I didn't have to adapt, didn't have to relearn how to be around people.'

'The cops never found that person, the one who ran by you?'

'No, they never believed me. They just thought I made it up to suit my story. They told me they couldn't corroborate my story, that there had been no witnesses.'

'But there was a witness,' I said. 'That person was a possible witness. Or even a possible murderer? They just never found them. Or maybe they did find them . . . but it wasn't in certain people's interests for them to be officially found.'

'Do you really think you can help clear my name?' he asked.

'I'm sure as hell going to try,' I said. I started packing up my notebook; the morning was already gone. 'We need to find that person. But first I think we need to talk to William's alibi. Where did they go? They're not a minor any more. Maybe they're ready to talk now.'

35

CLEO

Getting to know the neighbours

That evening, I was still processing the events of the day. Work had been exhausting and relentless. I changed into a soft low-cut t-shirt and cashmere track-suit bottoms, the next best thing to pyjamas. When my doorbell went at exactly 8 p.m. I had completely forgotten that I had invited Dave – my neighbour – around.

'I'm so sorry, Dave, I completely forgot. The news about Marley, my god, can you believe it? Come in, come in, I'm sorry, you'll have to take me as you find me tonight . . .'

He looked shocked as well. 'She was so lovely. I can't believe it,' he said, sitting on a stool at the island. 'She must really have been struggling to do something like that . . .'

'Do you really believe it was suicide?' I asked.

'I find it hard to believe – she loved that kid but the police said they found her keys on the balcony so she had clearly gone outside and locked the door with the intention of killing herself. It didn't stop them asking me my whereabouts last night.'

I could imagine. I'm sure Dave would be number one on their suspect list if they did deem Marley's death to be suspicious.

'I just keep thinking maybe I could have helped her more, you know, if she was depressed. She was totally on her own. And now her poor little girl is orphaned ...'

'It just doesn't bear thinking about,' I said. I opened the fridge and pulled out two beers, popped the lids. 'Let's go into the lounge.'

Dave was friendly but polite, open but reserved, which made me think of the old-fashioned respect men used to have for women. And he was disciplined. I had seen this with my own eyes when I woke up early every morning and saw him already working out. I thought discipline said a lot about a person's character. Sure, there was usually something motivating it, no more so than in my own life, but that wasn't a crime last time I checked.

'She seemed so happy too, to have finally gotten an apartment, a safe place for her and her kid to live ...'

'I know. It's so tragic. How are you finding living here?' I asked him.

'Yeah it's great,' he said. 'Clean, warm, dry. I've never lived anywhere like it.' He laughed, but it wasn't funny when I thought about it. 'I haven't really done anything with it yet, nothing like this anyway,' he said, looking around at my place. 'This is like something you'd see in a magazine. Were you just born knowing how to do this stuff or do you take a class in decorating? I still don't know how to do much more than put a table and a bed in a room.'

'I paid someone to do it,' I said. 'And they definitely ripped me off. I think they just make up numbers when they come into a building like this. They know you can afford it and I don't have time to haggle.' I tried to see my place through his eyes. Books and paintings, mirrors and lamps, blankets and sculptures, everything perfectly placed. I had always envisioned how my apartment would look when I was a kid, what I would have in each room, how it would feel, and everything had turned out exactly as I had wanted. I was in full control of my life, of my surroundings. I felt uncomfortable suddenly. There was a world between my life and his. We were neighbours, but could we be friends?

'What would you like to do with your apartment,' I asked, gently encouraging him to answer.

'I'd like to do it right, which is why I haven't done anything yet. It still feels like an empty rental, a place anyone could live. I need to make it feel like a home but I don't really know where to start.'

'What about last night, the party, did you meet anyone, get to know any neighbours?'

He laughed. 'It was a bit like first day at school. People are a bit standoffish here, they either know you or they don't. They assume if they don't know you, you're not worth knowing because surely they already know everyone worth knowing, right? So, it means a lot that you invited me up here for a beer. What about you? Do you like living here? This is next level altogether.'

'Well,' I said, 'if you'd asked me as a kid what my dream home would be it was definitely this – a skyscraper condo on the Upper West Side. I loved looking at all those little squares of light, all the lit-up windows, and inside each and every one of them was a whole person, a whole life ...' I felt myself meandering and pivoted back to the story. 'I grew up in a house so I guess I was attracted to what was different. I actually lived in a brownstone in Brooklyn before this, so I'm still adjusting to living here, being able to see everybody, being seen by everybody. I miss my brownstone. It was so lovely but the commute was killing me. I haven't quite been able to settle in here yet. I don't know why but this place feels like it has lots of ghosts. Maybe it's just all the reflections in the glass. I keep thinking I see something moving just out of my eye-line. When I look, there's nothing there. It gives me the creeps. I've lived in really old buildings and have never felt like this. Here it feels like there are ghosts and shadows everywhere. I feel like every time I try to make the place feel more comfortable, more homely, the building rejects my advances. It spurns my attempts at womanly home-making.'

'Well, I think you're doing an amazing job,' he said. 'I grew up in a brownstone too ... except it was broken into thirteen apartments, so probably a different kind to yours.'

I laughed. He was funnier than I expected. Maybe we could overcome our differences and be friends.

He stood up and looked around. 'You have the place really nice. Really homely.' He walked around the room, stooping to investigate various ornaments and items. 'These are lovely,' he said, picking up some old-fashioned big gold rings. I chastised myself for the fleeting mistrust that beat in me when I saw him pick up the rings. I knew how easily they could be slipped into a pocket.

'Family heirlooms,' I said. 'I'm going to grab us more beers. And I haven't eaten all day. Will you save me from myself and share a pizza with me?'

'Sure, that would be great,' he said. 'Are you sure, though? I'm happy to leave you to your dinner. I don't want to outstay my welcome.'

'Don't be silly,' I said. 'To be honest, after everything that's happened today, I could do with the company.'

I ordered the pizza and gave him another beer. 'Cheers,' he said, and the sound of his bottle against mine rang in my head like cut crystal.

36

EDDIE

A phone is unlocked

I was sitting in Vivian's apartment. I had called around
to see him. I knew he'd be upset and I also knew he'd
be the last person anyone would think to check in on.
And, as usual, I was looking for any excuse not to go
home, not to re-enter the draining chasm of memories
that was my apartment.

'Do you really think she killed herself?' he said.

'I find it hard to believe. But the police say it's the
only explanation. The door was locked from the outside. It must have just all got too much for her.'

'I don't believe it,' he said. 'She loved Flo. She would
never leave Flo.'

'Well, they say you never know in these situations,'
I sighed. 'What about your CCTV?' I asked, nodding

towards his glowing screens. 'Was there anything on that to suggest that it was something other than suicide?'

'Nothing much. People were coming and going all the time but Bryant never hooked up the full camera count on that floor. He said it was extra and as that was the social housing floor he wasn't paying for it. So there's only one camera just at the elevator. Here, I'll show you.'

'*Jesus H* . . .' I said. Fox was something else. He really didn't want to make it attractive for these people but what he didn't realise was even the shittiest apartment in his building was better than the nicest apartment they could afford by themselves. He was so out of touch with reality, he thought something like that would put them off.

'Look here . . .' he swiped to the date and hour ' . . . this is Cleo going to Marley's apartment. That's Dave. His apartment is on the same floor as Marley's. There's another guy then, this guy in the baseball cap . . . Then there's you . . .'

'I saw him, that guy. He was so shifty . . .'

'If there is a suspect, it's him. I think he's hiding because of the baseball cap and the way he averts his face and has his collar up. We don't know who he is or where he goes afterwards but he doesn't come back to the elevator, ever. So he either stayed in someone's apartment or he went down the emergency exit.'

'Does anyone know who this guy is?' I asked.

'The police have interviewed everyone on the floor but nobody can recognise him from the footage. Samsara Bentwell said she thought it looked like Dave but anyone can see it's not Dave's build.'

'She seems like a real piece of work,' I said. 'Such a snob. I need to speak to her for my article, though. She was best friends with Juliet . . .'

'I think she wants all the cost-rental tenants out. She was stirring things up at the last residents' meeting. She thinks they don't belong here. Whoever this guy is, though,' he said, pointing his finger at the mystery man in the cap, 'is important. I'd say essential to ruling Marley's death suicide or something more sinister,' he said.

I stared at the zoomed-in freeze frame of the man until it started to blur. 'I'd like to talk to him. I wish I could remember more about him but all I remember is he was very clearly trying not to be seen.'

He scrolled forward again . . . 'And then there's you coming back again a few minutes later. What were you doing there?'

'I had Marley's phone and her wallet. I wanted to drop them back to her . . . but she didn't answer.'

I pulled the phone out of my bag. 'I was going to give them to the cops this morning but when I saw Bentwell in the lobby, talking to the detective, it just made me think of everything that happened with the

166

Juliet case and how maybe the police have motives that are not always justice-driven. Bentwell's so powerful. When I saw him this morning, it felt like he was giving orders, tying things up. Do you think I'm paranoid? You probably think I'm crazy ... but for some reason I'm not too confident that they want to find an alternative explanation for her death. I thought maybe we can find something. It all just takes me back to the Juliet case. The police don't always have powerless people's best interests at heart. And Marley had no power. She's completely disposable to them, the Foxes, the Bentwells. They'll stop at nothing to get what they want, to protect themselves. I've seen it all before.'

Vivian took a shaky breath. 'I agree. I know they're capable of anything really to protect their interests ...' I waited. He seemed to want to get something off his chest. I had learned that in interviewing if you just wait, just let the silence build, often people will tell you something they didn't mean to. I looked at Vivian and he started to talk.

'You know the CCTV footage from the Bentwells' house that was mysteriously missing after Juliet's death?' I nodded; I didn't want to risk interrupting him.

'Well, it wasn't a power surge or a fault that wiped the tape ... it was me.'

I sat back. I really was shocked. I didn't know what to say, where to begin.

'What, Vivian? How? *Why?*'

'Because they know how to get to everyone. The Blacks, the Bentwells ... they stick together. There was incriminating material on that CCTV. It showed an argument between Juliet and William, then an argument between her and Mr Bentwell, and then Samsara ... what it categorically did not show was Dave killing Juliet ...'

'Vivian *why*, you could have cleared Dave's name ...'

'They blackmailed me. My wife was sick, and Bentwell and Black made it clear they would blackball me all over town and we'd have nowhere to work or live. They're so powerful, Eddie. You above all people should know that. Besides, I honestly never thought that Dave would be found guilty. There was no evidence so I thought it was a victimless crime.'

'Have you ever thought about coming clean,' I asked.

'It's too late now,' he said. 'It's not like it would help anyone ...'

'Dave might beg to differ ...' I said. I could see he was upset. 'Look, Vivian, I'm not judging you. I know exactly what the Bentwells are like and how they operate. I'm not going to say anything to anyone. We'll find another way ... I just can't help but feel that Marley's death is somehow connected to Juliet's.'

'I feel the same. She would never have killed herself. It seems like the Bentwells, the Blacks and the Foxes all cast a very dark shadow wherever they go. Anyone in that shadow can become collateral damage.'

I ran my fingers over Marley's phone, which was encrusted with tiny crystals and covered with cute raised stickers of gummy bears and cherries, probably something Flo had added to the phone. The screen was cracked but still functioning. When I touched it, it lit up with a picture of Flo and Marley. I felt a lump in my throat.

'Where is Flo now?' I asked.

'She's staying with a woman from the shelter. I can't look after her and do this job. They've said they'll help out until they can find something ... it's just so unfair on her, Eddie. I can't believe Marley would do this to Flo. It doesn't make sense.'

'She wouldn't.' I gave his shoulder a squeeze. It was as comfortable as I got with physical affection.

I hit the phone screen again. Twenty-four hours ago, Marley had everything going for her. She was a fighter. She had got herself this far and she was excited about the future. Why would she give up now, just when things were getting good? Now she was in a morgue and her little girl was orphaned. I tapped in the passcode 1-2-3-4 and the phone punished me with a haptic buzz. Worth a try, I thought.

'She did *not* seem suicidal when I interviewed her yesterday. She seemed hopeful. And she was fine at the party last night, right?'

'I agree,' Vivian said, dabbing his face with a tissue. I tried 4-3-2-1. Buzz. Wrong again.

'I'd go so far as to say she was looking forward to the future.'

'I know,' Vivian said.

'Something about it just feels ... *off* to me,' I said. 'We need to figure out who that guy in the elevator was. And if anyone else has access to the property.'

I punched in 0-0-0-0. The phone unlocked with a rewarding smooth click.

'Vivian,' I said, and held up the unlocked phone to face him.

'How did you do that?' he asked.

'I'm a journalist, Viv. It's what I do.'

37

CLEO

A social invitation

A few minutes later, there was a knock on my pool-terrace door. Strange.

'Samsara! Come in . . .'

Samsara recoiled when she saw Dave. 'Oh hi . . . I probably should just have gone downstairs and put a note in your cubby but I could see you were home so I figured why not just walk across the terrace?' She handed over a bottle of champagne. 'Housewarming gift.' She smiled.

I could see how this looked to her. Soft music was playing and the lights were low. I kept my private life private so Samsara would probably jump to the wrong conclusions and might spread those conclusions all throughout the building by sundown.

I tapped the bottle with my rings. It was a tap of uncertainty but it came out harsh, like impatience. Appearances can be misleading. Samsara looked tame but she was wild. Easy does it. I may be able to crush prosecutors and exonerate murderers but I know how dangerous someone like Samsara is. Slippery, duplicitous, charming, but no one gets to be chair of the PTA for five years running *and* treasurer of a New York Co-Op board without being cut-throat. And her PR firm represented everyone in Manhattan because of who her father was. I needed to tread carefully here.

Dave had stood up.

She turned to him. 'I'm Samsara,' she said. 'I live just across the pool.' She turned back to me. 'I'm sorry, I didn't realise you had company, Cleo, or I would not have taken the liberty but ...'

She placed her chess piece down so I was forced to make my move. 'Oh please, you're not interrupting. Not at all, please won't you come in? Join us. We were just talking about poor Marley, how tragic the whole thing is ...'

I did a quick stock-take of the apartment through Samsara's eyes and was happy it looked beautiful and sophisticated. I thought I detected a flash of jealousy. I knew Samsara's apartment was more Park Avenue family traditional than my single-woman glamorous.

'Dreadful news. That poor, poor girl ...' Samsara said. 'She must have been so desperate ...'

'We were just talking about it,' I said, pouring Samsara a glass of white wine and gesturing for her to sit down. I didn't bother offering her a beer. I knew a woman like her would never drink beer.

'And what will happen to her apartment, do you think?' I asked Samsara, who I knew would have already started campaigning the board.

'Well, I imagine the board will make a decision,' she said. 'It will probably go up for sale.'

'Won't they have to replace it with another cost-rental tenant?' Dave asked. 'For the planning laws, I mean?'

She scrunched up her face. 'I think that was only necessary for the planning approval. I don't think there's anything that says those tenants need to be replenished *ad infinitum* if they move out or, in this instance, meet a tragic end. You would know more about the legal ins and outs of that, Cleo ... did the police talk to you? They practically interrogated us. It actually reminded me of, well, Juliet Fox; do you remember the case, Cleo?'

Dave shifted uncomfortably. I demurred. I didn't want this to turn into a nostalgia fest for what was a very dark time.

'What did they ask you?' I said.

'I found them pretty hostile,' Samsara said. 'Aggressive, almost.'

'They didn't let me leave the building until they had

173

interviewed me . . .' I said. 'I was late for a hearing with a real stickler of a judge.'

'Ridiculous,' Samsara said testily, taking a huge mouthful of wine. 'Really, so unnecessary. The poor girl killed herself. Why do they have to treat us all like criminals?'

'I guess they're just doing their job,' Dave said. 'They'd look pretty stupid if it turned out that she hadn't killed herself and that they had neglected to do due diligence. It's inconvenient but it's just protocol.'

Samsara gave him a cool glare and said, 'Well, you would know better than me. Anyway, I won't disturb you any longer. I really just intended to pop in with this bottle and to invite you to drinks at our place. We usually have an end-of-summer get-together . . . William and I started doing it the year we got married. A way to reclaim that time of year from the dreadful memories of the past. You know our friend Juliet was murdered when we were all still in college,' she said pointedly to Dave. 'It's our way of trying to celebrate her life. So, can we expect to see you?' she said, turning back to me.

'Oh, oh well, that would be great; what do you think, Dave?' I said, turning to him, and Samsara's face darkened. She hadn't intended to invite him but I was determined to include him, even if just to make the evening more fun for me.

'Of course, thank you,' Dave said. 'Great to get to know the neighbours.'

'Wonderful,' Samsara said through gritted teeth. 'I'll be in touch ...'

I escorted her back out through the terrace doors. As I watched her retreating blonde head I felt the urge to smack it off the tasteful terrazzo tiles.

38

EDDIE

A journalist never forgets

I left Vivian's apartment when he started to yawn. I couldn't in good conscience keep an old mourning man up after his bedtime just because I didn't want to go home. When I let myself into my apartment, the old sadness welcomed me. I wasn't a bit tired so I went to the box files I kept on my bookshelves and pulled out the one marked Juliet. Inside was every single article I had ever written on the case, from news reports about her death right up to the investigation and trial and beyond. I had also collected cuttings from my own paper as well as the other nationals on the case. It had gotten national coverage at the time – a young, pretty, rich girl murdered in cold blood on one of the wealthiest streets in Manhattan. There were very few blogs at the time, but lots of podcasts and newsletters and YouTube channels had since revisited the case over the years, each with its own implausible take on what might have happened. A little quality control was a marvellous thing. I made some tea and sifted through the clippings, refreshing my memory. I was convinced that Marley's death was somehow connected, a sure sign I was losing my mind – she wasn't even born, but somehow I couldn't shake the feeling that everything that happened in the Sky Building was connected and nothing was coincidental. And I was more sure than ever that Dave had been an easy set-up for the murder. There's no way he did it. Too many things didn't add up. There were so many assumptions and so little evidence. Certainly on the night in question, he had been more interested in keeping Juliet safe and defending her, it seemed, than in harming her. But to Juliet's friends, people she had known from childhood from the same prep schools and summer camps and holidays, he was an outsider, not to be trusted.

What struck me now, going back over my notebooks from interviews at the time, was that so many details were not followed up by the police. Juliet was promiscuous. I know, I know, I'm not victim shaming, I'm just saying the girl got around and seemed to have several boyfriends that we knew of at the time. And yet those people, and the ones we might not have known about, were never run to ground. It was like the police just wanted to close the book quickly. They never even found a weapon. The one piece of evidence that was required for a murder. If Dave had killed her and stayed with her screaming for help, wouldn't they have found the weapon nearby? Well, they never did. The police had come up with some story at the time, about it all being part of Dave's grand premeditated plan to trick them into believing he was innocent when actually he had masterminded the whole thing. That might be how things happen in TV shows but it's not how they happened in real life. I had covered enough murders to know.

Unsurprisingly, the police didn't investigate William Black too thoroughly. His father was one of the biggest lawyers in Manhattan and he was represented by the Bentwells, one of the biggest firms in the state. Unless they had him standing over Juliet with a bloodied rock in his hand there was no point. There were no dash cams, Ring doorbells or social media back then, but these were wealthy houses in a wealthy area, so there had to have been something on CCTV, some security footage ... And what Vivian had told me about the Bentwells' CCTV the night of the murder was deeply suspicious in and of itself.

Why had they not leaned on William more heavily? He was the spurned ex-boyfriend. He had had a public row with her *the night of her murder*. He lived on the street where she was found. He had been seen at the scene of the murder. The investigators had pushed this aside because he had come up with an alibi, one that clashed with others' accounts of when he left the party. Why had they accepted his alibi? And who was it anyway? *Why had Dave's legal aid not dug into it?* Well, I knew why. Legal aides were so demoralised it was hard to find one who cared and hadn't lost all faith in their own ability to do a job, especially against the might and resources of a firm like the Bentwells. They were tooled up. And they were influential. Nobody wanted to be the lawyer who put the Blacks' kid behind bars for murder. Try and have a career in law after that. No, thank you.

The holes in this case were big enough to do somersaults through, but somehow they hadn't been enough to keep Dave out of prison, which told me powerful people were working powerful influence back then, and possibly now too. I yawned. I was going around in circles. It was time to leave it alone for tonight. I had let this story take over my life once before. I shouldn't let it do it a second time.

39

CLEO

Never ask a question you don't already know the answer to

'I guess we're going to drinks with Samsara,' I said, and Dave made his eyes wide with disbelief. 'You wanted neighbours, well now you've got them.'

He laughed. 'I should be careful what I wish for.'

I sat down heavily and sipped my beer. All lightness was gone from the atmosphere.

'I actually knew her a long time ago,' Dave said.

I played dumb. 'Samsara? *How?*'

'We graduated the same year, in NYU. I dated one of her friends ...'

'Huh, I never would have put you with them ...' I realised how crass that sounded. 'Sorry, I just mean, well, they're such snobs and you're, well, not.'

'She doesn't even recognise me . . . I've bumped into her a few times in the lobby and she always looks suspicious, completely tenses up.' He laughed. 'As if I'm going to mug her.'

I groaned. I could just imagine her turning her diamond rings in towards her palm and tightening her grip on her Birkin.

'I guess I just don't register on her radar. If you're not in their circle, you're invisible. It's kind of disappointing, really. You'd think someone like that might have a wider view of people . . . It's amazing how someone can be given every advantage in the world and still be so insular. I don't know, it was a long time ago but she doesn't really seem to have changed.'

I shrugged. 'I'm a few years younger than her, and obviously our families knew each other. I do remember her swanning around NYU, though.'

The doorbell went. 'Pizza!'

By the time I had laid out the pizza and napkins, I was feeling a bit tipsy. The lamplight in the room was lovely and glowing. The view outside was spectacular; everything was twinkling and shimmering in glass. I saw my reflection looking back at me and it felt right that it was blurred and wobbly. I turned on some music. Shirley Bassey's voice began.

'What the hell?' Dave laughed. 'Is this your music?'

'This is my jam.' I smiled and swayed a bit to the strings and the bombastic Bassey. 'I listen to this on my

AirPods before I make a closing statement,' I giggled. 'It gives me big power energy.'

'Oh my god, my mother played her over and over when I was a kid. We had this little turntable that was like a suitcase but we only owned two records, and Bassey's hits was one that was on constant rotation. I literally haven't heard this in decades. What are you doing to me?!'

'She was an incredible singer,' I said. 'What I really love about her though is that I can be someone else when I listen to her. It's nice to be someone else sometimes, nice not to be me . . .'

I flopped back down on the couch beside him. A puff of air exploded from the cushion. I was slightly out of breath and closed my eyes.

'What's not nice about being you?' he asked.

'Oh, you'd be surprised,' I said, keeping my eyes shut. I risked asking him a little more about himself.

'So tell me where was your brownstone,' I said, gently ribbing him.

He told me about his young life in Harlem, his mom and siblings, his scholarship to NYU to study engineering and architecture, his dream of designing houses, homes.

'I had so much idealism back then. I just seem to have lost the heart for it. That's why I really love your place,' he said. 'It feels like an actual home . . . a representation of *you*.'

182

'There's still lots to do,' I said. 'I need to put up that shelving over there for one thing, and hang some paintings and pictures, but have you tried to get a tradesman in Manhattan these days? They say they'll come, you take the morning off work to wait in for them and they don't even ring to tell you they're not going to show. It's worse than being on the apps,' I laughed. 'You expect to be ghosted by dates, but not by your handyman.'

He laughed. 'You're funny. So you're on the apps?'

I smiled at him. 'I am not. Despite what people will tell you, you can't have it all. I couldn't ask anyone to take second place to my career, and I love my career more than I've ever loved any human being and I won't compromise on it … it's just the nature of the job. I mean, sure I'd love to have a marriage, kids, but it hasn't happened, and I have to accept that it probably won't happen. There's very little expectation on my part.'

'Hmm,' he said. 'That's usually exactly when you do meet someone, just when you're not looking. Isn't that what people say?'

I smiled a tight smile that communicated exactly what sort of bullshit I thought that was.

'So what exactly do you do, that keeps you too busy for relationships?' he asked.

'Lawyer. Defence. The worst kind,' I grimaced. 'I help people get away with murder, or that's what the *New York Times* said when they profiled me.'

He whistled to show he was impressed.

183

'I prefer to think of it as saving innocent people from the broken justice system.'

'Wow, I sure could have done with someone like you in my life when I was younger . . .'

'Oh yeah,' I said. Then I asked the question I knew I shouldn't. I already knew the answer – of course I did – but I wanted to see what he would say. I wanted to know did he trust me yet. So I went ahead and asked the question – 'Why's that, then?'

As a criminal defence lawyer, I had an innate sense of when someone was lying and when someone was telling the truth.

'I was in prison.'

No response.

'A long time ago.'

Silence.

' . . . for something I didn't do.' That was the most important piece of information.

Still I said nothing. I knew these moments were often crucial, delicately balanced, and if I said something I risked shutting him down. So I let him talk and waited.

'I was sentenced to seven years, but got out in three after they factored in time already served and good behaviour. It doesn't sound like much time to serve in the grand scheme of things but it completely derailed my life.'

He stopped, but I knew now was not the time for me to speak. I waited. He broke first.

'I'm sorry, Cleo, I've ruined a really lovely evening but I think we're going to be friends and this is not something I'd like to keep from you so it's better you know. I think I'll go home now. Thank you.'

I found my voice. 'Oh please Dave, you haven't ruined anything! You forget I spend all day listening to stories much worse than that,' I said. 'Have you thought about getting someone to look into your case? There are a lot of not-for-profits who help unfairly convicted people appeal their cases ...'

'I've thought about hiring someone to go back over things but it's just too expensive, and I'm not sure I have the stomach for it either.'

I thought for a moment then said: 'What would you say to a trade?'

'A trade?'

'You hang those paintings and shelves for me,' I said, 'and I'll take a look at your case for you? Sound like a fair swap?'

'You would do that for me?'

'Sure. I've got my own investigative team and a *pro bono* department that works on cases just like yours.' I pulled out my phone. 'Put your number in there for me.'

'Are you serious? Thank you so much, Cleo.'

'No problem,' I said. It really was the least I could do.

40

EDDIE

A journalist edges closer to the truth

The next day I rushed through my work so I could get into the archives. I had decided I didn't care if the Juliet case took over my life again. What did I have to lose? A few hours binge-eating Doritos while watching sub-par detective shows? It wasn't like Cassie was waiting at home for me this time around. Time seemed to move differently when I was alone in my apartment, dragging its heels like a weary old man. The air seemed cooler, the light colder. It felt like my blood was silting in my veins when I was there, strangling my ambition, hope and dynamism, dead.

I wasn't sure that this feeling was anything to do with the place. I think it had something to do with being lonely. Some people lost limbs and claimed they could still feel them, even years after their arm or leg was amputated. That's how I felt about losing Cassie and our life together. It was like my phantom life, one that I could still hear the echo of from time to time. I wondered what things would be like now, if I had listened to Cassie at the time, done what she asked of me, what she begged of me, and dropped the Juliet story, stepped aside, handed it over, or even left journalism for good. But I was an addict. Cassie had gently taught me how to be a person, how to trust my instincts, my talents . . . but she had good instincts too. They told her that the Juliet story would bring us nothing but trouble. She knew that tragedy begat more tragedy if you cared to wallow in it as I did. And her instincts told her I'd never change. I was an adrenaline junkie. I couldn't blame her for leaving but I still felt the hologram of that other possible life glitching over my real one from time to time. Would we still be together if I had done what she had asked? What would we be doing? Probably going for dinner with one of her sisters, or looking after her elderly father. Would we have had kids? Maybe one? A boy probably, a classic only child, who we'd treat more like our friend than a kid. Or would he be freezing us out, like any ordinary teenager?

I thought about fresh starts. Maybe that's what I needed. I thought about moving, finding somewhere new to live, but I couldn't muster the energy. Nor could I afford it. Besides, wherever I moved I presumed my problems would just be waiting for me. I still really missed having someone in my life. I'd never had a friend like Cassie before or after. Maybe that's why I had been thinking about Cleo again. She was the closest I had come to having a relationship again after Cassie, but even when we had gotten close, I always felt like there was a guard that Cleo never quite let down. Years of defending criminals probably did that to a person.

I turned my mind back to the story and tried to get the facts straight in my head:

Juliet dated William, both rich kids, perfect for each other.

Juliet had a lot of relationships, some of them secret. Who were they with?

She lied to William about Dave, and lied to Dave about William. Were there others she lied to?

At the party, William and Dave fought.

Juliet left with Dave, Dave walked her home but came back because he had her phone in his pocket, which is how he found her dead.

On his way he had passed William, drunk in the alley, but William denied it and produced an alibi, most likely fake. Who was this alibi?

Dave bumped into someone running away from the scene. Was this a witness or the murderer?

That person was still out there, had gone through their whole life, these past twenty years, staying silent ... How did that person live with themselves?

Sure they may have been young and afraid back then, but what were they now? Upstanding members of their community, no doubt. Possibly married, with kids, a job, a life? Did they ever think about Dave, how they might have saved him?

I had written about it all at the time, tried to sow doubt where there was doubt, but it was all swept away in the end. I flipped back through the archives ... There wasn't a single mention of the alibi in all these reports. Who were they? As a minor their name had never been released. But their name would be in the police reports. I needed to find out who had vouched for William that night.

41

CLEO

A lawyer takes on a personal cause

Between our investigations into the historical assault allegation against Bentwell and now trying to help out Dave, I was drowning in work. I didn't need to refresh my memory about the Juliet case but I googled the story anyway. Everyone remembered it. Whether you read the news or not, the story was inescapable. Everywhere you turned back then, Juliet Fox was the story. Her beautiful symmetrical face gazed out from televisions and newsstands – the young, blonde, beautiful, rich woman with the world at her feet. Murdered women were somehow so much more fascinating when they were heiresses of wealthy property developers, somehow much more tragic, more compelling, and more of a waste of a beautiful life than the ordinary women that were murdered every other week. It was also somehow much more urgent that a killer be found, convicted, and punished. Police and Juliet's family made desperate pleas for help – *if you saw anything suspicious . . . if you were in the vicinity of . . . if you have CCTV at your property in the area . . . a reward . . .* There was a wide-ranging investigation and a quick arrest of the man who tried to save her, who was quickly put under suspicion. Her boyfriend. Dave. I tried to push out of my head that it was always the boyfriend. I reminded myself that Juliet had at least two boyfriends.

I scrolled through article after article. I had forgotten how prominent she and her group of friends had been in the press at the time. They were presented as a brat pack who were all forever tainted by the murder. There were endless photos of Samsara and William, and Dave too looking more and more gaunt and guilty with each passing month. Another picture of Samsara at the trial. She still had that same smug look even twenty years later, but I just realised her nose was *totally* different now. I couldn't help laughing.

I was not attractive back then. I was what they called an ugly duckling, a late bloomer who had only really bloomed with the help of New York's finest Park Avenue cosmetic surgeons and dermatologists, and the loss of 25lbs. Bit by bit, I transformed myself from a plain Jane into one of New York's army of wide-eyed, sculpted, wasp-waisted pneumatic-breasted soldiers. At a certain point in my career I looked around and realised all of my peers had had work done. And the fact that I hadn't was holding me back. If I wanted to be at the top, if I wanted to be the best, I had to use every tool available to me. And so over the years I had fixed everything from my hair, my hairline, eyelids, nose, marionette lines, jawline, lips, neck, breasts, waist, tummy, vaginal rejuvenation, glutes and ankles. I hadn't done it all at once, of course, but if you looked at a photograph of me in my twenties as an intern and me now in my forties, I was practically unrecognisable.

It used to be that only movie stars were expected to look like movie stars, but now, everybody had to, from the girl on the subway to the doctors and lawyers and accountants and hairdressers: everybody. It was just another expectation of women now. Power was supposed to liberate women from having to look a certain way – they had influence and money – but actually now it was considered a failure if we didn't have power, money *and* looks, because if you didn't have looks it suggested that you didn't have *enough* money to buy them, which ultimately equated to *failure*. It was crazy but it was the norm, and I could benefit more from joining them than trying to beat them. I know I was invited on certain news shows and talk shows because I was 'camera friendly', and it had helped increase my profile and my fees. I treated every court appearance

like a fashion show and I had an extraordinary ward-
robe of outfits that I tried never to wear twice in front
of the news cameras.

The real irony in all of this was that I had never quite
managed to conquer the relationships quadrant of my
life. I had dated but never liked anyone enough to invest
my precious time on second or even third meetings.

I scrolled on. The reports became fewer, occasionally
prompted by 'fresh leads' or the suggestion that 'police
still looking for third person in Juliet murder'. I noticed
the by-line on that one – Eddie Wright. Finally, the
only news article left was the one documenting Dave's
release from prison three years later, which passed by
with barely a ripple.

Most people just wanted to forget. But Dave couldn't
forget because he was innocent. If I was to clear Dave's
name, I knew I'd have to come up with fresh forensic
evidence. I needed to pull the unidentified DNA profile,
and the evidence file from the crime scene, and get my
external investigator working on it. I usually used Alice
but I needed absolute discretion for this one. So I called
Smith. Smith didn't come into the office. I kept him exclusively for my personal cases, ones I didn't want the
office to know I was working on. Every lawyer needed
an investigator like that.

'Smith, I need your help,' I said, when we met.
We always met. Never spoke on the phone, never by
email. We were sitting on a park bench just inside the

south-west edge of Central Park. 'I'm looking into an old case for a client,' I said, passing him an A4 envelope. 'He got sent down for three years for the manslaughter of Juliet Fox, the developer's daughter. Do you remember the case?'

Smith nodded.

'Twenty years on, the guy is still looking to clear his name, which tells me he didn't do it. He lives in my building now, and, well, I said I'd see if there's anything I can do. I got him to give me a sample.' I handed him a smaller brown envelope. Smith knew what I meant. It was Dave's DNA profile. '... and this,' I said, adding a second envelope, white, padded, 'is a sample of the DNA profile collected from the crime scene, the one they never identified. Don't ask me how I got it but I do need it back within the week. The case is officially closed, so it won't be missed, but I'll sleep easier, and so will my contact, when this piece of evidence is back where it belongs. We need to work fast on this one. The less anyone knows the better. Just run it all and see what flags pop up; anything raises your antennae you let me know, OK?'

Smith never questioned me, even though I was crossing a lot of lines.

42

EDDIE

A trap closes

I woke to the sound of my phone buzzing.

'*Hello?*'

'Eddie? It's Dave ...'

I sat straight up in my bed. *Please gods of journalism don't let him back out on me.*

'Hey, it's great to hear from you, what can I do for you?'

'I think I found a lawyer who's willing to look into my case, *pro bono*. She thinks I have a good chance of overturning my conviction ... She's a real hotshot too.'

'Oh yeah,' I said. 'Well, that's just great. What's her name?' I was already pulling the notebook and pen on my bedside locker towards me but I didn't need to write down the name.

'Cleo Fry ... have you heard of her?'

I laughed in disbelief. '*Everybody* has heard of Cleo Fry. She has the highest hit rate of any defence lawyer in the five boroughs. Cleo Fry doesn't lose. How the hell did you manage to get her?'

'She lives in my building. I took her trash out for her. I guess it pays to be polite.'

'This is fantastic, Dave. If anyone can make something move with your case it's her. She's so connected.'

It felt like Cleo and I were being flung together no matter how hard I tried to stay away. Everywhere I turned on this story she was there. Was this the universe trying to tell me something? I looked different now than I did then, when she had liked me enough to want a relationship with me. And our age difference seemed more pronounced now; she was still young, barely forty, while I was in my fifties. Jesus, I needed to get my head back on the story.

'I can't tell you how happy I am to hear that,' he said.

'Hey,' I said. 'I'm just headed to the office – you wanna grab a coffee at Connolly's before work?'

'Sure,' Dave said.

'Great, see you in ten.'

I stood up and put on the jeans and shirt that lay in a rumpled pile on the floor.

Slowly, slowly, catchy monkey.

*

He was sitting in the same booth we sat in last time. I loved that army discipline.

'This is great news, Dave. It feels like you might get some momentum now. If anyone can find a break in your case it's Cleo.'

His hands were trembling. 'I feel that too. I'm afraid to let myself get excited but I feel it ... I've started dreaming again. It's as if my subconscious has been flung open and is spilling out into my dreams. I thought I had dealt with everything – the court case, the wrongful conviction – I was in therapy every week while I was in prison, learning how to deal with the injustice, and then every week after I came out of prison, trying to cope with the trauma, readjusting to "normal" life, attempting to catch up on everything I missed out on, trying to speed-live through my twenties so I could position myself where I should be. I used to have a recurring dream where I didn't go back to give Juliet her phone, where I just went home and had a rock-solid alibi. It was torture.'

I got the impression that Dave didn't even see me, like he was talking to himself more than me.

'I've started dreaming about the person who passed me in the alley that night, the person who I think was Juliet's killer. My therapist told me the reason I couldn't identify the person was a common trauma response. The mind isn't capable of coping so it shuts down. And yet my mind keeps reminding me that someone else *was* there. My mind is desperately trying to show me that person's face but all I can see are the eyes.'

'That's something,' I said. 'Eyes are the fingerprints of the soul. Do you think you would recognise those eyes if you saw them again?'

He shrugged. 'I think a DNA match would be a much more acceptable method.'

I sipped my coffee. 'A lot of people were hurt by that murder. A lot of people would be interested in seeing justice done. Me included.'

'It's like Juliet's ghost is in the foundations of the Sky Building, coming through the walls, trying to talk to me, asking me to help her, whispering through the air vents, begging me to do her justice. I tried to save her before. The only person I can save now is myself. And a lot of people don't want it stirred up again. It's so weird seeing Samsara, Bryant Fox, Bentwell, William Black ... all those people from my past. Do you know I don't think William Black even recognises me? I know I look different now – I'm bald for a start and my body is very different. Back then I was just a lanky indie kid. But I don't think it has anything to do with my altered appearance. People like William Black never remember people like me. It's as if they can see class. Is there a skill for that, like the elitist equivalent of synesthesia?'

I laughed. 'I hope not!'

'I just feel like they have face blindness when it comes to anyone from my social stratum. I become interchangeable with all the other working-class faces he encounters on a daily basis. They have no need to remember the faces of the people that delivered their packages or made their lunch or fixed their plumbing or cleaned their bathroom . . .'

'Maybe that's why nobody can remember the witness from the alley that night . . .'

'Maybe. I just feel so triggered by the whole thing. I keep thinking I'm somehow going to end up falsely charged and imprisoned for some crime again. Just being around these people feels dangerous. I have to keep telling myself they can't hurt me any more.'

I sipped my coffee again. *Oh Dave. They can always hurt you more.*

43

CLEO

An emergency phone call

I was just finishing for the day when my phone rang. 'Dave? How are you?'

'I need your help, Cleo. I'm at the police station. They want to question me on suspicion of Marley's murder. They say they have a witness who saw me go to Marley's apartment on the night in question. I need your help, Cleo. It's happening again. Someone's trying to frame me for something I didn't do.'

His voice was bordering on hysteria. 'Dave, don't speak to anyone. Which station are you in? I'll be right there.'

What on earth?

'Eighth Avenue. Someone has given a statement saying they saw me in the corridor, after you had gone home, and long after I had gone to bed.'

'Dave, this is ridiculous. This is just one person's word against yours and I wouldn't be surprised if it's just a calculated way to get you out of the building. What about the unidentified man who got out of the lift that night? Have they discovered who he is yet? His unknown provenance would be enough to throw doubt on any spurious case a prosecutor could build against you, so don't panic.'

I knew Samsara was behind this. She was trying to get him out since the day he had moved in.

I heard him exhale down the line. 'Can you let Eddie the journalist know. She'll help too. Please help me. It's happening again.'

'Just trust in the facts and the process for now, OK?'

'I've been here before, Cleo. I've trusted in truth and the law and reason before, and look where it got me . . .'

'Yeah, well, you didn't have me on your side back then. Sit tight. I'll be with you shortly.'

The guy in the lift was bothering me. Something about him on CCTV had felt familiar.

44

EDDIE

I just can't get you out of my head

My phone rang. It made me stop in my tracks. I hadn't heard that designated ring tone in years. Kylie Minogue's 'Can't Get You Out Of My Head'. I had designated it to Cleo's number when we were dating and she had never broken our agreement to give each other space, so I hadn't heard it in a long time. Why was she ringing me now?

'Eddie, Dave's been arrested on suspicion of murdering Marley. I'm on my way to the police station at 8th Avenue now but he said to let you know.'

'Fuck. I'll meet you there.'

I was full of concern for Dave but I also couldn't help noticing the note of excitement at seeing Cleo. And I hated myself for it.

45

CLEO

Déjà vu

They brought me to a tiny interview room, where a few minutes later they brought Dave. He had the haunted look of someone who had been through a harrowing experience. He had PTSD. I could see he was terrified, likely somewhere else in his mind.

He sat down. 'It's OK, Dave. We're going to sort this out.' I turned to the detective who was wearing a shirt that had seen a lot of life since its last encounter with a washing machine.

'Before we begin,' I said, 'I will be filing a complaint about how you have kept my client in a cell like a common criminal when he is not charged with anything and not under arrest. He is here voluntarily to assist with your questions, and you led him to believe that he is a suspect in a murder, despite the fact that to the best of my knowledge there has been no murder, rather a suicide. So, speaking to that, I will be filing a formal complaint. Now, how may we help you going forward, detective?'

'We had a tip-off that your client was seen in the vicinity of the deceased around the time of her death.'

'A tip-off,' I said. 'From a reliable source?'

'Anonymous. It came in on our tip line.'

I stifled a laugh, and some fury too. Some days I really struggled to keep my rage in check. So Dave had been hauled in here, because someone (most likely Samsara) had called in and tipped detectives off about his criminal record and they saw fit to drag him in.

'OK, do you want to continue with this embarrassing charade so you can justify your jobs or shall we leave it here and stop wasting each other's time?'

The detective had the good grace to look sheepish. 'We just want to rule your client out of our investigation. A couple of questions and then everybody can go home.'

Dave visibly relaxed.

'Where were you on the night of Marley's death?'

'I was at the party and then I went to bed. I met Ms Fry in the lift and she saw me go into my apartment.'

'And did you leave your apartment again that night?'

'I did not.'

'Can anyone attest to that?'

'No, I live alone.'

'Are we done here?' I asked. I kind of loved this bit, where I got to be a complete ball-breaker and there was nothing anyone could do about it because I knew everyone's rights, inside-out and backwards.

He nodded his head and I stood up.

'Just one question, detective – has your suicide been upgraded to a murder investigation?'

He shook his head, no.

'That's what I thought. Next time you want to speak to my client, contact me.' I flung my card on the crappy table. 'Let's go, Dave.'

He looked absolutely shattered. Eddie was in the reception area and leapt up. 'Dave, is everything OK? What happened?'

'Keep walking,' I said. 'We'll fill you in on the way back to my place.'

'Try not to worry, Dave,' I said. 'This is just some disgruntled resident trying to make your life difficult, you can be sure of it.'

But what if it wasn't? What if Marley had been killed. And what if somebody was trying to stick it on Dave? Again.

46

CLEO

A Pandora's box is opened

After saying goodbye to Dave, Eddie and I were left alone in the lobby. We had seen each other quite a bit since the party and I wondered if she might be open to me again. I had always thought of Eddie as the one who got away; despite the fact that she had told me she wasn't interested in a relationship, it had never felt like a true rejection. Her reasons were to do with her own past, her aversion to getting hurt again, her sense that her job came first (I mean, I could relate), so I had taken it more as a case of bad timing. But maybe now, all these years later, the timing could be right?

'Do you fancy a beer?' I said casually. Then added, 'I could really do with talking this over.'

She shrugged. 'I could do a beer.'

We got to my apartment and she whistled, as I knew she would. 'To think I might have been mistress of all this . . .'

'Did you just quote Austen at me?'

'I have hidden depths,' Eddie said. 'I presume I take my shoes off?' she asked as I kicked mine into the custom-built sunken shoe recess. 'Yes please, if you don't mind.'

I opened some beers. I knew she preferred beer to wine and I wanted her to relax. I filled a huge bowl of chips and some dips and put them on the table. 'Just give me a sec, I need to get out of these clothes.' I came back in a v-neck t-shirt that plunged low and some jersey shorts. I threw my hair up in a messy bun and joined her on the couch, looking out onto the sky pool and the skyline beyond it.

'That is some view. But also you can see everybody – is that Samsara? Is she just standing there drinking a bottle of wine on her own?'

'She does that most nights. It's really sad.' I hit Chet Baker on my phone and the whole apartment was filled with his trumpet.

'Wow,' Eddie said. 'This place is very cool.' I knew that Eddie liked jazz.

I pushed the bowl of chips towards her and she shoved a few in her mouth, while dipping another handful in the sour cream. I also knew that Eddie liked food.

'So I've been going back over Dave's case and I keep coming up cold. The only thing that will move this forward is the alibi. I can't help but suspect that the Bentwells have this all tied up. If I could find a way to get access to their case files . . .'

I leaned towards her, touched her hand. She didn't pull away.

'Be careful, Eddie. Bentwell is very powerful and very connected. You've experienced what that feels like once before.'

'I know, but this one just feels so personal. I feel like if I can resolve this I can live with everything I sacrificed – my career, relationships, even second chances at happiness . . .' she looked at me.

I curled my legs under me and sat up so I was looking straight at her. 'Maybe you can still have a second chance at happiness . . .'

She met my eye and the air tingled. I never hesitated when an opportunity presented itself – not in the courtroom, not in life, and not in love. I leaned in, and kissed her, brief and light, to test the waters. When she didn't pull away, I kissed her again, deeper this time. I pulled her towards me and her hands moved up my legs, my waist, my breasts. I let her push me down on the couch. I cleared all thoughts of Dave, Bentwell and the Juliet murder from my head and hit the remote to lower the interior lights so that we made love in the shimmering blue light of the sky pool. But I couldn't shake the feeling that someone was watching me.

Afterwards we took blankets and some more beers to the bedroom and I opened the doors onto the terrace so we could listen to the water and the traffic down below.

I didn't want to scare Eddie off again. I wanted her to stay the night, and as she was already in my bed I said nothing. She told me everything Dave had told her, which aligned with what he had already told me, including the detail about the person he saw running away from the murder scene. 'According to him the police never found this person,' she said.

I took a long swig from my beer. 'Or perhaps they already knew who that person was. Never underestimate the Bentwells,' I said. 'I've worked for their firm, I know what they are capable of.'

She nodded. 'God, I hadn't thought of that.'

'What's most interesting to me is that he told us both the same story, no variation, which suggests to me that he's telling the truth.'

A moment of comfortable silence passed before I said, 'You know I don't kiss and tell, but I may have overheard something that might interest you ...'

'Go on ...' Eddie said. She was wide awake again.

'I may have caught sight of a brief. I could be mistaken and you definitely didn't hear this from me but I thought I read something about a historical case of sexual assault being brought by a woman ... against Bentwell Senior.'

'You serious?' she asked, sitting up in bed. 'I spoke to two young women years ago about Bentwell Senior. It's one of the things that got me bounced from news to features. They said I had an unhealthy obsession with Bentwell, a vendetta. If I didn't then, I sure as hell do now. I'd so love to take him down now ... Back then it was a case of he said/she said, and Bentwell had friends in high places. The order to spike the story came from the very top. Different times though now, huh?'

'Different times indeed,' I agreed. 'If you could re-member the names of those two women you spoke to at the time, I know a lawyer who'd be very keen to get in touch, an associate of mine; she's trying to build this case against Bentwell. She might even be so grateful as to keep you appraised of her progress and I might be so grateful that I'd have to thank you personally ...'

She laughed. 'It's so great to have someone to talk to about this, you know,' she said. 'Somebody who un-derstands?' She nestled back into me and her breathing was even and long.

I smiled. 'I'm interested in it too,' I said. 'If Dave is innocent, I'd like to help him clear his name. It's what I do, it's *why* I got into this career in the first place.'

'Oh yeah,' she teased. 'It wasn't so you could buy a place like this and live a life of luxury? What are these sheets made of anyway,' she said, lifting my bed linen off me and exposing me. I grabbed her and pulled her on top of me so she was looking into my eyes. 'Maybe

I did it just so I could sleep with hot women,' I said, and kissed her deeply. She laughed and rolled over onto her back. 'I just wish I could speak to the alibi, or the witness. I feel like they would unlock everything.'

'Wow, you're worse than me. You never switch off. It would be good to hear another take. As it stands we only have one side of the story ...' I said. 'How Dave remembers it. And there are always three sides to every story.'

47

EDDIE

A pearl hidden on the ocean floor

Days turned into weeks and I wasn't getting anywhere fast. I was enjoying nights in Cleo's bed,
and the gnawing empty loneliness that was my constant companion was melting away. I could get used
to this. Marley's death had fallen from the news and
the residents' minds and the police had not come back
to Dave. Nor had they even bothered to ask why they
hadn't found the phone of a twenty-year-old woman,
which told me they had no interest in investigating this
case. But I was still certain she hadn't killed herself. I
had kept her phone but it had yet to reveal any secrets
to me. My search for the alibi's name was hitting brick
walls. I was sure I knew it at one point, that I had heard
it mentioned by a loose-lipped cop or clerk, but when

I reached for it my mind responded with blankness. I was sure the name was buried in my mind like a pearl with years of sand washed over it. It was there. I just needed to brush away the sediment. I just needed the right trigger. It would come to me eventually, I knew it would. But I needed it to come *now*. I had once known the name and I had to trust that the boys in the basement would eventually do their job and send it up from my subconscious to my conscious mind. The only thing I remembered for sure was that the alibi was underage, which is why the name was never made public.

In the evenings, I pulled my boxes of files and notebooks apart, in the hope that I might have written it on a scrap of paper, but they revealed nothing. In the days, I spoke to cops who had worked the case, buying them donuts and coffees and burgers and curly fries and cheese fries and chilli fries and more coffees, and had even tried a few twenty-dollar bills, but still I didn't get the name. One of my best cops told me he would go into the evidence files and get me the interview transcripts but when he went there he said they were empty, the files were missing. What the fuck? Why would the files be missing?

In the nights, I lay wide awake staring at the ceiling. I thought I could see the shape of the name in my mind's eye but it remained tantalisingly out of reach. My phone buzzed. I picked it up. Why was I getting a message in the middle of the night. But there was no notification, no alert. It wasn't my phone. And then I remembered. Marley's phone. I had left Marley's phone constantly charging on the floor by my bed. I may have had her PIN but I didn't have a PUK to unlock it if it shut down, so I didn't want to risk it running out of battery. I picked up her phone. There was a notification from an app, 23andMe. I had gone through all of her messages, her socials and her emails over the past weeks, searching for something that might give me a lead but hadn't gone through all of her apps. I opened the notification, which was a reminder message saying she had two new matches. I wasn't familiar with the terminology but it said – '10 per cent DNA Shared: Relationship – half-cousin/nephew/niece'.

The second match was '25 per cent DNA shared: Relationship – half-sibling'.

I scrolled down to the previous responses, which had several other matches with varying degrees of strength.

'50 per cent DNA shared: Relationship – parent/full sibling.' Oh my god. Had Marley found her mother? Or her father? If so, why had she not said? I checked the date of the results. The night Marley died. My hands were trembling. This felt like the breakthrough I had been waiting for ... I couldn't believe what I was reading. It had to be a mistake. I went back and clicked on the 50 per cent match, and there I saw the details of Marley's mother. The name I had been seeking for weeks now, the name that had sat just out of reach on the periphery of my mind shimmered to the surface like a pearl emerging from the sandy seabed, shining at me as if it had always been there, just waiting for the right tide to reveal it. Rachel Little.

I knew the name Rachel Little from the police reports I had read. Rachel Little was the alibi. And Rachel Little was Marley's mother. I felt a shiver down my spine. What on earth had Marley gotten mixed up in? I didn't believe in coincidences. I clicked on the contact details. Only a c/o address – Bentwell and Sons.

I clicked on the most recent matches. I actually thought I might be having a stroke. I took a sharp breath. My head was spinning. None of this made any sense.

So Marley had found her mother on the day she had died. Coincidence? And Marley's mother happened to be represented by the Bentwells. Coincidence? And Marley's peripheral DNA matches all led back to one source – the Bentwells. I knew first-hand what the Bentwells were capable of. Oh Marley, what slumbering beast had you awoken?

PART TWO

48

RACHEL: BEFORE

A cruel summer

That was the summer everything came crashing down. We should never have gotten involved with the Black family, or any of those families. People like us got scorched just by being in the vicinity of people like them. They lived at a different altitude – it was all too bright, too big, too much. But before everything went wrong, before my mother died and Juliet was killed – or was that the other way around? – being around the Blacks felt like living in a dream. Certainly to a sixteen-year-old girl from the Bronx.

Mom and I were still sharing a fold-out futon in our studio apartment in Woodlawn, which was the last stop before Yonkers, or so people liked to joke. It wasn't that far away from the Bentwells ... just over half an hour on the 4 train, but because it was the last stop in the Bronx and full of immigrant communities, people liked to look down on it. I liked it, though. It was home. The mostly-Irish neighbourhood we lived in reminded my mom of her own mother, who was from Galway. It was tight. People still knew each other's families and looked out for one another.

During the long summer holidays I tagged along with my mother to her work. She said it was to help her but I knew it was because she didn't want to leave me alone all day. I was old enough to handle myself but Mom didn't trust people, too many immigrants she said, even though she was one of those very immigrants. I always felt safe in Woodlawn. I liked the people, they were kind and caring, but mom said it was dangerous for a young girl to be alone in New York City, that there were things I didn't know about the world yet, things I didn't know about *men*. 'This is New York City, Rachel – anything can happen.'

I laughed but relented. I knew she worried. And she was right. There were things I didn't know about men. But I would have been safer in Woodlawn than in those gilded buildings that she cleaned. Anything could and did happen. I just never thought those things would happen to me.

My mother had worked for the Blacks for as long as I could remember. The Blacks had always been kind to us, passing on hand-me-downs, books, clothes, sports equipment, which I loved, although the practicality of Chanel swimming fins was lost on me, as we didn't have a swanky pool or tennis or country club membership to go with the accoutrements. They gave my mother a cash bonus every Christmas but even though she had known us for so long, Mrs Black never allowed us to forget the demarcation between *us* and *them*. She was the benefactor, and we were to behave like the grateful recipients of her generosity at all times, rather than employer and employee. She was so pale that she was almost translucent. She dressed in equally pale shades of grey, pink, ivory, and her hair was a similarly leached shade of blonde. The faded pearls at her throat seemed to blanch any remaining colour out of her. She was only a few years older than my mother, but she looked as if she was a whole generation removed.

Sometimes we cleaned for their neighbours too, the Bentwells and the Foxes. My mother had been sick the previous year and lost a lot of work, so she was glad to pick up some extra cleaning work from the Blacks' wealthy neighbours. The Blacks subcontracted my mother as if she were a lawnmower that they could lend out whenever they were feeling generous. The Foxes were different, somehow more ordinary, even though I knew instinctively none of them were normal. Bryant Fox was the most famous property developer in the city. His buildings went up like prefabricated doll's houses and then the financial storm blew the roofs off like a wicked fairy tale. Yet the Foxes', the Bentwells' and the Blacks' roofs somehow stayed on nice and snug. Mr Bentwell I had only met once, and it wasn't an experience I wanted to repeat.

Most days, my mother and I took the 4 train to 59th and Lex, then cut across the park to the beautiful brownstones on the Upper West Side. I loved tagging along. It wasn't that I loved cleaning but I did love being in those epic, ordered, breathtakingly beautiful mansions, with endless space, hidden rooms, ante-rooms, places for everything, books and reading nooks, secret gardens and terraces, and *history*, so much history. I thought of the people who had lived here over a hundred years before, the fingers that had brushed this very banister rail. It blew my mind. Our own studio was one white plastered room that held no mystery at all. Or else it was the kind of history you wanted to forget, to whitewash over. While Mom was scrubbing the shower stalls and bathrooms, I liked to pretend I lived in those houses. I was supposed to be dusting and polishing, but instead I would jump on the plump couch, put my feet up on the ottoman, or run my finger along the spines of the DVD library and pick what I would watch if I could. I liked pretending that everything in these houses, the endless food and clothes, the jewellery and books and art and *things*, were also mine. I marvelled at the glass extensions at the back. Some families had even dug out their basements and converted them to light-filled gyms and saunas. I loved these rooms the most. My experience of growing up in NYC was living in rooms with little-to-no light; everything was overlooked or in the shade of another bigger, better building. But not these places. When you walked into these homes, the air was clean and dry, regulated and purified. The light streaming in through the windows warmed you to your bones, while the smell of exotic plants that grew in decorative pots filled your senses. Our studio always smelled of damp laundry and we never felt heat like this. It was always either freezing cold and damp, or boiling hot and humid, the drip-drip-drip of the air conditioning unit rammed in the window never quite doing its job. The difference between how we lived and how they lived was so acute it made me feel desperate with longing. The houses on this street were owned by lawyers and doctors or Wall Street businessmen who came from generations of lawyers and doctors and Wall Street businessmen, and had owned these buildings before them. Why did they get to live like that, while we lived inside our four cold damp walls? Luck. Simple luck. That's why. Surely a person's luck could change.

Sometimes, on summer holidays, the kids who lived in the houses would be around too. My mom really disliked when that happened. She complained that they were under her feet or that they made her feel like she was under *their* feet when she was just there to do her job. Mom was proud and always taught me that people were people, that we were all as good as one another, worth the same no matter what our actual financial worth was. I believed that at the time, of course, because the alternative was too awful to believe, especially from our perspective, but I couldn't say anyone else in those houses held that philosophy.

That summer, the Blacks' eldest son, William, was stuck at home studying to repeat his exams, which he had failed. I was in awe of him, and his friends. None of the people I knew looked like this. They all looked like they had stepped out of a fashion catalogue. I stole surreptitious glances at them all summer as I cleaned and dusted. William rarely acknowledged me, except when he was very bored, and then he would deign to talk to me. I was still very naive, a young sixteen-year-old. Things were different back then. The internet was there but you needed a computer to access it. My mother kept me uninformed in that traditional Irish way of hers, afraid that if I knew the facts about sex, I would somehow morph into a harlot. The truth was I didn't know what I thought about sex. I had never even kissed anyone. I hadn't grown into myself yet, I was very self-conscious, embarrassed by my height and my general largeness, especially next to the girls William knew, who were all willowy with bird-like bones and delicate features, the kind of thinness that has nothing to do with your diet and exercise, and everything to do with genetics and eating disorders passed down from mother to daughter like a family heirloom.

'William is studying,' Mrs Black said to my mom that morning, 'but if you could bring him some lunch, try to cheer him up a little, encourage him to take a little bit of fresh air, I'd consider it a personal favour. I think he's a little depressed that he's missing out on all the summer fun this year, but his father says it's time for him to feel the consequences of his failing. He simply cannot drop out of school and Mr Bentwell can't solve everything for him. It's time for him to stand on his own two feet now. Five generations of Blacks have studied law in NYU and our son will not be the one to end that run. I've heard you're a bit of a scholar, Rachel. Is that so?'

I blushed. I couldn't help it. I was still a teenager, after all, and I loved being acknowledged in any way by these people. I was in awe of them and any kind of approval made me feel special.

'I'm a freshman in NYU,' I said. College had been a liberation for me. Finally I was free of the bullies who had picked on me for being too smart, too dumb, too frigid, too virgin, too grunge, too lesbian (which was a term used for anyone who didn't have a boyfriend). In college, I was free of that. I was invisible, which is exactly what I wanted to be.

'Aren't you young to be a freshman?' she asked.

'I was accelerated, there's a scholarship for kids like me if you can qualify for the grades, which I did.'

Mrs Black made an approving face. 'It's wonderful that these programmes exist for people like you, just wonderful that you can get an education, pull yourself up by the bootstraps. Mr Black and I are longtime donors of the college and it's so nice to see the money being so well spent.'

At lunchtime my mom appeared with a selection of sandwiches. 'Here, Rachel, make yourself useful and bring this up to the terrace to William for his lunch.' When I arrived on the upstairs terrace with the lunch tray, William was slumped on a faded sun bed, not studying. I loved this terrace with its beautiful old garden furniture. Even their old stuff always seemed beautiful while my old stuff just seemed worn-out, broken-down and dirty. The striped canvas on the sun bed was gently fraying, somehow still managing to look elegant. I thought of our plastic lawn chairs strewn around the communal dirt yard at the back of our building. I stepped onto the terrace as silently as I could, trying not to draw attention to myself, and put the tray down.

'Lunch is ready,' I said.

He looked up, surprised. 'Oh thanks. What's your name again?' he asked, halting my departure.

'Rachel,' I said as I slunk back towards the doors. He asked me this every time he deigned to make conversation, as if it were the very first time we met.

'God, I'm so bored. Stay, talk to me for a minute, will you?' he said, not looking at me.

I sank into the plump cushion of a sun bed opposite his, feeling the cushioning comfortable against my bare legs. He said nothing. I sat waiting. I noticed a ring glinting on his little finger, gold and black with a red ruby. And then another big gold one on the middle finger of his other hand.

'I like your rings,' I said.

'Oh these,' he said petulantly and stretched a hand out in front of him, shading his eyes with his other hand. 'I don't really like wearing jewellery. I think it's a bit, well, you know, but it's just our tradition. They're my dad's and they were his dad's before him and his dad's . . . well, you get the idea. My dad got these when he was eighteen and he gave them to me when I turned eighteen. And I'll give them to my son when he turns eighteen.'

'Oh, you have a son?'

He started laughing. He bent over, held his sides, squeezed his eyes until two soft crystals of tears seeped out. 'What? No! Of course I don't have a son. I don't have children. I mean *when* I have a son, I'll give him the rings.'

'But what if you don't have a son?'

He looked at me in a strange way. The doorbell echoed ceremoniously through the house and, a couple of minutes later, my mom appeared with a group of young, beautiful people behind her. 'William, some friends of yours ...'

They overtook Mom, streaming past her like she didn't matter at all. The boys were called variations of things like Chuck and Ted and Max while the girls all had names like constellations or proud historical figures – Cleo, Samsara, Juliet.

'William, your mom said you needed cheering up ... but not to cheer you up too much,' Juliet laughed and plopped herself down on top of his lap, her arm slung around his shoulder. Another girl, Samsara, squeezed herself into the tiny gap beside them. They were breathtakingly beautiful. I couldn't help but stare. I felt like an ogre in their midst. As Mom was leaving, William shouted, 'Oh Mrs Little? Bring some iced tea for my friends?'

I felt a weird divergence, hearing him speaking to my mom like that, while at the same time wanting to be one of them so badly. None of them even thanked her when she returned with the drinks so I said quietly, 'Thanks, Mom.' The girl called Cleo looked directly at Mom then and said, 'Thank you so much, this all looks delicious.' I liked this girl instantly for showing my mom basic respect.

'I'm going to be upstairs doing the bathrooms if you need anything, OK, hon,' Mom said, and I cringed. Now they all knew I was the cleaner's daughter. Samsara and Juliet stifled giggles. William took a sandwich and offered the plate to the others. The boys ate, the girls shook their heads. William took a bite, and made a grimace.

'Ugh, this doesn't taste of anything except butter. It's disgusting.' He was pulling the bread apart and wiping butter off one of the slices of bread using the other slice, making a mess in the process. A mess that my mother would have to clean up, no doubt. The sun beat down on my clothes and I felt a hot wave of shame rise up my body and into my face as I stopped eating my own sandwich. I put it down on the plate and put the plate on the garden table. I felt humiliated for liking my mom's sandwiches.

The girl called Samsara wrinkled her nose. 'Ugh, I think I'm going to vomit.'

She threw a sandwich and it landed on Juliet's tanned bare leg. She screamed as if a tarantula had just landed on her. 'Gross! Keep it away from me,' she said, flinging it across the terrace.

Cleo looked at me, then leaned forward, saying, 'I am hungry actually. I'll have one.' She smiled at me and started to eat and, just like that, the debate over the sandwiches was over. I felt enormous gratitude to her.

'So what do you do, are you in school?' she asked me.

'Me?' She was actually asking me a question about myself. 'Oh, I'm a freshman in NYU.'

'But you look so young . . .' she said.

I smiled. I liked her so I said, 'I'm on the . . .' I

lowered my voice, 'I'm on the accelerated programme for ... gifted kids from disadvantaged areas.'

Cleo smiled, saying, 'Good for you,' but one of the boys had overheard and boomed, 'Oh my god. Are you one of those geniuses? What's 9473 divided by 17?'

'557, give or take,' I said. 'And I'm not a genius. The accelerated programme is just another way for good students in public schools to get access to Ivy League scholarships.'

'You're Ivy League,' one of the other boys sputtered. 'What a waste,' he said under his breath.

I said nothing.

William realised the conversation had been about someone other than him for far too long and said, 'Well, if you ask me, college is one giant long pain in the ass. You're lucky if you don't have to go. Here I am studying in the summer when I should be on a yacht in Greece.'

Chuck stood up. 'Speaking of, we should get going if we want to get a good spot at the beach. Traffic is going to be hell. Wills, don't study too hard!' He slapped William on the back and the group filed out again.

Cleo smiled at me and said, 'Nice to meet you, tell your mom thanks for the food. We might see you around campus.'

If I ever got rich, I decided, I would be the kind of person Cleo was. Manners cost nothing, that's what Mom always said. I started gathering up the drinks and napkins and plates, the sandwich that had been flung across the patio, and piled them all on the tray. William didn't budge or even offer to help.

'Why does someone like you want to go to college anyway?' he said out of nowhere. 'What's the point if you're just going to end up cleaning houses?'

It felt like a punch. 'Well, *that's* the point,' I said. 'I go to college so I *won't* end up cleaning houses. I'll finish my degree, do a post-grad in NGO work and then hopefully get a job helping people. I want to work in the housing sector. You see, my mom and I—'

He cut her off. 'God, that sounds so *boring* but I suppose somebody has to do it. Juliet's dad does that too. He's a real-estate developer . . .'

'No, I don't mean I want to become a property developer, I want to help people to own their own homes, homeless people, disadvantaged people, people who have no credit rating or access to mortgages . . .'

'Oh God, *Yawn!*' he said. 'It's so hot. Do you want to finish our drinks downstairs? There's a little shade in the walled garden.' He gave the mangled sandwich a withering look, and flung it onto the tray I was holding with the other plates.

'OK,' I said meekly. I was pathetically delighted that he wanted my company. 'I'll just bring this tray inside . . .'

'Just leave it for the cleaner,' he said.

I put it back on the table and we walked through the

house and down through the basement, which led out onto a walled courtyard garden with fruit trees. Even with the extension the garden was huge. He pulled an apple from a tree, rubbed it against his shirt and bit into it. As he stretched up I saw a slice of tanned, toned belly appear between his polo shirt and his waistband. I was always pasty. I suppose several holidays a year kept you that golden. He took another apple and handed it to me. There was hedging towards the end of the garden, with a little gazebo in it that led through to a hidden walled garden. 'I didn't know this was here,' I said, delighted by the secret space. 'It's so pretty.'

'Yep, I like it in here, it's peaceful and shady and nobody can find me.'

We sat down in the leafy space behind the garden, with our backs against the sun-warmed boundary wall that led onto the alley behind. 'So what's college like for you, then? Do you have a boyfriend?'

I was slightly taken aback by the question and felt myself blushing to the roots of my hair. I had never had a boyfriend. When I thought about having a boyfriend it made my stomach curdle with fear. My mom told me when I met the right person it would feel good. I shook my head, hoping to shake away the red tinge that was suffusing my skin. 'No.'

He laughed. He had one leg straight in front of him, and leaned his forearm on the knee of his other leg, which was drawn up towards his chest. 'God, I'm so

232

bored. I wish I could be at the beach with the others.'
He looked at me and before I knew it he had leaned
in and kissed me. I froze. My stomach told me I didn't
want to do this. My stomach always told me when I
was in danger but my mind told me to shut up, stop
being a baby, told me that you did not say no to people
like William Black. It was just a kiss. I didn't want to
get my mother into trouble. *Don't tell.* So I let him kiss
me again, roughly this time, let him put his sweating
hand over my breast, which hurt so much, let him push
it around roughly as if it wasn't a part of my living,
breathing body at all. It hurt so much it brought tears
to my eyes. After a few seconds my mind floated up-
wards like an escaped balloon. My body stayed on the
grass with William. I wondered about all of the girls
he had done this to. Then wondered – did he do this to
the other girls, the girls I had just met – Samsara, Juliet,
Cleo? Or would he dare? Did he feel like he could do
this to me because I was the cleaner's daughter?

Afterwards I felt like I had been cored out by one of
the implements my mother used for slicing and grating.
He casually threw his half-eaten apple into the shrubs,
as if nothing had happened. And then he started to
laugh.

I didn't know what to say.

'What's funny?'

'Oh nothing,' he said, still chuckling to himself. 'It's
just, you taste just like I thought you would.'

'Like what?' I asked.

'Like the bread and butter sandwiches the cleaner made.' He laughed harder now, meaner. I felt the tears rising and when I heard my mom calling my name over the wall I was so relieved to be able to break away and run all the way back to the safety of the house, tears stinging my throat and eyes.

Later that day I was standing in the hallway waiting for my mom to finish. I saw William's rings, the gold ones, sitting on top of a sideboard and picked them up, turning them this way and that in the light; they cast pretty patterns in the sunshine. Mrs Black walked in to the hallway and I jumped, dropping the rings on the sideboard with a clatter. 'Sorry, I was just looking . . .' I said. My mom appeared a moment later and we left together.

After that day, William never even looked at me again. But that didn't bother me because by the end of summer my mom was dead, and so was Juliet, and I never wanted to see any of them ever again.

49

EDDIE

A journalist goes in search of an alibi

My whole body was trembling with excitement. I googled Rachel Little immediately but there was barely anything on her. An address for a building that was now demolished, like so many old buildings in New York. There were a couple of news references to her in college – a debating competition, a softball tournament – but the links led to broken web pages. After college, the trail went cold, meaning she had probably done what a lot of these young, privileged kids did: got married, changed her name to her husband's and dropped out of the working world in favour of a life of good deeds, charity fundraisers and competitive eating disorders. But what were the chances? Marley's mother was the alibi I had been searching for in Juliet's

murder? And now Marley was dead too. I kept goog-
ling different iterations of Rachel Little's name and of
Juliet's name but there was nothing.

I was so amped up I nearly called Cassie to let her
know what was going on before I realised that would
be absolute madness. But somehow I wanted to tell her
that it hadn't been a total waste of my life, a waste of
our marriage, that I was finally getting closer to the
story. But I didn't call Cassie. I called the most obvious
point of contact: the Bentwells.

'Uh, hello there, I'm trying to get in touch with a
client of yours and wondering if you have a forwarding
number or address for her please ... Of course, her
name is Rachel Little ... thank you, I appreciate it.'

The woman asked me to hold. A few minutes later
she came back to me. 'That's not an active account,
ma'am. The last time we dealt with that client was
twenty years ago. And the only piece of information
on the file is the lawyer who dealt with her ...'

'Can I speak to them, please?'

'Uh, that lawyer no longer works here at Bentwell
and Sons ...'

'Can you give me a contact?'

'Hold please ...'

I was so close. Please don't cut me off now. She came
back on the line. 'Do you have a pen? The lawyer who
worked on that file was Cleo Fry; you will find her at
Fry and Associates. Do you need a number?'

My whole brain was lit up like a Christmas tree. 'No, no, thank you. I know the firm.'

Cleo answered on the second ring.

'I've got a lead,' I said. 'Marley's phone. She had submitted her DNA to a genealogy site and she got a hit. In fact, she got several hits.'

Cleo was uncharacteristically quiet on the end of the phone.

'Go on . . .'

'As you know, I've been searching for the alibi for weeks now. I knew if I saw the name I would remember it. Well, guess what? I just saw the name . . . in Marley's DNA match. Rachel Little is the name of the alibi. She's also the name of Marley's mother. But the only contact I had for her was a forwarding address for the Bentwells. So I just called them and asked for a contact. They didn't have one but they did tell me the name of the lawyer who worked on her case. Cleo, it was you!'

50

CLEO

A journalist enquires after an old client

As far as I was concerned, Rachel Little might as well be dead. In fact, I really wished she was. But here she was back in my life after twenty years.

'Eddie, I was an intern in Bentwells during that time period. They gave me the most inconsequential cases, and they put my name on anything. It didn't mean I was actually acquainted with the case or the person or anything like it. A lot of the time it just meant I had filed the case.'

'Please, Cleo, this is the best lead we have.' I could hear how excited Eddie was. 'We've got her, Cleo. I really feel Rachel Little is the key to the murder, to clearing Dave's name and maybe she's the answer to Marley's death too. Do you know the DNA match came through the night of Marley's death? Surely you have a number for this woman in your files? Or you can get access to her file? There has to be a way of contacting her.'

'I can't promise anything but I'll do my best. I can put in a professional request to the Bentwells, say I'm trying to get in touch with one of their clients on behalf of one of mine ... but Eddie, let's not put the cart before the horse. We don't even know if this woman is alive. Let's wait and see.'

But Eddie didn't know how to wait. My phone rang an hour later.

'Any joy?' she said.

'Eddie, I have a job. And clients. Clients who pay me. I can't just drop everything because you want me to chase up someone from decades ago. I will check my archived files at home. But you are going to have to wait until then, I'm afraid ... Don't get me wrong. I really admire what you're doing for Dave and I want to help him too, but even if we do track down this Rachel woman, even if she does admit to being a false alibi – which would be a huge risk for her legally – she most likely does not know who the real killer was ... I just don't want to see you disappointed.'

Eddie sighed heavily.

'OK, fine,' I said. 'Come by my place tonight and we'll see what we can find.'

'You're an angel, Cleo,' she said.

'Yes, and you are lucky that I like you. I'll be home from eight. Call any time after that.' I wish I didn't want to please her so much but she was the only person I would do this for.

By lunchtime I had reason to email Eddie.

From: cleo@fryassociates.com
To: steadyeddie687@gmail.com
Subject: FAO: Rachel Little

Eds, I found an old email for Rachel Little in my files and took the liberty of contacting her. She got back to me and says she's not willing to speak to anyone. She doesn't want to be drawn back into the case – she says it was the most traumatic time of her life and she wants nothing to do with the Bentwells ever again. Call over tonight anyway and we can talk through next steps. x

Cleo.

I knew what I was doing by calling her Eds, the name I used to call her, and by adding an 'X' at the end of my email. I was letting her know. I still thought we were good together. And I wanted things to work this time.

51

EDDIE

Things fall apart

It's true I became obsessed. I know that now. Hindsight is a wonderful thing. But I could trace my problems back much earlier than the Juliet Fox case. You had to go back a very long way to find the beginning of this story. Before sky pools and luxury apartment buildings. Before the poor and hardworking were locked out of the Upper East and West Sides, back to when the grid was still peppered like a terrazzo tile of all sorts of people. I had a long memory. It's what made me a great journalist. For the beginning of this story, you had to go back to the day my mother OD'ed in our one-bed with the tub in the kitchen, back to the rich yuppie college kid who supplied her and the law firm who got him off the hook for manslaughter.

241

It's why the Juliet case bothered me so much. It just felt like the Bentwells doing what that law firm did to my mom – getting rich kids off the hook. I don't mind saying I was triggered. It's why I couldn't let go, even when my whole life was falling apart.

I do have some memories of life being normal as a kid. There are even a few pictures of me at the age of nine, ten, eleven years old, when my mom was still a mom and I was just another happy-go-lucky kid who didn't know how good I had it. We had a routine, she paid our bills, she fed me and made sure I got to school, but the summer I turned twelve, my dad died, and instead of finding a job, my mom found a boyfriend who told her he'd look after us. But instead of supporting her in her grief, in her newfound life without my dad, he turned out to be an addict and, instead of showing him the door, she joined him. Oblivion was soothing, I guess, and her boyfriend got her so consistently drunk and high that she forgot about the bills and the rent and the studio ... and me. So I became the responsible one. The boyfriend was gone by the time I was thirteen, but his habits stuck hard. My mom found she liked being oblivious more than she liked reality. I managed to set her up on disability, filling out forms I didn't understand, starting a direct debit payment system for the rent so we at least would have somewhere to live. Friends stopped inviting me to their homes, and the shell of my body became softer and bigger, a more protective space that I could disappear into, muffling the world outside.

The studio was painted the most depressing dark green – it's still the same shade today, and I wonder what a therapist would have to say about that – shiny, inch-thick paint. The room was already dark but that green paint made it seem even darker inside. It was made up of two rooms but it was barely more than a studio. The kitchen doubled up as the bath/shower. I was a teenager and already self-conscious about my body so I never used our shower, preferring to wash at the kitchen sink, a little birdbath, splashing under my arms, my face and rubbing water from the back of my neck over my head. I wasn't sporty but I played sports so I could use the showers at school at some point every day. My mom had no such inhibitions and I regularly came home to find her passed out in the tub. I used to pull the plug so I knew she wouldn't drown and would then wake up to the sounds of her teeth chattering and her voice cursing me. She had been a good mother once, and I tried to remember her like that. Most days, I left for school before she woke up, but I could always smell the acrid, peculiar stench emanating from the bedroom where she slept. I had long since moved to the couch. I stayed late in school and when the doors closed I moved on to the public library until 10 p.m.

Most of my friends were still being collected from school by mothers at this stage. By the time I got home she would be drunk again. Some days she was just sober enough to remember she was a mother and to make some semblance of an effort at being one. Other days she was so drunk she didn't know who I was, and fired insults at me, telling me to get out of her house. Well, I liked to think she didn't know who I was. It made it so much worse to think she knew I was her daughter and felt I should sort her life out for her. As if anybody could do that.

I ate whatever I could. I had no idea of nutrition. My hygiene was questionable, I didn't know how to do laundry. It led where you might expect. I was taunted and bullied but it didn't get to me. I was already numb.

The apartment was a mess. I did my best but I had no idea how to keep a house. Nobody had ever taught me. I would attack it in fits and starts, sweeping madly or scrubbing a mouldy corner, but I was always beaten back by exhaustion or the relentless creep of the condensation that ran down the walls in winter as I cranked the heat to little effect, or the humidity that broiled the building in summer. By my final year in high school I was barely there.

When I found her dead one night at 10 p.m., with a young guy passed out on the floor beside her, I called the ambulance and then the police. One of the cops had recognised the guy and called in a lawyer, who came and got him out of there. That was the first time I came across the justice system. The guy got off, an innocent college student led astray by an influential older addict, caught up in the chaos of this woman's unseemly life. They painted it as if this kid had been trying to help and had got pulled into the maelstrom as opposed to running a small drugs business on the side of his art history degree. At the time I was too preoccupied staying out of social services' eye-line and clinging on to our rent-controlled studio to do anything about it, but I never forgot.

The rent on the apartment was small enough that I could cobble it together with odd jobs. My best subject in school was English and my isolation had made me watchful: two excellent qualifications for the world of journalism. I had already been accepted onto the Columbia degree but when I was refused the full scholarship I knew I wouldn't be able to afford to take up the offer. So I did the next best thing – I got a job. I sent letters to every local newspaper in the city until I found someone willing to let me do odd jobs and from there I worked my way up, moving from local to state to national press, finally landing at the *New York Post* after winning an award for solving a double murder cold case that had left the police stumped. I was the best investigative journalist in the state. Officially. The job at the *Post* came with golden handcuffs, stating the contract was inviolable under any circumstances until I turned sixty-four. I was so sure that it was the beginning of my life. I met Cassie that same year and I was in love and feeling that everything was possible for me. I was living beyond my wildest dreams. I never imagined the parabola would have curved so catastrophically that it would land me right back where I started in my grim childhood home.

It was so obvious to me back then – as it still was now – that they didn't have their guy, that the guy they had was a fall-guy so the guy who had actually killed Juliet could carry on with his privileged life. I made as much fuss about it as I could. I butted heads with investigators about the evidence that didn't add up, wrote about it, published it, called them out for having an unidentified DNA profile from the body, an unidentified suspect at the scene and wafer-thin alibi for William Black, who had been seen arguing with Juliet that very night. None of it worked. The cops got shirty with me, while the lawyers stuck to what they did best – getting rich guilty people off the hook. I found out later that the Bentwells had tried to put me down after the Juliet case was over. Tried to sue the paper, tried to sue me personally, tried to have me sacked (even their legal resources couldn't undo my iron-clad contract).

I dug so deep I came across a quiet story from two young women who claimed Bentwell had groomed and raped them when they were teenagers. When they told me that he was still doing the same to young college students hopeful of interning in his law firm, I knew I had the story of my career. What I didn't realise was how far the Bentwells' influence reached, right into the newsroom of the *Post*. My editor refused to touch it. *It's just she said-he said.* That never stopped us before, I argued. But the Bentwells were too litigious, it wasn't worth it. These women's lives weren't worth it.

Plus, I was biased. My editor had heard me speak about the Bentwells in bars after hours, knew I thought they were dirty to the core. I couldn't deny it. Nor could I let the story lie. I dug so hard and deep that I blinded myself to everything else. They got tired of me the way you get tired of a mosquito, and squash it. And they did the same to me in the end. I pushed them too far.

I got an anonymous tip-off, offering me a meet with William Black's alibi. I was so desperate to speak to the alibi that I never stopped to ask myself who the anonymous tipper might be, and what was in it for them. I never got to meet the alibi but they did manage to make it look like I was trying to tamper with a state's witness, and got me and my newspaper investigated by the police, and eventually got me thrown off the news desk. The paper couldn't fire me as they couldn't actually prove any wrongdoing, but they could do the next best thing, which was to put me on the social diary.

And until a few weeks ago, I thought I had accepted my fate ... but it turns out it's nearly impossible to escape the grooves life has ingrained on your path, to climb out of the ditches you don't even know you're in. The past is the place that understands who you are, without explanation, and it can call you back again and again. Even if you never want to go there. An unresolved past will keep calling until it's laid to rest. That was why the Juliet case had such a hold on me, and that was why I found myself answering its call one more time, twenty years after it ruined my life the first time.

The Bentwell name seemed to follow me at the worst moments of my life. And now, here I was again, wondering why the name Bentwell was at the centre of my investigation into Marley's death and at the centre of her search for her parents.

I needed to get to the bottom of the Bentwell connection, so I decided to cut to the chase and go direct to the source. I dialled the number for Bentwell & Sons.

'Oh hi, I'm doing a family tree for my dad's fiftieth birthday and I'm trying to find some relatives that we have matched with on 23andMe and the DNA matches have redirected me to your offices. Do you have someone who deals with this?'

'Can I take a name please ...'

I couldn't do it under my name. I was a walking red flag and would be cut off from the start. Likewise, I couldn't do it under Marley's name. I took a chance and thought of the young women who had contacted me all those years ago with their complaints about Bentwell assaulting them.

She typed a few words, paused then said, 'Putting

you through now. Hold, please . . .' I waited for the call to be transferred.

'Bentwell and Sons genealogy research department, how may I help you?'

52

RACHEL: BEFORE

Never trust rich people

The week after William took me into the secret garden, Mrs Black asked my mom about a 'small sum' of money that had gone missing, as well as a couple of William's rings, very important family heirlooms. The sum of cash was $200. I remember thinking *that's* what she considered a small sum? It would have kept my mom and me going for weeks. Mrs Black wanted to know had my mom seen the money or the rings anywhere while she was cleaning? William was certain he had left them on the sideboard in the entryway but had not been able to find them.

'This is ... delicate,' Mrs Black had said, taking my mom by the elbow and steering her into Mr Black's study. 'William said he saw Rachel taking the money and the rings. And I did catch her handling the rings recently. I don't want to embarrass her but maybe you could talk to her, convince her to return them? I'm sure you understand we trust *you* completely, but we cannot tolerate theft.'

My mom was horrified. She came out to the hall again and called me into the living room. 'Rachel, did you take money or rings? Have I not taught you right from wrong?'

'What? No! Mom, you know I would never do that!'

'William says he *saw* you,' my mom said. 'Why would he lie? What reason has he got to lie about something like this?'

I thought maybe he would lie because he wanted rid of me, maybe he felt guilty about what he had done to me, but I couldn't tell my mom about it.

'I didn't, Mom, you have to believe me.' I started to cry. My mom knew me, she knew I wasn't capable of something like this. 'I did pick up the rings, but it was just to look at them. The gold one with the emerald. It was so pretty, I just wanted to look at it but I put it back. Mrs Black, you saw me put them down when you came into the hallway. I left them where I found them. And I don't know anything about money.'

'OK, hon, it's OK, I believe you. Wait in the hallway for me and I'll be right out.'

After I left the room, I heard my mother say to Mrs Black, 'I'm sorry, but she says she didn't touch them and I think she's telling the truth. I'd know if she was lying. She's a good girl, she's never done anything like this in her life. Honestly, I think even if she did have the impulse she would be too frightened to ever do something like that. She knows how seriously I take things like this.'

'But then who is lying, Mrs Little?' Mrs Black said, and I could hear the curl of her mouth in her words. 'Why would William lie? Perhaps you should talk to her later in private, in your own environment.'

'All right then, but I don't know if I'll get a different answer.'

It was obviously a ruse. William was ashamed of his behaviour and didn't want to have to look at me any more.

As we sat over dinner in our studio that night, Mom asked me again whether I had taken the money and the rings.

'It's OK, Rach, you can tell me, you won't be in trouble.'

'But Mom, I didn't, he's lying. He doesn't like me. I think he's using it as a way to get rid of me.' Then another thought struck me. What if Mrs Black wanted rid of us. What if she had seen William and me, maybe had seen something on their security footage. She wouldn't have liked it. She would put an end to it, however misguided she was about what 'it' was.

'But *why* would they want rid of us,' my mom

asked. 'My work is excellent. They've never had any complaints.'

But I couldn't tell her.

Later that evening, Mrs Black called to the studio. Mom and I were dressed for bed and it felt so strange to see Mrs Black standing there amongst our shabby things in her lovely clothes. She asked Mom if I'd changed my mind and when Mom said no, she took a thick envelope out of her handbag and gave it to her. Six weeks' wages, enough to tide us over until Mom could find something else, she said.

'I cannot tolerate theft, Mrs Little,' she said.

I cried myself to sleep that night and between crying wondered how we would survive now.

53

EDDIE

A seed of doubt

I had gotten sidetracked by the alibi but I still had a deadline for the feature on Juliet's anniversary and I had made arrangements to speak to Bryant Fox and Samsara that afternoon, which meant I couldn't visit Bentwell and Sons until tomorrow.

I met Fox in the restaurant and coffee area on the ground floor of the Sky Building. I knew this was going to be a tough one. He probably saw me as the journalist who had stood in the way of his daughter's justice, but I hoped the fact that he was talking to me meant that there were no hard feelings.

We ordered coffees. The restaurant was largely empty now that it was after 3 p.m.

'So you work social diary now? That's a surprise,' he said.

'Yeah, I'd love to say it's less drama than the crime beat but I can't honestly tell you that. Congratulations on this building, by the way,' I said. 'It's an incredible achievement.'

I had to tread carefully with Fox. These guys were like ageing actresses; you had to flatter them and reassure them at all junctions. If you said the wrong thing, hinted at their insecurities, you were in the enemy camp before you knew it, without having had a chance to ask your actual question. It might have been easier if I looked like some of the other female journalists working on the paper but unfortunately I didn't have that tool in my arsenal. So I spoke to him on a business level. I flattered him with compliments about the architectural feat, the planning row, the apartments that had been handed over to the social housing sector and let him wax lyrical about his social ideals before I risked moving closer.

'I'm aware that it's your daughter's twentieth anniversary coming up soon,' I said gently. 'The paper would like to pay our respects to her and your family by doing a commemorative piece, linked to the building and your new charity, of course, which might be seen as her legacy in some ways. Building this sky-rise here, on this location, so close to where she died, it must feel like an homage to her in some ways. Would you talk to me about Juliet, about how her death has informed your work, and the projects you have taken on since, your desire to help other people with projects like the cost-rental one attached to this building? And before we begin I just want to say all of the reporting I've done on this case has only ever been motivated by discovering justice for Juliet.'

Fox gave a tight smile. 'I've always known that, but thank you.'

'So, twenty years is a momentous anniversary. Can you tell me a little about what it means to you, to mark Juliet's anniversary with the building and the charity?'

'Anniversaries are always painful. It's hard not to think about the kind of person she would be now. I would be a grandfather. That's painful too.'

'Of course, and I don't want to make you relive your trauma. Can you tell me a little bit about what you remember about her now, twenty years on, perhaps your fondest memories of her?'

He spoke about what she was like as a child, the kind of woman she was becoming, her studies and her hopes for her future. I felt sorry for him actually. All of the usual bombast was gone, all of the concern about appearing down to earth with humble roots. I liked him better for it. He said her death inspired him to live life differently, to seize every day. Our time was nearly up when I dared ask what I really wanted to.

'This is a sensitive question, and I have no evidence of this, but I do have an intuition and have always suspected that the police did not get the right person for Juliet's murder. Do you have any thoughts on that?'

'The police did a fantastic job getting swift justice for my daughter,' he said. 'That man has served his time and my wife and I forgave him a long time ago.' He pressed pause on my phone recorder. 'Off the record, I trusted the process of justice, I let the courts do their work, but I didn't think Dave killed her at the time and I don't think so now. Juliet hadn't told us about him so I had never met him, but from what I saw in court he was a good guy. I believed him when he said he didn't kill her. If he had done it why would he have called the ambulance, tried to save her? He did not kill her. But I don't think William Black was capable of that either, even if he was blackout drunk. He's not a killer, for god's sake. Obnoxious, yes, but a killer? No way. So yes, I think your intuition is correct. But until someone comes to me with proof, I won't criticise the police on the record.'

Samsara arrived just as we were finishing up.

'Bryant,' she drawled, 'how are you? I'm so happy to help with this commemorative piece about Juliet. It's hard to believe it's twenty years.'

'It really is,' he said. He turned to me. 'Ms Wright, if there's anything else you need, just get in touch with my PA. I'd be happy to answer any follow-up questions.'

Samsara slipped into the seat Bryant had just

vacated. Her body was the result of lifelong denial that left her sinewy and pale. Her clothes signified what she wanted them to – the same as her thinness – that she was wealthy enough not to wear logos and that she had the kind of brutal self-discipline that came with going to certain schools and growing up in a certain social class in New York. I felt sorry for her too.

'Samsara, thanks so much for meeting me.'

'Of course, anything for Juliet.'

'That's a great outfit … I wish I could wear something like that.' Absolute rubbish. You wouldn't catch me dead in the weird collection of bandages that hung from Samsara's bones.

'How are you enjoying being a resident of the most exclusive new address in town?'

She smiled serenely. 'Well, it's the last word in luxury, obviously, and the views are to die for.'

'You live in the triplex, right with your husband and son?'

'Correct,' she said. 'William Black – he works with my dad now – and our son, Josh. He's going to college in the fall, which is why we thought it was time for us to downsize.'

I tried not to scoff. Downsize to a 6,000-square-foot triplex? 'Wow, what was your previous dive like?'

She smiled tightly. Everything about Samsara seemed tight.

'I'm just kidding,' I said. 'Honestly, congratulations.'

'Thank you. We're also celebrating our twentieth year together this year too, so it feels like a special year. A sad one too, what with Juliet's anniversary.'

'Can you tell me about Juliet?'

'We were best friends. This is painful actually to talk about. We don't really ever talk about her because of how tragic her death was. But I'm happy to speak to you, for Juliet,' she added.

Her eyes seemed a little unfocused. Something occurred to me. 'Say, this is my last job of the day and I could murder a beer. Would you like a proper drink?' She lit up. 'We could share a bottle of wine ...'

'Excellent idea,' I said.

She downed half the glass in her first mouthful. She immediately became less agitated. I didn't touch my glass but let her believe we were drinking together as she worked her way through the entire bottle.

'Can I ask you about that night, about the night Juliet died? What do you remember of that night now?' I asked. She took another large gulp of her clear drink and paused. Perhaps I had been tactless, obvious.

'That night was supposed to be the beginning of our lives,' she said, and I breathed a sigh of relief that she wasn't batting me away, 'but instead it ended in a tragedy that changed everything.'

Talking to her was like talking to a bad actress. Everything she said seemed studied, fake, but it was still quotable.

'If anything good came of it all, it was the fact that it brought me and William together.'

'A shoulder to cry on,' I suggested. I needed to be very careful here, to speak as little as possible.

'I guess so. We got married and had Josh within a year. People said William had a broken heart and that's why he married me, as if that wasn't the most offensive thing you could say,' she said, topping up her own glass now. 'I was one of the most eligible girls in our circle . . .'

'It's just that nobody was good-looking in comparison to Juliet,' I offered.

She laughed bitterly, studying me for a moment, as if from on high. 'Exactly. Everyone was just a minor planet in the orbit of her blinding sun. When William and I got together after Juliet died it seemed natural. We were both frightened and shocked, and we clung to each other in the aftermath.'

'I'm sure it was the right thing to do for you both. It was such a trauma for people so young to have to go through. Forgive me if this sounds callous, but young people need to forget trauma, put it behind them, get on with their lives.'

Samsara smiled her tight smile again. 'Thank you for saying that. People were not so kind at the time. They were judgemental. They said we should move away, make a fresh start, live somewhere more anonymous, that we should be respectful to Juliet and her family by hiding ourselves away … as if we had something to be ashamed of, as if we had killed her! But this was our home too and we needed our families.'

'Do you think it affected your lives, or were you able to move on? Did it change you?'

'Oh, it changed us all. I think William took it particularly bad. He was under suspicion at one point but his cleaner's daughter finally came through with an alibi. She had been at the house that night. But I feel like something died in William that night: his emotions became fractured, or he couldn't access them – he couldn't go there after Juliet died. But that's been problematic for him, I think. He pushes all of his emotions down and then they bubble up at the wrong moment. Look at what happened at the party the night Marley died. That was embarrassing, shouting at a little girl and her mother who was barely more than a kid herself. At least he had the good sense to disappear. Marry in haste, repent at leisure, that's what Granny had said to me at the time but, you know, I was in love and there was no talking to me.

'William went to work at my father's law firm after doing a masters at Harvard law school (Daddy wouldn't accept anything less than Harvard, even from his son-in-law). William's father was a bit miffed but he understood it was good for our families. I gave birth to Josh and William started earning good money and that was the beginning of our life together.

261

We raised Josh, and went through the cycle of seasons and festivities with a rotation of holidays – January ski, mid-term European culture, summer Hamptons followed by island-hopping in Greece, winter sun in Mexico, interspersed with some religious rites and celebrations, and repeat *ad nauseam* until twenty years have slipped by in the blink of an eye. It was the kind of life most people dreamed of. And it was the kind of life I had dreamed of too, before Juliet died and drained all the colour from my worldview. I've had to work really hard to stay positive, to see the point of things, to continue with a career of my own. I didn't know how else to live, except to repeat the patterns I had been taught, sticking to the script. I realised I was traumatised by Juliet's death too. After she died, I begged God, or maybe it was the devil, for this quiet, ordinary life – marriage, family, work – unassailed by nightmarish thoughts of danger or murder or attacks of conscience.'

'What about your neighbour, the lawyer who lives in the pool penthouse ...? She told me she thinks the police might have got it wrong with the man they convicted of the murder.'

'Oh, you must mean Cleo. Have you noticed that her apartment is not a penthouse? They call it the "pool penthouse" but I think that was probably a marketing trick to drive up the price. The real penthouse is eighty-two stories up.' She tipped her head back and nodded towards the ceiling. She sipped some more wine. 'I'll let you in on a little secret about Cleo,' she said, dropping her voice to a stage whisper. 'She's not really wealthy ... she's just very rich. There's a difference, you know.'

Jealousy ... I wouldn't have expected it from the woman in the triplex. Nothing much changes, I thought. These people were still just looking for ways to make themselves feel superior. I was already feeling angsty from spending so much time in these dark corners of my memory, reading their files, researching their families, their lives ... and now I was back amongst the living, breathing versions of them.

'What's your relationship like with the Foxes now?' I asked. I thought I had sensed a *froideur* between her and Bryant.

'After Juliet died and William and I married, our families slowly drifted apart from the Foxes.' She picked up the bottle of wine but it was empty. I signalled to the waiter and he came by and filled her glass. She took a huge swallow.

'How come?' I asked.

'I think they thought we had moved on quickly. We were just kids. And I think they were upset that there was an issue with our CCTV, which looked directly onto the alley.'

'What issue?' I asked. 'I thought there was no CCTV coverage of the night?'

The alcohol had loosened her up but she was on red alert now. 'No, I'm getting confused. Of course, you're right there was no CCTV. It's all so long ago now. Not worth dwelling on,' she said.

54

EDDIE

The department of covering up

I just about made it to the Bentwells' office for 5 p.m. for my appointment with the genealogy department. I was hoping I wouldn't encounter anyone who might recognise me. When I gave my fake name and appointment details I was surprised to be led to a room with two attorneys, a file and an NDA.

'This is a non-disclosure agreement, which we will need you to sign, and then a one-off payment of $150,000 will be made to your account if you fill in your bank details on this page. No mention can be made of your or any offspring's biological connection to Mr Bentwell, or of this payment. If you initial, here, here and here, and then sign here, we can authorise the payment immediately.'

Jesus Christ.

'Wait,' I said. 'Do I get to even read this contract?'

'It's all standard, but please feel free to go through it. We'll be in the next room; you can just come find us when you are ready to sign. We need to witness your signature.' They stood up and left.

I quickly photographed the contract then followed them out. I told them I'd need to think about it some more. 'Just to be clear, there is no room for negotiation of the sum. Mr Bentwell has a set budget for these issues and will injunct any attempt to speak publicly about his private business.'

I rushed home with my heart in my throat. I felt something I hadn't felt in a long time: fear. When I got home I opened Marley's 23andMe app and clicked on the weaker matches she had connected with. I knew I had to be careful of how I asked the question if they had signed NDAs. I messaged them one at a time, asking them whether they had ever heard of the Bentwells genealogy research department. The answers came back quickly. Several of them acknowledged they had heard of such a place. It was obvious what was happening here. Bentwell was paying hush money to women he had impregnated, and their offspring – *his* offspring. And one of those women was Marley. Had he also paid her mother to provide an alibi for William Black? Had Marley refused to be silenced? Was that why she was dead? Combined with the rumoured charges of historic abuse against Bentwell, this story was front-page news.

55

RACHEL: BEFORE

An apology rings false

After the Blacks let us go, it was as if they had cast a voodoo sickness spell on Mom. She had been sick on and off over the previous few years with a bad chest and we put it down to the black fungus coating the back wall of our studio. But when the Blacks let her go she got sick again, first with the same old cough that wouldn't go away, and then with what we thought was pneumonia. When she arrived at the ER they did some tests and all the doctors could say was they were very sorry. Lung cancer. Stage 4. Palliative treatment only.

I picked up some work with the Bentwells and the Foxes, appealing to them directly. I knew it was irrational but I put my mother's deterioration down to the stress of being unjustly fired by the Blacks. She had been so distressed, more distressed by the insult to her reputation than the loss of income. She was an honest woman. When I wasn't cleaning for the Bentwells and the Foxes, I was at my mom's bedside, which is where I was when Mrs Black arrived unannounced one afternoon. She had heard from Mrs Bentwell that my mom was dying.

'Hello, Rachel,' she said, coming in and sitting beside Mom. I was frozen. I hated this woman. In my mind, the stress and shame she had heaped on my mom was responsible for her decline.

'How are you feeling, Mrs Little?' she asked Mom, who was awake but heavily dosed with painkilling medication.

She smiled politely. Always polite until the end. I wanted to rant and rage at Mrs Black but I knew it would upset my mother, so I stayed cool.

'She doesn't have the energy to talk much now,' I said, by way of explanation. 'She's too breathless.'

'Ah, I see. This must be very hard on you, Rachel. You were always such a support to your mother, helping her out at the house.'

I ignored her. 'Did your son ever find his rings, and the money that went missing?' I asked, bitterly.

She inhaled sharply, then schooled her expression into one of lightness. 'Oh, those,' she replied, with a little laugh. 'Yes, you wouldn't believe where they did eventually show up … in William's room! Teenage boys are so careless with precious things. But all's well that ends well, I suppose.' She smiled.

I felt my head tingling. Was this really her idea of something ending well? It was all a silly misunderstanding for the Blacks. But it was life and death for me and Mom. It never would have occurred to her to come clear the air with Mom, offer her a reference, for sacking her, *apologise* for accusing me of theft. And now Mom was dying.

'Well,' she said, 'I don't want to tire your mother out. I just wanted to come and say that we are all thinking of you and that we're all so sorry.'

I couldn't help myself. 'For what?' I asked coldly.

Mrs Black knew what I was asking. Sorry for ruining our lives? Sorry for making up some convenient story to get rid of us so your rapist son could move on to his next victim? Sorry for causing my mother so much stress she was now dying?

She did the little laugh again. 'Well, sorry that this has happened to your mother, of course, that she is so poorly. Goodbye Mrs Little, and thank you for everything you did for us.'

I needed to be sure Mom had understood that I had never stolen the rings and that Mrs Black knew that too. She had come to clear her conscience of her treatment of us before Mom died. Well, she had come to the wrong place for absolution. I would never forgive her or her family. She let herself out and I didn't bother walking her to the door.

'I'm so sorry, Mom,' I whispered. 'I can't believe they treated us like that. They never, ever believed us. They didn't even consider that their perfect son might have been responsible for his own lost property. All of those things meant so little to them. They were always throwing them around, they didn't care if they lost them or not. They would just replace them every time. They just wanted an excuse to get rid of us.'

'I always believed you, Rachel,' my mom said. 'You'll never be like them.'

She smiled, and squeezed my hand and slipped away. She never regained consciousness.

After Mom's funeral, when I went to talk to the undertaker about coming up with a repayment schedule for the bill, he told me that the funeral had already been paid for.

'By whom?' I asked, shocked.

'Let me just check here … ah yes, here it is. A Mrs Black … paid in full. Was it not expected?'

I didn't know whether to feel relieved or enraged. I was a little bit of both. Relieved because I had no way of paying for a funeral and enraged because the Blacks had put their awful mark on this too. It was all a way of paying off their guilt. These people thought a conscience was something that could be paid for; like a carpet-cleaning service that washed away stains, so too could a conscience be rehabilitated. Just increase the payment to match the size of the guilt. And now I would have to feel indebted to them for this thing I had not asked for. Well, I would not be grateful to them. And if they thought this absolved them they were wrong. They would never be able to erase their debt to my mother. I would never forget. That was the moment at which I decided my one goal in life would be to become completely independent of people like the Blacks so that they could never have this kind of power over me or my family ever again.

The rest of the summer had been rough, really rough, so when Mrs Bentwell texted to say they were having a party for the students and would I come, my initial reaction had been no way. Not on your life. I had had enough of these people. But after a while I began to see there might be some benefit to accepting the invitation.

56

EDDIE

A journalist gets a tip

I was sitting on my ancient couch working through what I knew and what I suspected, and trying to parse the two. I was also trying very, very hard not to think about Cleo. Reconnecting with her had been so good. I had spent several nights at her house. We had talked so much, had dinner. And the sex was great. I had forgotten. Maybe I was finally ready to move on. I could get used to having someone in my life. I realised now that I didn't want to be alone any more.

I looked around my place and realised it was holding me back. It was not a home. It was a place where I kept bad memories, and kept myself in stasis, a pod I climbed into at the end of every day. I had no sense of comfort, safety, no routine, no sense of hope, no items that brought me peace and no rituals of sanctuary. This place was a holding cell for my ambitions, a place that kept my dreams earthbound. When I came home here I felt like a ghost returning to a purgatory of its own making, condemned to live in a place that held only sad memories; another thing to run from. When I was with Cleo, I felt like life was in colour again. That was probably one of the things I missed most about being married: the sense of belonging, of having someone to come home to, a sense of life and movement and activity and connection. I smiled, I laughed, there was a sense of anticipation. I was excited about my life and work again. And she shared in my passion for my work because she was the same. She never complained that I was working too much. She didn't get tired of talking about the stories I was working on and she seemed to work as much if not more than I did. We were well matched. The sense of sheer pleasure I got from being next to her was intoxicating. I had to admit to myself that I was falling in love with her this time. Too quickly, sure, but it wasn't like we were absolute strangers who had just met. I was tired of putting up blocks to the things that might make me happy anyway. I didn't want to slow down this time. I wanted to run towards her and everything she made me feel.

Sitting here in my hollow little flat with all its re-minders of my late mother and my childhood, and the empty feeling it gave me in the pit of my stomach, threw things into even starker relief. I just wanted to pack a bag and run to the Sky Building, into Cleo's arms. Every time I left work these days I had to force myself to walk past the Sky Building and home to my studio. I had already slept there three times this week.

I switched the TV on to distract myself from the desire to text Cleo or call her or ask her if she was up and if she wanted company. I knew it was futile. I knew that I had already fallen for Cleo in a way I had been too afraid to the last time. The TV flickered blue in the darkness. I heaved myself up out of the chair, put a teabag in a cup and poured hot water on top of it. My mind turned to Rachel Little again. Cleo still hadn't had any further response from her. I really needed to convince her to talk to us. I dialled Cleo's number.

'Can I tell you what I discovered today? I think it's something we should share with your colleague who is working on the Bentwell case. Bentwell, Samsara, Samsara's kid, all showed up as matches on Marley's 23andMe account, as well as a host of others. When I called Bentwell and Sons and enquired about a DNA test that directed me to them, I was invited to meet with their genealogy department.'

'Wow, you have been busy,' she said.

'It's a hush money scheme to silence women Bentwell got knocked up. I sent messages to the other matches asking them if they had heard of the department and they all knew about it. I think Bentwell was Marley's father. I think he had something on Rachel Little that made her give William Black an alibi. Maybe it was just that he was the father of her child or that he knew her secret ... These women can't break the NDA for an article, but they could break its terms for a sworn affidavit. It looks like Bentwell is covering up sleeping with a lot of young women and getting them pregnant. There's clearly a database because when these women or their adopted kids go looking for their parents on DNA sites, the matches re-route them back to Bentwell. It's a closed circuit.'

'Eddie ... this is *huge*.'

'It's sick is what it is. When I rang the offices using the name of one of the girls who came to me with the story of Bentwell assaulting her all those years ago, I was given a meeting offering me $150,000 if I signed an NDA. I took photos of the contract and told them I needed more time to think. So I've got the evidence of the proffered NDA, which is a huge story by itself. I'm going to take it to the news editor. Trudeau won't let me run it. He was a friend of Juliet's family growing up. All of these families know each other. But the news editor will like it, I know he will. And he'll fight Trudeau for it. Cleo, I really wish we could speak to Rachel ...'

'I know. We can keep trying. She might change her mind. Look, why don't you come over? I don't want to be alone tonight.'

Of course, I came running.

57

RACHEL: BEFORE

A girl takes an ill-advised path

The night of the party, I stayed on the periphery, as I always did, going unnoticed, and yet, noticing everything.

Juliet was there, at the centre of it all, with Dave. Handsome but so obviously not one of them. He was one of the few people who spoke to me that night actually, him and Cleo, the only people in that group who acknowledged my existence. For everyone else, I might as well have been a ghost.

I never expected to stumble on everything I stumbled upon that night, but the consequences were long-lasting.

I had actually gone looking for Dave, hoping for some company.

I walked around the lake's edge but as I approached a small demesne, Dave emerged, brushing past me brusquely, and told me to turn around. He didn't look back to see if I heeded his advice. Of course, his warning had the opposite effect. My interest was piqued, so I walked on into the demesne. What I saw there was simply unbelievable. And, it occurred to me, also very powerful leverage. Juliet and Mr Bentwell . . . together. Was she yet another young woman he preyed upon? I heard footsteps behind me and I stepped back quickly into the hedging. Samsara passed me by in a plume of tulle. She didn't see me. She never saw me, whether I was hiding in the hedges or not. Being invisible had its advantages, I suppose. But I saw her, saw her horror as she took in what was happening in front of her, saw her tears as she turned and ran away. I took out my flip phone and took a video. If I had learned one thing with these people it was this – proof was the only thing they understood. Without proof, there was no holding these people to account. I was a fast learner. I stayed and I watched and I recorded until I couldn't stomach any more.

58

EDDIE

The dam weakens

The next morning, Cleo was absentmindedly trac-
ing the line from my hip to my ribcage as we
discussed the Bentwell case her colleague was building,
and what the NDAs meant.

'Do you think your women will talk to my associate?' she asked.

'I guess it depends if they trust her. But I think if
they realise there is another woman taking a case they
might be persuaded to testify. From what you've told
me about your colleague's client, their experiences are
pretty similar. Sounds like the dam might be about to
burst on Bentwell.'

'Nothing would make me happier,' Cleo said.

'OK, I need to get ready. I need to file a piece and then

I'm doing a follow-up interview with your neighbour, Samsara, this afternoon. Anything you want to tell me?'

'Nope. Samsara will tell you everything. She likes to talk.'

'OK, have a good day ...'

'Wait,' Cleo said. She hesitated, and I was unsure of what she was going to say. I got a pang. I had finally started to think that my life could accommodate a relationship, that Cleo and I could have something real together. Did she want to pump the brakes on us? 'Just say if this is too much but ... do you want to come over again tonight?'

My relief was palpable. I did. I really, really did. 'Sure,' I said.

'Great,' Cleo said. 'See you later.'

59

RACHEL: BEFORE

A girl becomes forgetful

The day after the murder, the Blacks summoned me, as if I was still their employee. I was living in the studio in Woodlawn, subsisting on my college grant. They sent a town car, which took me all the way back to the Upper West Side. Because obviously they couldn't speak to me on my turf. Everything happened on their terms. When we got to the Blacks' home, Mr Bentwell was there too, as was William. The Bentwells were acting as the Blacks' legal representation.

Mr Bentwell spoke: 'I'm sure you've heard the dreadful news, Rachel. We just have a few questions about last night. We're trying to get things straight. The police are interviewing everyone and we want to help where we can. Where were you last night, after the party, Rachel?'

'I was home. I went straight home.'

'At what time?'

'Just after eleven, I think.'

'Did you speak to anybody, can anybody corroborate that information?'

'Well, as you know, Mr Bentwell, I live alone since my mother died, so no, there is nobody who can back me up but I'm sure people would have seen me leave the party; there were still lots of people there.' I knew absolutely nobody would have noticed me leave the party, considering nobody even noticed I was there.

I was scared. Bentwell was so imposing, intimidating, completely in control. I hadn't seen him since before my mother had died. And the Blacks were not my favourite people either. The last time one of them had got me in a room by myself things didn't exactly go well for me.

'I can't remember anything unusual about last night,' I said. 'I just went to the party and then I got the 4 train straight home. After all the fighting and drunkenness from … well, William, I didn't want to stay. I just wanted to get out of there. It felt a bit dangerous and tense, not really like a party at all.'

'About that,' Mr Bentwell said. 'I feel that calling it fighting is rather overstating it, don't you?'

'No, I wouldn't say so,' I said.

'And you're sure you were home by eleven? Because, it's just that I am almost certain that I saw you on my CCTV lingering near the alley and I wondered if that was because you had come back here with William, to watch a movie. William says he has a hazy memory of you guys crashing out on the couch watching old movies on TCM. If that was the case, it couldn't have been you on the CCTV because both William and you would have been safely indoors? Can you remember . . . ? Try to think carefully, now,' he said.

I was flabbergasted. He was blackmailing me into giving a false alibi for William by suggesting he would use whatever CCTV footage he had to incriminate me.

'It's so easy to get confused at a party,' he said, 'especially when you've had a glass of champagne. Easy to get turned around about times and places and chronology . . . As Mr Black remembers it, you and William got back here at around eleven p.m., had some pizza and zoned out in front of some old movies. Our driver dropped you home at about one a.m. . . .'

My mouth was slack with shock. I understood now that he was writing a narrative for me. One that the Blacks needed to protect William and one that Bentwell thought they could secure.

Mr Bentwell was still talking. 'We see this a lot in court. People are shocked by shocking events and think they remember one thing but it's just the shock; it does funny things to their memory, to their sense of time. It's just our mind playing tricks on us because we're scared. People will swear they remember something one way but then the prosecutor comes in with CCTV or video evidence that clearly refutes what they have been saying and, well, there's no arguing with CCTV . . .'

He poured himself a glass of something umber-coloured from a crystal bottle. He took a slow sip and nodded his head a couple of times.

'You're a very clever girl, I can see that. I know the human impulse is to want to help where we can, to offer muddled-up memories in some misguided sense of assisting, but in a situation as serious as this the truth must never be compromised by the unreliability of memory or our unpredictable hearts.'

He changed the subject. 'You said you're still living in Woodside, Rachel?'

'Yes but the whole block is being redeveloped, by Juliet's dad actually, so I have to be out by Halloween.'

Bentwell nodded as if he was thinking, as if what he was about to say hadn't been already agreed upon before I arrived.

'OK, here's what we're going to do,' Mr Bentwell said. 'Mr Black and I, we're going to look after your living arrangements from here on in. It's what your mother would have wanted and it's the least we can do for you, in her memory. We all thought of her as one of the family, you know. You'll need to concentrate on your studies, not worry about paying rent. Every scholar needs a benefactor so you must allow us to do this for you. We'll find you something close to NYU. I know Bryant has lots of units around there. Now, I'm so glad we had the opportunity to do this. You can rely on us. And we know we can rely on you, Rachel, to let the police know that you and William were at William's house after the party last night until around one a.m. It must be a relief for you to remember this now as it sorts out your alibi too. You don't want to get mixed up in this case. We've seen how the police can be, well, I hate to say it, but they can be a little biased when it comes to people from certain areas, like the Bronx. And we wouldn't like for that to happen to you. We know that you and William had nothing to do with Juliet's murder, and we would hate to muddy the investigation, or to put you in jeopardy by having no alibi. So, do you want to tell us what happened again, from the start, as you remember it?'

I was equal parts impressed and appalled. But I knew it was better to be practical here. Give the alibi, get a place to live, put it all behind me. And I always had the footage from the demesne if I needed to use it.

I looked at Bentwell and smiled, a smile cold with fury, and I spoke slowly. 'William and I went back to his house, after the party ...'

'Good, very good.' He smiled. 'The police are questioning a young man who they are confident is responsible for the murder. There are a lot of eyewitnesses who said he was aggressive at the party, and that he pushed William into the pool and that he left with Juliet.'

Oh god, they were talking about Dave.

'He was the last person to see her alive, he was the last person witnessed with her and he was the one who conveniently *found* Juliet's body.'

'Dave? They've arrested Dave?'

'I've been in law for forty years and believe me when I say, Rachel, sometimes we don't want to believe the facts but when it all lines up like this, you simply have to accept it. But it's nothing for you to worry about. You have your alibi, and William has his. And Mr Black and I are going to look after you. Now, Emilio will drive you wherever you want to go. Good girl,' he said, putting his hand on my shoulder and squeezing.

My body froze at his touch, and at those familiar words. They were the same words he had said to me every single time he had raped me.

60

EDDIE

Keeping secrets

S amsara's triplex was different to Cleo's. It was like a luxury spa. Recessed lights glimmered every-where – beneath skirting boards and steps, cupboards and mirrors. Every step was like walking on rays of light. But something about it felt cold, like a pristine afterlife, except this place was totally soulless.

She hesitated only momentarily before gesturing to-wards the white couch. I sat on its edge; I didn't want her to throw me out for dirtying the place.

'Thank you for speaking to me again ... what was it you wanted to add?'

'Please, sit down. Can I offer you a drink?' I remem-bered how much she had put away at our last meeting so I said, 'Sure, whatever you're having.'

She poured two ice-cold glasses of wine and joined me in the living room.

'What I'm about to tell you has to be off the record. This is just for background, OK?'

I nodded. 'You have my word.'

'There was a lot of inaccurate information around the time of Juliet's death. Her parents wanted to protect her reputation, and theirs as well, I suppose, but I don't think they did anything to help the actual investigation.'

'What do you mean?' I asked. My glass sat untouched but Samsara sipped hers. 'Juliet was not a saint. None of us were. She was just a young girl, in college, experimenting, having fun ... She didn't deserve to die but she liked to take risks; she liked excitement, and attention. She was heedless and she had a lot of secrets. The fact that more than one person had motive to kill her tells you everything you need to know.'

'But why were the police only interested in one suspect then?' I asked.

'Well, I'm not saying everyone *knew*. I didn't say anything at the time ... I was just a kid really. And I loved Juliet. You know what teenage girls are like, we keep each other's secrets. I honestly thought I was doing the right thing keeping hers. Her parents must have guessed a little but they had no idea how wild she was. Besides, I was convinced that Dave did kill her. My dad had sat me down and told me there was

287

no doubt about it; William had told me too. But it was possible somebody else had reason to kill her.

'Juliet had made plenty of enemies. She had a way of rubbing people up the wrong way, or she didn't care if she offended people or if she trampled over them, and I think that's why she ended up dead. She never believed anything might backfire on her. She always felt that she was more powerful than any enemy she could make; she didn't need to be diplomatic because her daddy was rich and influential. But people always think it's the people in power you have to worry about. What they might do to you, how they might use their power to control you, but actually, in my experience, it's the people with no power that you need to beware of. They're the dangerous ones. They're the ones with nothing to lose. I think she made the wrong enemy. She pushed someone too far.'

I leaned forward. '*Who?*'

She ignored me. 'We had been looking forward to the party all summer,' she said. 'Juliet usually hosted it but I was hosting it that year. Again, this was something that she was doing her best to sabotage. I had hoped the party would establish me as an adult, not just the silly little girl I'd always been treated as. I was desperate to redefine myself on my own terms. To step into the life of a woman. But the minute Juliet found out I was hosting she started dismissing end-of-year parties as passé, childish, something she herself had grown out of. She took ages to RSVP and made sure people knew she was thinking of not showing up as an attempt to damage my numbers. It was, unfortunately, just snippy, jealous behaviour that went on all the time amongst girls at that age. You must remember we were still in that schoolgirl mindset. It wasn't just her that was like that, we all were, but she was definitely the most influential amongst us.'

'Yeah, that wasn't my school experience,' I said. 'I wasn't ever part of those cliques.' Samsara laughed as if I had made a joke.

'We were young women with every privilege and luxury; we could buy most things. But status? We had to fight for that. That's why it mattered so much. Everything else came so easily. Primacy was power. Juliet had always been number one. It was infuriating because she didn't even have to try. She was good at everything and everything came naturally to her. Her life was just *easy*. She was an A student, a brilliant hockey player and every guy she wanted seemed to fall at her feet. She had everything. But it wasn't enough. She was insatiable when it came to male attention. She always had to prove she was *the fairest of them all*. It didn't always equate with popularity.'

'Why not?' I asked.

'Well, because she stole everyone's boyfriends, and then got bored of them a few weeks later, threw them away like the skins of hollowed-out fruit. No man was

off limits; the more taken, the more loyal and monog-
amous, she just saw it as a bigger challenge. She had
even been with married men, much older than her.
Older than her father. She was desperate for validation,
I suppose. It never sat right with me. People thought
she was innocent because of the way she looked, but
she was calculating. And she could be really cold. I had
seen her cut people out of her life completely, ghost
them. But she learned from the best, her father, Bryant
Fox. There was little she hadn't been taught indirectly
by him about seizing and manipulating power to her
benefit.'

'Did you tell the police this?'

'Don't be ridiculous. My dad said it would be disre-
spectful to speak like that of someone who was dead.
He said it would embarrass her parents. He said it
would be different if the police needed help finding a
culprit but they already had the guy who had done it.

'I think Juliet was out of control that summer, worse
than ever. She had even started flirting with some of
our dads. I thought it was gross at the time but I understand now that she was railing against her parents'
expectation that she would marry within the next
year or two. It was her way of having some agency, I
suppose.' She sighed. 'Even if everyone else got caught
in the crossfire.'

'What do you remember of the night she died?'

'She was determined to ruin the party that night.

She was acting as if she had outgrown us all. She had always behaved as if she was better than us, that wasn't new, but there was something new in how she held herself apart now, smiling on us like we were children and she was so much further along in her life, like I was hosting a tea party and she was going to cocktail parties. William was the most eligible guy in our group. Everyone thought they were going to get married but then she had turned up at the party with the scholarship guy, who had surprised everyone by finishing first in the class. Not that it mattered, really. Straight As can't get you a table at *The Leopard* and pick up the cheque at the end of the night, right?'

I nodded, smiled.

'Still, Juliet didn't seem to mind. In fact, she seemed crazy about him. I remember being secretly pleased that night by her very public bust-up with William. I knew that things between them would be irreparable after that. And I hoped that William might finally notice me now that Juliet was out of the picture. You see, even then I had feelings for him. I never realised she would be so *permanently* out of the picture, though. I felt so guilty afterwards.'

'Do you think you and William would have ended up married if she hadn't died?' I asked.

She paused for a long moment, considering the question carefully. 'I have asked myself that in less dignified moments. Because Juliet died I could never actually be sure that William was with me because I was his first choice or because we were both grieving the same woman. What can I say? I don't think *they* would have ended up married. I'd like to think William and I would have ended up together regardless. What's meant to be will be. Our friendship group certainly fragmented completely after Juliet died. Nobody really wanted to see each other again after that party. It was like none of us could face each other; we each became reminders of that night, of what it had done to us, and of what it had done to her. The few times we met up as a group after that merely highlighted the absence in the group, the hole at its centre – Juliet.

'That night I remember looking for my dad. I was upset by the row between William and Juliet: all the shouting and name-calling. I felt the party was a failure and I was cross with Juliet and William for making a scene at my party. My dad was actually very good on this stuff, putting it all into perspective. It was always him, not my mom, who managed to calm me down as a teenager. But I couldn't find him. Instead, I found Dave. He was really upset. He said he had just seen Juliet making out with some old dude. I don't know who it was. He didn't know either but I always wondered could that person have had something to do with Juliet's death?

'I saw her later that night and we had a row about it. I told her she was going to get a reputation. That was the last time I saw her. When I think of the last words I said to her ... I told her William was right, that she was a slut.' She put her hands over her eyes and dropped her head.

'Hey, you weren't to know she was about to get murdered ...' Did I actually feel sorry for Samsara? Was I really trying to make her feel better about herself? This was getting more messed up by the minute.

'The thing is, she was sleeping with so many guys that summer, people I didn't even know about. Any one of them could have killed her.'

'What you said earlier about powerless people having nothing to lose. What did you mean by that?'

'Juliet treated most of her friends with a certain level of disdain. She stole our boyfriends, our outfits, our ideas, our project work; it annoyed us but most of us just shrugged and carried on. It was just Juliet. And we could do that. We could find new boyfriends or buy new outfits. We had resources. But there was a girl there that night ... she was hanging around on the edges. I had forgotten her until all this talk of the anniversary but she was always there, like a goddamn creep. I don't know if police ever spoke to her.

'Do you remember her name?'

'Rachel. Rachel Little.'

61

EDDIE

Six weeks' notice

I was in a state of shock. My mind felt twisted and confused. Could the alibi actually be the murderer? Was that why she was willing to give the alibi to William? Because in doing so she would also provide an alibi for herself? I was unsettled so I went to Cleo's that evening to test out my hypothesis. She made a negroni for me and a martini for herself and I took the drink in three gulps, pushed it back at her and said, 'I'm going to need another one of those for what I have to tell you.'

There were perks to sleeping with someone who was tangentially connected to the story I was obsessed with. I could talk it through with her and she didn't get annoyed or tell me to shut up like Cassie had done.

In fact, she seemed as interested in it as I was. And I wasn't bound by the same confidentiality issues as Cleo. I could tell her everything, and I did. Obviously I swore her to secrecy. I had started to feel very lucky that we had reconnected. I had asked her recently what she saw in me. She was gorgeous, that wasn't up for debate. She was also smart and independent and rich. What's not to like? But me? She told me looks meant nothing to her. 'You're smarter than me, and you make me laugh,' she said. 'You've no idea what a rare combination that is.'

I filled her in on what Samsara had told me, that Rachel could clear Dave's name in more ways than one.

'No wonder she doesn't want to get drawn back in to this,' Cleo said.

62

RACHEL: BEFORE

A young woman betters herself

The return to college after Juliet had died was a brutal transition for many reasons. I wanted to forget everything that had happened – my mother, Juliet, the fake alibi ... My life had been nothing but trouble since my mother had started working for the Blacks. I wished we had never met any of them. I was grateful that the others had graduated so at least I didn't have to see them in college. I didn't know how to cope with the emotional fallout so I started to shut down, and threw myself into my college work. I ignored everything. Looking back, it was the worst year of my life, from the murder of Juliet to the culmination of my own problems that Christmas. But, I made it through. And figured out a way to move forward successfully – just don't look back, that was my motto now.

People said your college days were the best years of your life, but I couldn't wait to move on, to forget, to leave it all behind and make a totally fresh start. By the following spring, I had resolved to put the whole terrible episode behind me, settling into a pattern of work, sleep, work, sleep and shutting everything else out.

I had to run twice as fast and work five times as hard to keep up with the other students, of course. They barely seemed to have to work. Their lifestyles consisted of constant trips, nights out, parties and dinners, celebrations, as well as hosting drinks in their professionally decorated duplex apartments that their parents had paid for so they could have some independence, but not *so* much independence that they had to pay rent, or get a job.

I wondered when they had time to study or go to classes but they always seemed to come out on top. Maybe it was because they didn't have to work in their spare hours, to make up some spare cash like I did. At least I didn't have to worry about rent, thanks to my deal with the devil. I still had to burn the midnight oil to study, to get assignments in on time, to finish projects and cram for exams. But I knew the only way to free myself of these people was to stand on my own two feet.

63

EDDIE

File under 'surprise'

Cleo's phone buzzed and I jolted awake. It was 5 a.m. I hadn't meant to spend the night but I liked waking up beside her. It was starting to feel like home. She groaned and read her phone. Another thing Cassie would have complained about, phones in the bedroom, messages at all hours, but I knew Cleo's job didn't stop at 6 p.m. and start at 9 a.m. and neither did mine.

'It's a message from the board of the building.' She read it aloud:

'It has come to our attention that there is a record of a historical criminal conviction attached to the name of one of our residents, who is also currently being investigated for a suspected crime. The board will conduct a full audit and investigation and come to a

decision as to whether this will affect their tenancy in the Sky Building. We will be in touch within four to six weeks.'

'I wonder who that could be,' Cleo said theatrically and rolled her eyes.

'Poor Dave. We need to clear his name fast. We are so close now. Do you think they'll evict him?'

'If they can, they will. Bryant and his investors didn't want any social-housing tenants in the first place and he has a reputation for getting what he wants. He definitely won't be replacing Marley with another social-housing tenant ... and if he has the opportunity to remove Dave, he's going to grab it.'

'Shit, Cleo, we have to help him. He's been through so much already ...'

'I'm trying!' she said, holding up her hands.

She got out of bed in an impossibly lithe movement. Pilates, I thought.

'Help yourself to the shower, coffee, breakfast. I need to use the gym but I'll be back in thirty minutes.' And with that she was gone. I was awake so decided to get up and shower in her enormous bathroom. As I dried myself with a towel that was softer and fluffier than anything I had ever felt in my entire life, I idly snooped in her bathroom cabinet. Expensive creams and perfumes, pill bottles labelled with all the usual city girl stuff – Xanax, Ambien, Valium.

I put some coffee on to brew then stared into her

refrigerator for a minute. Mounjaro and fruit and yoghurt. I shut the fridge again. I padded through the apartment, which took quite a bit of time. It really was vast. Her office had real big swinging dick energy. Very male in here. I liked it a lot. Leather-topped desk, lots of drawers, a few art deco antiques. Neatly ordered files. I pulled the drawers on the desk. The small top one was locked but the bottom ones slid open in an obscenely smooth way. So expensive. Just files. On the opposite wall was custom-built filing hidden behind beautiful navy lacquered doors, inlaid with mother-of-pearl.

I opened the filing drawers and marvelled at the design and the organisation. I thought of my battered cardboard boxes that housed my 'files'. I ran my finger along the organisational tabs, ordered from A to Z. Before I knew what I was doing my finger was travelling across the letters to 'L' then flipping through the category until it stopped on 'Little, R'. I closed my fingers on the file just as I heard the door to the apartment go. I dropped the file, shut the cabinet door and hustled back to the kitchen.

Was I actually now searching my girlfriend's apartment? Was this who I was now? Did I want to be alone forever? I needed to get a hold of myself.

Cleo walked into the kitchen a few seconds later, mid conversation on her phone. 'OK, Dave, I need you to take a breath,' she said. 'This is a process,' she was saying. 'I've seen this before. They absolutely can't discriminate against you for a past conviction and you're assumed innocent until proven guilty on the current investigation so they can't do anything until that is concluded. Plus they haven't charged you with anything there, which only means there is zero evidence. So, all is working in your favour. And you're living here now, which puts you in a very powerful position, and we are working on clearing your name in the meantime. I have two investigators working on it ... The six weeks thing is not in any way meaningful. This will likely take eighteen months before anything is decided and we'll have cleared your name long before that so sit tight and try not to worry.

'Dave, Dave, I'll have my associate draft a letter of response. Don't worry, you have a right to live here and if we open an appeal into your conviction, citing new evidence, the board won't be able to move forward with any decision until your appeal has been resolved, which will buy us even more time. And you know I'm going to clear your name, right?

'... Well, forensics have moved on for one thing. And *people* have moved on. You've no idea what a guilty conscience can do to someone over the course of twenty years. Eddie and I are working on this together. We're getting closer to the alibi ... My investigator has run some DNA tests and they have come back with some really solid leads. We're working on it, you have to trust me, OK? OK, good. So I'm hanging up now.

I'll see you at Samsara's tonight for our neighbourly drinks, remember? You need to be there – your absence will only make you look guilty. OK? OK.'

She looked at me and I smiled in what I hoped was an innocent way.

'Coffee?'

64

CLEO

Loose lips sink ships

I went to Bentwell and Sons on my way home. I had a client meeting scheduled. I was often in Bentwells' offices. If I was number one, they were the next best firm to represent you, so we were often opposing numbers in wealthy cases. As the elevator arrived, Bentwell himself stepped out as I was stepping in. We collided momentarily and I laughed.

'I beg your pardon,' he said. And it felt like a Pavlovian bell. I remembered where I had last heard those words. And I knew now why they had seemed so familiar to me.

65

CLEO

The night closes in

I sent Eddie a text telling her to come to my place as soon as she was finished her diary for that night. I really needed to talk to her about what I had discovered.

Meanwhile, it was Samsara's party. I had been softening towards Samsara but was incensed by the board's pending action against Dave. The board were throwing him into limbo and acting like they got to decide on *his* life. I suspected Samsara was behind it – who else? She was the only one who knew about it. She had been speaking all about it at the party. But what did she have to fear from someone like Dave? Even if he was guilty, which I don't think he was, he was least likely to do anything. He had a parole officer. He was on a watchlist.

I knocked on Samsara's terrace door.

'Cleo, how are you? I've set up the table on the terrace as it's such a beautiful evening – are you OK with being outside?'

'Oh sure, that's fine.' Try, Cleo, just try to be civil.

Samsara poured champagne and laid out olives and nuts, which none of us ate. Dave arrived a little later alongside some other neighbours. He looked incredibly uncomfortable and out of place, towering over everyone. It was like seeing a lion in a cage; there was clearly nowhere he'd rather be less. I didn't want to upset him. I wanted Samsara to see he was just a person, just like her.

The sky was turning indigo and soon it would be dark but the humidity meant we could sit out here all night if we wanted to. The illuminated sky pool rippled in the breeze, which was picking up, and it reminded me of how the earth looks from space, an impossibly bright-blue light in a thick blanket of stars. The terrace was decorated with tasteful linen flags flickering on delicate strings of fairy lights. There was something unsettling in how the pool rippled.

We did the small talk, our work, our lives, Samsara's kid and how he was acing his biology exam, marriage, schools, the best grocery store ... it was deathly dull.

An hour passed and Dave stood up suddenly, making his apologies. 'I'm so sorry, guys, but I think I'm going to hit the road. I'm not very good company at the moment. The Marley investigation and this stuff with the board is just getting me down. I'm sorry, Samsara – thank you, so much, for the lovely evening. It's such a nice gesture, and I hope we can do it again when things are less stressful.'

'Of course,' she drawled and took his hands in a way that seemed affectionate but actually forced him to stay at arm's length.

'Goodnight, Dave,' I said. 'Try to get some sleep. And try not to worry.'

66

CLEO

Burn after reading

My phone rang and I saw that it was Smith so I said, 'Excuse me, I have to take this.'

'So I got the medical examiner's file for Juliet's death. One thing we did not hear about – she was pregnant. But at the time they only tested the pregnancy against William and Dave, neither of whom were the father.'

'Jesus,' I said. This brought another suspect into play.

'I also ran the police DNA swabs from the victim. First through the police database. No surprises there. A match for Dave. But then I got my contacts on the other DNA databases, genealogy, private paternity testing companies, 23andMe and guess what? We got a hit on the swab from Juliet's head wound. That's important because it means it can't be ruled out by someone who was at the party. Then I ran the pregnancy profile against the match and guess what – they're connected.'

'*Who?*' I nearly screamed.

'I'll forward the results to you now.'

My phone pinged. I had to read the results twice to be sure. I looked across the pool at the apartments all lit up, and saw the faces of the names on the text message. I rang Smith back. 'I want these results hand-delivered to me tomorrow. Our usual place. Destroy all other copies.' I hung up and texted Eddie.

> Looks like we've definitively cleared Dave's name.
> DNA matches on the unidentified profile and on
> Juliet's baby . . . get over here ASAP. Your story
> just got a whole lot more interesting.

67

EDDIE

The beginning of the fall

After I filed my diary it was later than usual. I had turned my phone onto 'do not disturb' so I could concentrate. My mind was not really on my actual job any more. I was so preoccupied with investigating Marley's death and trying to clear Dave's name and trying to pull the Juliet anniversary feature together that my daily job was suffering. The last thing I needed was a lecture from Trudeau. When I switched my phone back on I saw Cleo's message. Jesus Christ. She had done it.

I ran, or attempted to run, the few blocks to the Sky Building. The wind had picked up and litter was whipping around the streets. I felt like I was being held back by a strong arm. In spite of all my intentions to keep Cleo at arm's length, I was happy with what had happened, with where we were. I was excited. We had done it together. We were a great team. I enjoyed our dynamic. It felt like we were two detectives in a cosy crime novel, sitting up in bed late at night discussing cases and theories. Truth be told I had never been happier. It felt so different to go back to her place after work, to eat and talk and drink beer and make love and fall asleep and wake up to do it all over again. It felt like a contentment I hadn't ever known. I hurried my steps against the wind. I couldn't wait to speak to Cleo.

68

CLEO

A confrontation

The others took Dave's departure as their cue to leave too. 'I'll help you clear up,' I said. I wanted to speak to Samsara alone.

'What the board is doing to Dave is unforgivable,' I hissed. 'Not to mention in breach of Dave's rights. It's a mistake, and it will backfire on the board and this building. Dave will be able to take a case.'

'Stop it, Cleo, we both know that Dave can't afford to take a case against us. That's preposterous.'

I couldn't hold back. The time was now.

'I'm representing Dave. *Pro bono*. So yes, he can afford to take a case and I don't think you want to go up against me, Samsara. Why are you bothering with this witch hunt? Why are you torturing Dave? You know he didn't kill Juliet and you know he didn't kill Marley, and you're putting the board and the building in danger of a damaging and costly suit.'

Samsara coughed out a little outraged laugh.

'I'm not targeting Dave, the board requested that this investigation be brought. Some of the residents don't feel safe. It's the board—'

'Yes, but who told the board?'

I could feel my fury building. I was ready to clear Dave's name, if only to piss off this sanctimonious woman in front of me. She acted like she owned the whole building. Didn't she realise she wasn't the only powerful person here? Besides, Samsara was only here because her father was rich, not because she had ever achieved anything herself. I took some moments to get my fury under control before it burned right through me. I had learned many years ago to harness my anger and use it in a targeted way.

'You need to back off and drop the investigation. You know he's not a threat to anybody and you know you can't win this. Not against me. Don't you think he deserves some good luck in his life, after everything that's happened to him? And I thought you said this would be a PR disaster anyway; have you changed your mind on that front? If it gets out that the Sky Building is a place where socially disadvantaged residents either kill themselves or are evicted, it won't look good. I imagine it's not something Bryant Fox would be interested in dealing with either. I'd be very surprised if Bryant even knows about this. I'm sure he'd squash it immediately if he did ...'

Samsara's face went a funny shade.

'I don't know why you're targeting me with this, Cleo. If the board decides to investigate someone it's not my fault ...' She was pathetic.

'You're the only one who knew about his conviction. He's been a model resident, he's paid his debt to society and he's an army vet, he's helpful to the residents, he doesn't disturb anyone and above all of that the most important fact here is that he was falsely convicted and it won't be long until I have absolute proof of it, so believe me it will backfire if you continue with this witch hunt. He'll be eligible to sue. And who do you think the board will turn on if that happens?' I asked.

'He shouldn't be *here*,' Samsara said. 'And I don't want him here.'

'Why not, what's the big deal ...?'

'He doesn't belong here. He makes people uncomfortable with his tight t-shirts and his tattoos. He'd be happier somewhere else too, in his own environment, with his own people.'

'Jesus, Samsara, do you hear yourself? What are you so afraid of? What do you think is going to happen? He's a human being like you and me; why are we the only ones who deserve to live in a place like this?'

'He's a convicted killer ...'

I laughed. 'You can't even say that with any con-viction, Samsara. You *know* that's not the truth. You know!'

She ignored me. 'There are children in this building,' she said. 'We can't have someone convicted of such a serious crime living in our midst, we can't put residents at risk like that ...'

'What you're doing is illegal. He has served his time, returned to the community, is living his life quietly and lawfully ... He has a human right as well as a legal right to move on with his life. He's paid his debt to society. You trying to use that against him is discrimination.'

'He killed a woman—'

'He didn't kill her and you know it,' I cut her off.

'Why do you keep saying that? I know no such thing. I know what the law has decided. I put my faith in the American justice system to keep me and my family safe.'

'Well, you're right to do that because the American justice system will always keep families like yours safe. But you were there the night Juliet was killed. I've read the case notes. The evidence was botched, a set of DNA was never identified or attributed; there was a very shady alibi for your husband from a woman who disappeared into thin air and seems to have been Marley's biological mother.'

'WHAT?' she said. 'How do you know this?'

'That doesn't matter. What matters is Dave was an obvious stitch-up and I am this close to proving it,' I said, pinching my fingers together. 'And I know that Marley didn't kill herself. And I'm going to find out who wanted her dead and why. What I know for sure is it's all connected. And you're right there in the middle of it all ...'

'Have you lost your mind, Cleo?'

'If you try to get Dave out of this building, I will dig up every ghost from your past.'

She did the little laugh again. 'I have no idea what you're talking about.'

'Well, allow me to spell it out for you, then,' I said. 'Times have changed since Dave was framed for the murder of Juliet Fox. Forensic science has moved on. Eddie and I have been investigating both Juliet and Marley's deaths and we have found some very interesting results; they tell a very different story about that night, a new story, one that implicates your entire family.'

'Bullshit,' Samsara said. 'You're lying. If you had anything, you wouldn't be standing here talking to me. We'd be in the police station.' Feigning nonchalance, but with eyes narrowed, she asked, 'What evidence have you got?'

'My favourite kind,' I said. 'D – N – A.'

'I've never even given my fingerprint to my iPhone. Nobody has my DNA. If you want it, you'll need a warrant. And I'd like to see you try that.'

We were almost nose to nose now ...

'You are already in a DNA database, or didn't you know? I found you and your precious son. Wonder what his college application will make of his DNA and his mother's being a partial match for a dead girl's crime scene. You were there that night.'

'I told you, I've never given my DNA to anyone.'

'Well, your DNA is on 23andme.com ... and so is your dad's and so is your son's, and they are all linked not only to Juliet's murder, but to Marley's death too.'

She looked possessed. 'What have you done?' she hissed. I stood still as she hurtled towards me. Fight or flight abandoned me and my stupid body chose the third option – freeze.

'I haven't done anything,' I said. 'I just investigated the evidence.' She was bearing down on me now. She wasn't stopping. I felt like I should run into my apartment but that felt silly too. Surely Samsara wouldn't do anything.

'The truth always wants to be known, Samsara, and if twenty years in law has taught me anything, it's that the truth always finds its way out; slowly or quickly, it always comes out in the end.'

'You have *destroyed* my family ...'

She sounded like a demon; I took a step back from her, putting the table between us. 'I haven't done *anything*. I've just done my job. Dave came to me and asked for my help in clearing his name. I just looked at the evidence, something your family tried to obscure from the start. This is what I do, Samsara, and I'm really good at it. I've dedicated my career to righting wrongs, trying to claim back some justice in this screwed-up system ... it's not personal.'

'Oh, it is *so* personal,' she growled at me and moved to come around the table. I shimmied around so that there was still a full table between us.

'Samsara, this is silly. It's over. I know about your dad and Juliet, I know what they were up to. The police didn't know that Juliet was pregnant with your dad's baby, that she was refusing to have an abortion, that she was trying to blackmail your dad. That would give him a pretty strong motive for murder, wouldn't it? It might even implicate you.'

Samsara was struck dumb.

I went on. 'Dave went to prison for a crime he didn't commit.'

'Better him than people like us,' she hissed. She still looked ready to attack. 'Besides, my DNA at the scene proves nothing. We were *all* at the party that night. We *all* had our DNA on Juliet ... the police said so at the time, they ruled us all out. How is it different now?'

'Because your DNA is on the swab they took from Juliet's head wound,' I said.

'Nobody knows what happened that night,' she said. 'There were no witnesses.'

'But there *was* a witness,' I said.

317

'The person in the alley? They never found them ... Nobody even knows who that was.'

'But they're out there, Samsara,' I said. 'And they can be found. You forget, we were all at that party that night. I may not have been in your inner circle but I saw what went on that night. The backstabbing, the cheating, the lying ... I'm pretty sure there were at least ten people there who had a motive to kill Juliet ... At least I have the decency to feel guilty about not speaking up at the time. I've been trying to make up for it my entire life by helping people like Dave.'

A man's voice came from behind me. 'You were *there*?'

I spun around.

'Dave! Wait,' I said. 'I can explain.' But he crashed out of the terrace.

I stared after him then turned back to Samsara, but I had forgotten the rule about never turning your back on a predator. I was met with a blow to the face that sent me spinning towards the pool.

69

VIVIAN

A storm is coming

A storm warning meant I had to check the terraces were secure before I clocked off for the night. The umbrellas would be whipping in the breeze and there was a risk of flying debris if everything wasn't properly secured.

As I stepped out of the service lift onto the terrace I wasn't quite sure if I was imagining things. I saw Samsara knock Cleo in the face with something heavy and watched as Cleo dropped like a stone into the sky pool. I couldn't believe my eyes as Samsara scrambled onto her – I thought she was going to pull Cleo out but instead she seemed to be holding her underwater.

Jesus Christ. I grabbed the stone Adonis from its plinth and ran to the pool.

70

EDDIE

Red and blue make violet

When I entered the lobby, Vivian was not at his station but it was late. I took the elevator up to Cleo's apartment but she was nowhere to be seen. I walked through her study but she wasn't there either. I pulled at the filing cabinets but they were locked now. I walked back towards the pool terrace doors and could barely process what I was seeing.

The garden furniture was in disarray and broken glass crunched under my shoes. At first I thought the storm had trashed the terrace but then I saw what looked like blood on a sharp corner of the art-deco edging of the pool. Everywhere I looked I saw more blood. And then I saw Vivian, soaking wet and breathing heavily on the tiles. A blonde woman was lying perfectly still by the edge of the pool, and another was in the pool, a trail of blood leaching from her head like a watercolour wash.

'Cleo,' I screamed and ran towards the pool. 'Vivian, what happened?'

'Call nine-one-one,' Vivian said grimly, and I called it in.

PART THREE

71

JULIET: BEFORE

An ambush

I knew straight away that Dave was different. Not just on the obvious level of class, money, education, but on another more important level too. The boys I dated were from my world. They didn't see me as a person. They saw me as one of scores of beautiful, thin, well-bred, rich girls that they had on speed dial. Dave looked at me as if I was the most beautiful woman in the world. And he spoke to me like a friend. None of the guys from my world did that. We had sex and then they spoke to their guy friends about it, usually spread some bad lies about me and then it was over. I never had actual relationships, or friendships, with the guys I had sex with.

Dave was different. We had conversations about

architecture and engineering, books and films and the world and ideas. I knew it couldn't go anywhere but I didn't have to worry about that right away. I was in college. I was allowed to experiment. I knew my father would make me settle down eventually, but it wouldn't be with boring William Black. I was determined of that. However, it would likely be someone equally dull. Which is why I was having as much fun as I could right now. I didn't tell Dave, obviously. I knew he was in love with me and I didn't want to be unnecessarily cruel. But this was my summer of fun. I was seeing as many guys as I could before I had to get serious.

Samsara had dubbed it our slutty phase. If we were going to get married by the time we were twenty-five, we were going to make the most of our single days. I didn't want any regrets. Nobody was off-limits, we told each other. It didn't matter if we hooked up with guys who had girlfriends or wives – which really was breaking girl code, I know – but all bets were off this summer. We could date anyone, older, younger, guys from the wrong side of town, busboys from the diner or buskers from central park, everyone was game. Of course, there was one conquest that I couldn't share with Samsara.

I was getting bored of Samsara's dad anyway. Maybe because he seemed to be getting bored of me. Ever since I told him I was pregnant he was on my case, constantly badgering to see if I had organised my abortion yet.

That's why I decided to bring Dave to the end-of-year party. At the very least it would shake things up a little. William knew something was going on. I had him on ice for the past few months, phasing him out, hoping he would get the message, but the day before the party he *still* thought we were a couple so I tried to spell it out for him.

'I think we're going in different directions, William,' I had said. 'We're too young to settle down. I want to enjoy my college years. Date a little, have fun, be a little wild. If we can't do it now when *can* we do it? And you might like to do that too.' I tried to appeal to him but the fact was the guys got to do that anyway, while maintaining girls like me as their steady girlfriends, the best of all worlds. He seemed genuinely upset so I said, 'Who knows, maybe in ten years' time fate might bring us together again.'

It didn't help. He looked shattered. 'I just can't believe you're doing this, Juliet, all so you can sleep with other people? I thought we were good together?'

'We are, William, we're just too young to settle down. I want to focus on my study and take life a little less seriously for a while.'

And so it was that Dave walked into the party thinking that William was an old boyfriend, and Mr Bentwell was just Samsara's dad, but actually what Dave walked into was an ambush.

72

EDDIE

A journalist creeps down the back stairs

We heard the sirens as the ambulance arrived downstairs and knew the police wouldn't be far behind them. Vivian seemed to realise for the first time that he was soaking wet.

'Eddie,' he said, 'the police are going to want to talk to me. Can you go downstairs? Quickly now, do as I say. Go to my apartment, and get me some dry clothes?'

'Of course,' I said.

'And Eddie . . . ? Can you check on the CCTV for me, make sure everything is . . . in order?' Vivian looked at me meaningfully then, holding onto my hand for a second longer than necessary, before he let go. 'You're one of us, Eddie,' Vivian said. 'Now go. Use the service stairs.'

'You got it,' I said, and I took his key and took the stairs that led directly to Vivian's fire escape and let myself in.

I went to his bedroom and pulled out some clean clothes and towels. As I passed the CCTV screens, I rewound the footage of the pool terrace and watched as I saw Samsara, Cleo, and then Vivian. I watched it once, twice and then a third time to be sure that I wasn't seeing things. And finally I understood what Vivian had meant when he said you're one of us. We had both seen how justice was served by the Bentwells to people like us in the past. And I already knew that the Bentwells had seen fit to delete CCTV on the night of Juliet's murder to protect their own – all's fair in love and war, I thought. Why not return the favour? I selected the time frame and hit 'delete'.

73

EDDIE

You can't libel the dead

DEATH OF AN HEIRESS

By Eddie Wright

Samsara Black, communications expert and scion of the Bentwell legal dynasty, died last night in what police are calling tragic circumstances. Following a party at the Sky Building, where Mrs Black lived with her husband William Black and teenage son, Josh, Mrs Black was found in the sky pool. She did not respond to emergency medical treatment at the scene and was pronounced dead a short time later.

A source who had been at the party said there was a tragic accident on the slippery terrace.

The building doorman, Mr Vivian Wyley, said he had gone up to the terrace to make it secure in advance of last night's impending storm and had discovered Mrs Black unresponsive in the pool.

Police are conducting interviews but do not suspect foul play.

The victim is being investigated for a possible connection to the Juliet Fox murder from twenty years ago.

In a separate development, Cleo Fry and Associates today filed a case against the late Mrs Black's father, Max Bentwell, who is being questioned about several historic allegations of sexual assault.

I loved the rule that you couldn't libel the dead. Call it poetic justice.

74

CLEO

A lawyer tells a journalist a story

I woke up with a blinding headache.

'You're lucky to be alive,' Eddie said.

'Why does it feel like someone has drilled holes through my skull, then?'

'Well, because that is kinda what happened,' she said with a smile.

The doctor looked annoyed with Eddie. She had a talent for rubbing people up the wrong way.

'You had a subdural haematoma,' the doctor said. 'We had to operate to release the pressure and drain the bleeding to avoid brain damage ...'

'Stop, please just stop,' I said. 'I don't want to know ... just tell me am I going to be OK?'

'We expect you to make a full recovery,' the doctor

said. 'But you need rest now. Don't stay too long,' she said to Eddie.

Eddie was sitting in the armchair by the bed. Did she never sleep?

The doctor left and a nurse bustled self-importantly behind me. 'You mustn't tire her out,' she said sternly to Eddie, reinforcing the doctor's warning but with a much more proprietorial tone.

'I won't, promise. I'm just happy she's going to be OK.'

The nurse pursed her lips and told us she'd be back to check on me shortly.

'Hey, how are you feeling?'

'Awful . . .' I said.

'Do you remember what happened?' Eddie asked.

I shook my head.

Eddie's face darkened. 'Samsara attacked you. I'm afraid she slipped and cracked her head. She had a massive subdural haematoma too, but hers killed her. They think she probably died instantaneously.'

'She fell? I don't remember anything . . . I remember the dinner. Dave . . .'

'If it wasn't for Vivian she would have killed you. He arrived on the terrace to do a security check – a storm was forecast and he needed to put the furniture away. He saw Samsara trying to drown you in the sky pool She had knocked you out with a statue, the art-deco one, you know the one you like – that's what

333

she hit you with. She was probably going to kill you if he hadn't shouted at her. She lost her balance, slipped and hit her head on the edge of the pool … Vivian was so preoccupied with resuscitating you that he only checked on her when the paramedics arrived.'

'Oh my god,' I said. 'She's dead?'

'Call it karma.' Eddie shrugged. 'She would have killed you if Vivian hadn't interrupted her. He saw all of it and told the police everything. They'll probably want to speak to you too,' she said brightly.

'And Dave?' I asked.

'He's fine but I think he's a bit hurt.' Eddie's expression changed as she scanned my face. 'Cleo, how could you have kept that to yourself, that you had been at the party too that night? He feels like you lied to him.'

I groaned.

'You have to understand, Eddie, I just wanted to forget it too, like everyone else. But it's probably time to tell you what I know.'

75

CLEO

When Cleo met Rachel

'I first met Rachel Little that summer. She was cleaning houses with her mother. It was just the two of them and life was clearly not easy for them, but I could also see that Rachel was smart, and nice. Of course William and Juliet were awful to them both. Being rude, asking them to do things for them. I was embarrassed by William and Juliet's behaviour so I always overcompensated by being extra polite and as kind as I could be to Rachel. I think that's how she ended up telling me what had happened to her. I think she felt she could trust me.'

Eddie nodded, encouraging me to continue. I could see that she was itching to take out her notebook but she just about managed to remember who she was to me in this moment.

'She told me she had been cleaning houses on the Upper West Side all summer with her mother. They used to separate, so they could clean twice as many houses and earn double the money. I knew Samsara's dad had a bit of a rep for groping young girls – everyone did. But unfortunately Rachel didn't have that inside knowledge until it was too late.'

'What do you mean?' Eddie asked.

'She worked in gym shorts and a vest because it got so warm cleaning the houses in the hotter months. She told me Bentwell had come across her in the kitchen one day. He was home unexpectedly and expressed his surprise that she was there. He asked her what age she was and, although she was sixteen at the time, she lied and told him she was eighteen. She didn't want to get her mom into trouble.

'"Older than you look", he told her, and she said she knew then that he was going to do something awful. She was afraid of him. The following week he was in the house again when she arrived. Standing sipping a coffee in chinos and an open-necked shirt. She told me he offered her some work on the side, waitressing at events for his firm, just serving drinks, checking coats ... but the pay was good, two hundred dollars a night, which was a lot of money back then, especially for someone like Rachel. I actually think that was part of his MO. He paid these young vulnerable women sums of cash that were just big enough to be irresistible to them. Just enough to make them believe they could put up with what he did to them. I've seen that detail come out again and again in the briefing for the case my associate is building against him. I think he knew these young women needed the money, knew they wouldn't be able to say no. He knew Rachel and her mom needed the money. It was a trap.'

'So when did it escalate, when did he actually assault her,' Eddie asked.

'He used to get his driver to drop her home after events. Then one night, she told me, he drove her home himself. He told her his driver had the day off and what kind of a man would he be if he let a young woman ride the subway alone at night? Anything could happen. Well, she would have been safer on the subway. That night he kissed her, told her she was a beautiful young woman and that he wanted to give her a bonus for doing such a good job, but she said it was implied in how he looked at her that this bonus was for the kiss. And you can probably guess where things went after that.'

Eddie's face was set in a grim expression. 'I always knew Bentwell was a filthy, low-life piece of work,' she said, 'but this ... he was an animal.'

I nodded in agreement. 'She said he raped her most weeks that summer, either in the house or in his car when he dropped her home. She didn't know how to get him to stop, she didn't know that was even an option.

How could she say no to him? Did saying no to him mean saying no to the extra work, to the extra money that made such a difference to her and her mum? Did it mean saying no to her mom's job, to their livelihood? She told herself when she went back to college it would all be over because she only helped her mom cleaning houses in the summer months. But then she realised she was pregnant.'

'Oh my god – Marley was Bentwell's child,' Eddie said. 'Jesus. It all makes sense now.'

I nodded. 'And Marley wanted to meet her father, very much. Things ran aground because, unlike the other women who came looking for him after he had gotten them into trouble, Marley didn't want his money. She wanted a relationship with her father, with Flo's grandfather. She wanted a *family*. But if the Bentwells acknowledged her as family, she'd have succession rights, and obviously that was something neither he nor Samsara could tolerate.'

Eddie looked both shocked and excited. 'So she must have told Samsara that night of the party—'

'Samsara had no idea that her son Josh had uploaded her DNA, along with his own, to the 23andMe website as part of his final-year biology project. That's how Marley matched with them, it's how she found them.'

Eddie nodded, 'and Samsara obviously got her dad to come around to Marley's that night, which is why he turned up in his baseball-cap disguise. Poor Marley, she probably thought she was about to have a family reunion,' Eddie said.

I nodded. 'But instead they killed her and made it look like a suicide.'

Eddie's eyes were glistening with tears. I don't think I had ever seen her cry before. 'Poor Marley,' she said. 'But what about the balcony door? It was locked from the outside . . .'

'Vivian has a master key, Fox does too, and so do a few of the board members, including—'

'Samsara,' Eddie finished with distinct distaste. 'Despicable woman. It's so obvious they've been doing this for years, literally getting away with murder. They put pressure on Rachel to give William a false alibi, simultaneously damning Dave. It's so obvious that Samsara did it even without the DNA evidence, the motive is obvious – Juliet had slept with Samsara's dad and was now pregnant. Sure that's a pretty awful way to treat your best friend, but she didn't deserve to be murdered for it. Samsara was utterly amoral,' Eddie said.

I shrugged. 'Black cat, black kitten.'

76

RACHEL: BEFORE

A blank space

I was unsentimental about the adoption. By the time I realised I was pregnant it was far too late for an abortion. So I was pragmatic. I continued my studies and allowed Mr Bentwell to arrange everything. I had the feeling he knew what he was doing. They took my details, took some samples, took my baby and I signed some papers. Bentwell made a large payment into my bank account and I signed an NDA. I saw it as a narrow escape. I had a choice to make – repeat the life my mother had had, raising a child single-handedly, with no education, poorly paid jobs and no security, or focus on transforming my life – get an education, a career, the kind of life I wanted, and give the child the life she deserved with a stable family.

That spring in New York, I told the midwife a story about getting drunk at a frat party and waking up with a hazy memory of the night before. All I could remember, I told her, was that I had slept with someone and by the time I realised I was pregnant it was too late to do anything about it.

I hoped my child's adoptive family would tell her a nice story about me, about how much I loved her and how I only gave her up because I wanted her to have a better life than I could provide. I hoped that they told her I loved her.

I channelled the pain into my studies, my career. I focused on becoming the best. Nothing less would do. Part of me hoped the child would never come looking for me, but that changed as I got older, as it became more apparent that I was never going to have another child. As the years went by, I found myself longing for my child, wishing she would find me. That's why I decided to do the DNA test. If she found her father, I could only imagine what his response would be. First it would be to dismiss the child, then to make sure that she had no claim to his fortune, no impact on his 'legitimate' children's assets, no right to succession. If he was the kind of man who could rape a girl in his kitchen, and pay her for the pleasure, he was the kind of man who could easily dismiss a child claiming to be his long-lost daughter.

I had only done the DNA test two years previously.

I did it on what would have been my daughter's eighteenth birthday, the day she would legally be able to make her own decisions about contacting me. I wanted to be available to her. There wasn't a day that had gone by when I hadn't thought of her, when I hadn't missed her. I marked her birthday every year. It drove me nearly mad. I never believed that I would feel this way when I gave her up. It had been damaging; traumatising. I had tried to bury it but, as the years passed, and as I failed to meet anyone, failed to have a child of my own, I thought of her more and more. And nobody told me of the hole she would leave at my centre.

77

EDDIE

Eddie tells Dave a story

'So Samsara murdered Juliet,' he said, in utter shock.

'There's a just a small matter of some paperwork before you are officially exonerated,' I said. He leaned forward and hugged me in a bear hug that made it impossible to breathe. 'OK, big fella,' I said.

I had secured the exclusive interview with Dave. He wouldn't speak to anyone but me. It was deeply gratifying, especially as Trudeau had wanted to put his pet crime reporter on the story.

The story made the front page, and we ran a huge investigative piece in the magazine that weekend. It was the highest-trending article on the website for a week straight.

'And Samsara's dad raped Rachel? And Marley was their baby?'

'That's right. Imagine how frightened she must have been. She was just a kid.'

'I know,' he said. 'I was a kid too. I was frightened too. These people were even more monstrous than I suspected.'

'Do you think you might come to see Cleo in the hospital, just once? It would mean a lot to her, I think. She feels really bad that she never mentioned the party to you. But I mean, they're all from the same ilk; of course they knew each other.'

'I don't know. It's just so confusing. I thought I could trust her. I just feel betrayed. How could she keep that from me? But also *why*? What did she have to hide?'

'I know, Dave, but maybe look at it this way – she is the only one who cared enough to try to clear your name, and it came at great cost to her own safety in the end . . . what did she have to gain from that either? Maybe you could cut her some slack. Keep in touch.'

As for me, I felt I could finally accept the story was over. I had done what I had always intended to do, and that was to clear an innocent man's name. We happened to get justice for an innocent girl in the process.

The police exonerated Dave and closed the Juliet case when they realised the DNA that was found in the wound swab was Samsara's. It was also backed up by Vivian's testimony. The board had dropped their investigation into Dave's criminal record and he was now working as an intern with an architectural firm, which Cleo had set him up with.

The CCTV of the swimming pool on that night had mysteriously disappeared but thankfully Vivian had been there at the scene, just in time to see Samsara slip on the wet terrace and hit her head, falling into the pool, where she was left until the paramedics arrived for Cleo, and the police could secure and clear the scene. Which meant Samsara's death was, unfortunately, all over social media. Because of the vantage point of the sky pool, suspended in the sky, it became a kind of attraction, as the crowds gathered beneath the perspex, staring up, while the people in their glass houses looked down on it all.

I felt like I could finally start living my life again. It was finally over. The crime editor had personally requested me back on the city news beat, my dream assignment, and I was in love. I felt alive again. Finally, I could let my demons lie and start to make a life of my own.

78

RACHEL: BEFORE

How I remember it

'Need help?' I asked, stepping out of the shadows of the alley as I saw William slumped at the back of his house ... The party had ended long ago and William had obviously intended to sneak in the back door to his house, but he was too drunk to manage it so instead had collapsed at the final hurdle. I despised him but he was in poor shape. I ought to help him. But he didn't want my help. He looked at me with disdain. 'No. Thank you.'

He shoved himself to his feet using the full assistance of the perimeter wall behind him and stumbled off towards the end of the alley. I watched him depart, let him get six, eight, ten feet ahead, before I started following him. I kept to the shadows, like I always did, careful to stay out of sight. I didn't need to be so careful; he was very drunk and lumbering like an ataxic toddler, weaving from side to side but making progress despite himself. I could hear the noise he made from twenty paces back. There was nobody to be seen, and yet it always felt to me that every lost soul in Manhattan was floating nearby in these alleys behind the Upper West Side mansions. I stopped and watched him progress a little further along, before he slumped against the wall and slid down to the ground again. He wasn't moving, but after about thirty seconds the rhythmic snores of a person in a deep sleep emanated from his body. When I heard a sharp voice further ahead, I swear my heart leapt out of my body. I pressed myself flat against the wall and crept a little closer, moving past the sleeping William on the other side of the alley, to the end, where I could hear people arguing. There was a man's voice; he was angry. I moved closer.

'You're too young to understand this, Juliet, but can't you see how this will ruin not just my life but your life too? You will regret this.'

I'd know that voice anywhere. Mr Bentwell. I crept a little closer. I could see them now, just at the entrance of the alley, a few feet back from the street.

I crept closer still and silently removed my phone from my pocket and started filming.

'You'll blow up our families if you keep the baby. Everything will change. And there's no going back with

347

a baby. Your life will change course. It won't be college, post-grad, engagement, wedding, babies ... Just take the pills, and your life stays the same, everything stays on track ...'

I tried not to gasp.

Nobody spoke for a moment. Then it was him again.

'How do you think your parents would feel if you told them you were going to be a mother? How would they feel if you told them it was mine? What do you think people would say? They'd call you a home-wrecker, Juliet. You know my wife. She's powerful, connected. She'll destroy you.'

I had to slap my free hand over my mouth to stop myself from gasping twice. Juliet was pregnant with Mr Bentwell's baby.

She snapped at him. 'I'm not going to tell anybody it's yours,' she said. 'I'm not stupid.'

'Our families are old friends, Juliet. Your father and I go back a long way. This would cause a rift, and would leave a blot that none of us would get past ... can't you see that?'

An impatient female voice cut across the calm tones of Mr Bentwell. 'Oh, for Chrissakes, Juliet, I can't ac-tually listen to this a second longer ...'

'Samsara, What are you doing here?'

'Don't worry, Daddy, I know all about you and Juliet. Weren't you aware? It's her summer of love ... she's sleeping with as many men as possible before she has to settle down with some unsuspecting rich fool like William. She'll probably pass the baby off as his. In fact, the baby could be anyone's so I wouldn't worry too much about it if I were you ... You probably have a one-in-twenty chance of being the baby's actual father.'

'How dare you, Samsara!' Juliet hissed. 'This baby is your father's, *your sibling*.'

Samsara gave a wicked laugh. 'It's time to stop playing games, Juliet. Why do you care about *this* pregnancy all of a sudden? Why not just do what you've done with all the others and get rid of it. *It's just popping a pill*, wasn't that what you told me last time? Why are you suddenly being so sentimental ... nothing to do with the fact that this time it's the child of a billionaire?'

'I have my own money,' Juliet said.

' ... sure, but most of it is tied up in development investment and trust funds that only unlock when you get married, when you have your first child, your second child ... but no clause in there about your first bastard, is there, Juliet? So what are you looking for here? A quick cash injection? Here's my cheque book – how much do you want to make this go away?'

'Samsara, we said nobody was off limits.'

'I didn't think I'd have to set a boundary about my dad, Juliet. I thought it was obvious that each other's dads were off limits! This was supposed to be a fun summer game but this is just ... sick!'

Mr Bentwell said, 'You told me you'd never had an abortion, Juliet . . .'

'Fine, if you want me to get rid of this baby, it's going to cost you a hundred thousand dollars. And you, Samsara, when are you going to stop being such a pathetic loser, eavesdropping on people? You have to tag on to people because you have no personality of your own . . . everyone says how boring you are. You can't even lose your virginity in a dorm full of twenty-something men. *That's* how boring you are.'

'Well, at least I'm not a slut,' Samsara said.

'You bitch,' Juliet said, and it sounded like she pushed Samsara.

Her scream was cut short by a loud thwack and then Mr Bentwell's voice: 'Samsara! What have you done?' After that a scuffling of feet, followed by silence.

I was shaking, terrified to move. I stayed where I was for a long time. I had no idea how much time had passed but when I eventually felt safe enough to creep slowly towards the edge of the alleyway, I saw Juliet, in the entrance, lying on the ground, totally still.

79

CLEO

Sometimes a story has no ending

I was meeting Eddie for dinner. We agreed on Thai. She had baulked at sushi and I had baulked at Connolly's, so Thai was a fair compromise.

We were going over our shared hatred of the Bentwells. It was a new favourite game.

'The Bentwells were fixers. They always knew exactly who to call, who to pay, how to make it all go away and everything was sorted quickly, quietly. For them, at least. I mean, I suppose I'm that person now if you think about it.'

Eddie made a horrified face. 'My girlfriend the monster.'

'What else do you know about Rachel Little? Is there anything else at all that would help me convince her to talk to me?'

'Eddie, it's done. Let sleeping dogs lie. We don't even need her. You've solved the mystery without her. She hasn't committed a crime and I don't think we should persecute her. The poor woman has been through enough.'

Eddie slurped her pad thai. 'You're right, I'm sorry!' and I decided to join in. I could almost be myself with Eddie, in a way that I couldn't with anyone else. I honestly believed she didn't care if I was rich or poor, didn't care if I was a lawyer or not, she genuinely seemed to just want *me*. Is this what it felt like to be loved?

We ate in comfortable silence for a few more minutes before I spoke again.

'You're a good person, Eddie. You finally did what you swore you would – you exonerated him.'

She squeezed my hand. '*We* did,' she said.

80

CLEO

No More Secrets

The summer was definitely at a close and I was looking forward to cosy autumn nights with Eddie. My buzzer went and I let her in. I noticed she was carrying a small suitcase. I smiled. 'Have you thought about my offer to move in,' I asked.

'I have,' she said, 'and I'd like to try. I mean, I'll miss my shithole and its bath-cum-dining-table, but these are the things we do for love ...'

'Love?' I asked. And for once Eddie was lost for words. I stepped into her arms and kissed her. She held me tightly.

'I'm just so glad it's finally over,' she said. 'And we can live our lives without all of these mysteries and secrets hanging over us.'

I smiled. 'How about we make this day zero, start all over again?'

'Deal,' she said. 'And no more secrets from here on in, OK?' she asked. 'We're a team.'

'Deal,' I said, and kissed her right back.

But there was still one secret. One I wasn't comfortable keeping from Eddie, but one I knew I could never share with her. Besides, what did it matter now? Dave was exonerated. Samsara was dead. And the dead can't talk. Thankfully. Sometimes secrets are just the price you pay for the life you want. And was it really a lie if there was nobody left to contradict it? If I try hard enough, sometimes I can almost believe things happened exactly the way I said they did.

By Thanksgiving, Eddie and I were settled into our domestic routine and we decided it would be nice to celebrate our first Thanksgiving together at home. It had been a crazy year and I had a lot to be thankful for. Dave and Vivian joined us. The table was set with red candles, foliage and plenty of food. The best part was being able to help Dave achieve his dreams, and to be able to help him get back on the road to his thwarted aspirations.

As we sat down at the table, Dave proposed a toast. 'I feel like I can finally start my life again, I can do the things I've always wanted to do. I'm secure and

I finally have hope ... and it's all thanks to you and Eddie. Thanks to you both for helping me, for always believing me.'

Then it was Eddie's turn. 'While we're on the topic of giving thanks I want to say how grateful I am to you, Cleo, for helping me get the closure I needed and to put this story away for good. My life has completely turned around this year. And obviously I'm so happy that this story, while it may have been responsible for ruining my marriage, is also responsible for bringing me the love of my life. I love you, Cleo.'

I looked down and shook my head. I felt so emotional. I was rarely moved like this and I didn't know what to do with my feelings. Had it really all turned out so well? How did I get so lucky?

'I don't deserve you, any of you. I never thought I would have a partner like you, Eddie, someone to share a home with, a family, and friends like you, Dave and Vivian ... I can't believe I've got everything I've always wanted.'

I felt a momentary pang for Samsara, for Juliet, so I raised my glass and said, 'To absent friends.'

81

CLEO

Christmas comes early

HEAD OF BENTWELLS LEGAL FIRM ON TRIAL FOR SEXUAL ASSAULTS AND SUSPECT IN MURDER

By Eddie Wright

The trial of Mr Max Bentwell of Bentwell and Sons begins in the south district today, where he is charged with allegations of historical sexual abuse with sample charges from nine women. The class action is being headed by Cleo Fry of Fry and Associates ...

It felt like all of my Christmases had come at once. I folded the paper and threw it in the trash.

82

EDDIE

Be careful when digging
not to trip a landmine

I had settled into a routine with Cleo, a relationship that was unexpected but had brought so much joy. We both liked working long and hard, we were both obsessed with our jobs, but we had found in each other a shared worldview and intelligence that fit nicely. Though we were comfortable with space, we ate together, slept together and caught a movie or a show if we had time. Sometimes we just walked through Central Park on the weekends. It was enough. More than enough.

We shared a partner's desk in the study now, where I wrote up my articles at night and Cleo wrote her arguments for court. It was a harmonious way of life.

To be honest, it made me sick how happy we were. We were truly disgusting.

With Dave exonerated and the story resolved, I had expected to feel differently. To feel relieved or at peace or something, but there was a niggle, like the story hadn't been resolved, like I hadn't done my job fully.

I trawled my mind to find the source of it. Did all the pieces fit together in the story? Yes. Why the uncertainty, then? Did all the pieces fit together too neatly? Maybe.

I scrolled back in my mind, through all the conversations I'd had over the past months, all the notes I had taken, all the copying and pasting of different versions of the same story onto each other until I had a collage that made sense. What was the thread that I hadn't pulled? I sat in the kitchen slurping noodles, sieving the information. I went for a walk but still nothing came to me. I woke around 3 a.m. and the lightbulb finally went on. I slipped out of bed, careful not to wake Cleo.

I padded into the study and turned on the shelf lighting behind the filing cabinets. I opened Cleo's customised cabinet. I flicked across to L, and found Little, R. I pulled the file. I think I knew before I opened that file what I would find there. I felt no surprise when I opened Rachel Little's old cancelled passport, and picked up her obsolete Driver's Licence. And when I unfolded the deed poll change-of-name application from twenty years ago, the face I saw looking back at me was Cleo's.

83

CLEO

RIP Rachel

Until that summer, I had believed that good would always trump evil, that truth would always overpower lies, that somehow doing the right thing would be enough. But those beliefs died along with the girl I had been that summer. That summer I learned that money and power win, every time. Which was why I stopped trying to be a good person and started working towards being rich and powerful.

After that summer, when I gave up my baby, I changed my name to the name of the only rich girl I had ever admired, the only one who had actually treated me and my mother like human beings – Cleo.

I chose Fry as a variation of the word free, because I hoped this new identity would liberate me. I won the coveted internship with Bentwells, thanks to the phone video footage I had taken. The internship was the springboard I needed to fast-track my success. I set up my own small firm as soon as I could afford to. Nothing slowed me down, not even Bentwell. In fact, he stayed out of my way. He knew I had leverage and I think he realised I was dangerous because I had nothing to lose. I devoured the law, dominated it, understood it, but more importantly I understood my wealthy clients, knew their weaknesses, their fears, what they would pay for, and I knew how to extract the maximum fee for my work.

At one time in my life, I saw guilty reminders of Dave everywhere, on the street, at work, in the line at Starbucks ... of course, I was imagining him. It was impossible for me to see him in the local coffee shop when he was in state penitentiary serving hard time for a crime he didn't commit, but I soon learned how to live with those demons.

Sure, I had now passed the burden of guilt to another innocent woman, Samsara, but it was the path that did least harm to fewest people, which was all I could hope for. Samsara had always believed she had been responsible for Juliet's death anyway, and she hadn't cared about Dave going to prison when she knew he was innocent. To use her own words, better him than me. Besides, Samsara was dead. It wouldn't hurt her either way. Eddie, sweet Eddie, didn't need to know the whole truth. She had *a* version of the truth and sometimes in life, just as in law, that was all you could hope for.

84

EDDIE

What we can live with

I dressed as quietly as I could. I needed to get out. If I saw Cleo now, I wouldn't be able to hide what I knew. My head was spinning. I grabbed my laptop bag and silently let myself out of the house. I took a cab to my office. I needed to think. I lay on the couch in the reception area running it all over in my mind until people started to trickle in at 5 a.m. I relocated to my desk. I really didn't want to see Trudeau.

'Hey Eddie, you're in early . . .' The back desk were finishing up their shift.

'Yeah, in the dog house,' I muttered and they laughed.

I was in a tailspin and had no idea what to do. If

Cleo was Rachel, was everything she had told me a lie? Why did I have to dig and dig and dig until I brought the whole sandcastle in on my head? I never thought I'd be happy with someone again after Cassie. And now I was in so deep with Cleo, I actually loved her, we had something really special and then I discover she isn't even who she says she is. Why did I never know when to stop?

But so what if she had a secret, I thought, desperation kicking in. Was that such a big deal? She changed her name to get away from the trauma these people had inflicted on her life? Was that a crime? No. And so what if she didn't tell me? Was that a crime too? Only against my ego. We had said no more secrets but Cleo had clearly made a decision to bury her old self, to not talk about it even with those who were closest to her. She had had a tough time, she wanted to start afresh, she *needed* to start afresh to get away from those people, that world ... even so, Cleo had lied to me, she had lied to Vivian. She had lied to everybody ... including Marley – her own daughter, who was desperate to meet her mother. Cleo was cruel.

But what was the difference between a lie and a secret? I was starting to think I didn't know any more. The real question was whether I could live with it.

I had to figure out whether it mattered to me or not that Cleo had given a false alibi, that she had put an innocent man in jail and that she had let her own daughter die without meeting her mother. Now *that,* I thought, was a crime.

85

VIVIAN

We live with demons

The door went and I looked up to see – speak of the devil – Eddie.

'Hey, Eddie, how are you doing . . . ?'

She looked a wreck. More so than usual.

'Yeah, didn't sleep last night. Do you have time for a coffee?'

I stepped aside and she walked in.

She told me what she had found out, that Cleo had changed her name, that she had been Rachel, everything she was struggling with.

'You knew?'

I smiled. She didn't miss much. 'I knew. Cleo's mom worked for the Bentwells around the time I was there so Cleo would be around from time to time. You two are so good together. Every couple has secrets, some even have a few lies … sometimes it's essential to keep the whole thing on the road. Take it from someone who was married for five decades. So she changed her name, so she did some things she's not proud of when she was a kid, so she didn't want to tell you about them? You can understand that, right? The way I see it she didn't have much choice in the matter. What is it about this that you can't wear?'

'She ruined an innocent man's life …'

'But the Blacks and the Bentwells gave her no choice. And she made it right in the end … she cleared Dave's name. You two were the only ones who lifted a finger to help him …'

'Twenty years too late. He lost his whole life to protect people like Samsara and William. He had a dream, and he was on his way to achieving it. She could have stopped him going to prison in the first place. She destroyed his life. That's the part I can't wear.'

'They would have destroyed her, you know that better than most, and Dave would still likely have gone to prison. He was found holding Juliet's body, after all. You know what these people are like. They destroyed you too for getting too close to the story, and you were a grown woman, a tough investigative journalist … She was just a kid. Imagine what that felt like for her. The way I see it she had no choice and she did her best to atone when she got the opportunity. That's the sign of a truly *good* person. And she loves you. And you love her. I can see it. I've never known her so happy. Don't let your black-and-white principles get in the way of your happiness, Eddie. This is not some crusading story you're writing. This is your life and life is not black and white. You above all people should know that.'

'I do. And I'm mired in it, Vivian. I thought my life had finally come together again – job, love, apartment – but now it feels like it's all a big mess.'

'This is life. Life is messy.' I broke off suddenly and went into a coughing jag that lasted nearly thirty seconds. Blasted cough was exhausting me. 'It's complicated. We choose our team and we support them even when they go through a losing season, even if they fail to live up to our expectations. This is what love is – for better *and* for worse. The only question is: can you forgive her her shortcomings the way she has forgiven yours?'

She arched an eyebrow.

'What? You think you're a perfect catch? That's why you're single all these years? She lets you be you. She lets you chase stories and become obsessed and ignore her and eat cold takeaway that's two days old because you can't prise yourself away from your precious work to have dinner with your girlfriend, who by the way *is* a catch. She's a unicorn, Eddie, so if you're going to throw her back in be prepared to never find another love like this.'

Eddie groaned. 'You're right. I know. The reason I'm struggling is I don't think I can let her go. I'm in too deep.'

Then she asked all of a sudden: 'Do you believe Samsara killed Juliet?'

'What makes you ask that? Of course I do. One hundred per cent,' I said. 'The DNA proves it beyond a doubt.'

'How can you be so sure?' she asked. That was Eddie all over. Always wanting certainty, always digging even when she had the answers. Good for a journalist. Not so good for a relationship.

'I told you I worked for the Bentwells, at the time of Juliet's death. They lived on the corner of the block where the Foxes lived. I was the Bentwells' doorman. Bentwell came to me that night, told me he needed access to the CCTV footage. I didn't ask why. He told me to get out but then he called me back in because he needed me to show him how it worked, how to isolate specific time codes, how to play them back, how to delete them. Their house was on the corner of the alley where Juliet was killed. He told me to delete the hour from eleven p.m. to midnight, and to make sure there was no backup saved anywhere. I assured him there was not. I saw Samsara hit Juliet with my own eyes.'

'Jesus, Viv,' Eddie said. She looked worried. 'That's a federal crime. If the police ever found out . . .'

'They didn't. Bentwell made sure of that. He told me

if I wanted to keep my job, or any job for that matter, I would do as he said and keep my mouth shut about it. So I deleted it, and when the police came looking for the CCTV the next morning I played dumb, told them some lie about the power sometimes shorting and the feed stopping. They didn't believe me but there wasn't a lot they could do about it. Once the fingers started to point at Dave, they seemed to lose interest in the CCTV anyway. They didn't need it any more. Cleo was just a kid. You're great together. Don't throw it away because she was forced to do something stupid. She's paid her debt.'

86

EDDIE

The calm after the storm

I let the door slam behind me. I didn't want any more surprises.

I heard Cleo shout ... 'I'm in the living room!'

I slouched in, leather computer satchel hanging from my shoulder, rumpled blue boyfriend shirt underneath a Donegal tweed blazer, black cotton chinos and Gucci loafers. I was improving or being improved. Cleo had been not so subtly buying me expensive items of clothing that she thought fit my style but would make me look a little more professional, a little more presentable. I had never understood how people could spend so much on designer clothes. But that was before I had owned any. I was starting to understand.

'Hey,' I said, as she turned her face up to meet my kiss. 'I missed you today.'

'That's sweet ... Did you have an early start?'

'Yeah, this story I'm working on. You wanna go out for dinner tonight? I feel like celebrating ...'

'Sure. What are we celebrating?'

'Me, letting go of being such an uptight, moralistic, truth-seeking pain in the ass.'

'Now that I can get behind,' she said, bouncing up onto her knees on the couch.

'Thank you for your support,' I said.

'But you know there's nothing wrong with wanting to find out the truth. It's probably a good trait for a journalist to have.'

'Yeah, I know,' I said. 'But I could say the same thing about you. You can defend people and clear their name without ever knowing the truth. Maybe reporting the facts is enough.'

'I do believe that is what my therapist would call "growth", Eddie!' She laughed.

'I hope so. I hope I'm learning when to let go ...' I pulled her towards me. 'And when to hold on.'

She kissed me and smiled with such genuine affection I knew I could get past any secret for her.

'In my experience,' she said, 'the truth is overrated anyway.'

87

VIVIAN

Us and them

It's funny how people remember 'the truth'. I had my truth, Mr Bentwell had his, Samsara had hers and Dave had his. But history is written by the victors and Cleo's truth was the one that won out in the end. And I found it was one I could live with because, well, my enemy's enemy is my friend.

Samsara wasn't the only person on the CCTV the night of Juliet's murder, but Mr Bentwell, for all his lawyering and his fancy degrees, hadn't watched the CCTV past the moment where Samsara had knocked Juliet out and he and his daughter had scarpered from the scene ... a few minutes later, another figure appeared. It was shocking but I found it was something I could keep to myself. Besides, could I ever be certain who had actually killed Juliet? William had shoved her against the wall. That could have done some unseen internal damage. Samsara had knocked her out cold. That could have been a concussion, the type that skiers get, where they seem absolutely fine immediately after the fact and then twenty-four hours later they're dead. But I knew the police wouldn't see it that way. It didn't matter in the end because Mr Bentwell had ordered me to clear the CCTV from the back-alley camera from the hour between 11 p.m. and midnight. He told me I had to choose between my job and my home, my livelihood, and following orders. I presumed there would be lots more CCTV from the houses around the streets so I wasn't too conflicted about deleting the file but I made sure to keep a copy. Call it insurance.

Eddie didn't know what was good for her, didn't know when to stop. She had discovered, through her own snooping, that Cleo was actually Rachel. Curiosity killed the cat. She was so sanctimonious; journalists often were when it came to other people, I found. She said she didn't know if she could forgive Cleo for not coming clean about William's alibi and casting doubt on Dave's conviction.

I gave her my ten cents. I told her I had known Rachel's mom when I worked for the Bentwells. She perked right up when she heard me say that. We became friendly after my daughter died. Well, I am ashamed to say that Dodi and I went through a rough few years and I sought comfort in the arms of Mrs Little. She was kind, we liked each other; we each gave each other something we both needed.

I guess that's when I first started to feel paternal towards Rachel. I needed a place to put those feelings after Lucy died. I never spent time with Rachel directly but I sometimes helped out with money if she needed something for school. It made me feel good again, to look after someone, to feel like a father. I kept an eye on Rachel after her mother died. I knew she would have wanted someone to look out for her daughter. I kept track of Rachel from afar, which is how I knew she had given a baby up for adoption. I kept track of the baby then too. I don't know why, but something in me felt connected to her. I knew her name, I watched her for years, joined her local church so I could get to know the family a little. She was a beautiful young woman. When I saw she had gone to a women's shelter I volunteered to help. She was my main focus in that shelter and over the years I got to know her and her own baby, Flo, until one day I came in and she told me she had the best news ever – she had won a place in the Sky Building cost-rental lottery. She brought me over to the notice board, showed me the ad that hung there asking for applications for the lottery. The ad also showed a list of positions that were open. I took a photo of the ad and went home and applied for the job of doorman. I couldn't lose her again. I needed a reason to stay in her life. And I made sure I got that job. I called Mr Bentwell, told him I was owed and so it was that an old man of questionable health got the job.

When Marley told me she was looking for her birth mother on the DNA website, I knew it was a bad idea. She said she had a lock of her mother's hair, the only belonging she had of her mother, and that she was going to get it analysed for DNA.

The Bentwells had destroyed too many people's lives and they had always gotten away with it. Which is why I reacted the way I did that night on the terrace. I couldn't let the Bentwells destroy Rachel's life twice. And Marley would expect me to protect her mother. So I did.

When the police came asking questions about Cleo, I found I could say what I needed to say to protect her. It wasn't difficult to tell them that Samsara had attacked Cleo – because she had. I had no guilt withholding the information that I had hit Samsara over the head with a garden sculpture, knocking her against the edge of the pool where she hit her head again before tumbling into the water. It was easy to say she had slipped while attacking Cleo. And when Eddie had asked what had happened I found it easy to ask her to go to my apartment under the pretence of getting me some clean clothes. I knew Eddie would always protect us over them.

88

EDDIE

Curiosity killed the cat

It was not such a shock when Vivian died. His health had been bad for as long as I had known him. What was a shock was when I was named his executor. It made me sad to think that Vivian didn't have any family or even friends closer than me, a random journalist he had known for just a few months, to look after his personal effects. I couldn't help but feel that Marley would have been his executor if she hadn't been killed by the Bentwells.

Being the executor of a penniless old man was not as glamorous as being the executor of a wealthy one. My job was really just to clear out his apartment, decide what to trash and what to send to goodwill. It was tough to know what to do with all of his mementos of his beloved wife, Dodi, and their late daughter Lucy. While these things had held so much value for Vivian, without his memory to infuse them with life they were just tatty old things. I placed them carefully in a bag. If I was going to throw them away, the least I could do was to treat them respectfully. My phone buzzed. Cleo. I smiled as I read the message.

> Thought we could have dim sum tonight? I'll pick it up on the way home if you grab a bottle of wine and put it in the fridge?

I typed back:

> Sounds great, see you later. X

I still couldn't quite believe that I had gotten a second chance at love. I had never been happier. I held back a polaroid of Vivian with his wife and daughter in happy times. I'd put it on our fridge. That way they could live on in this world for a little while longer. I moved to Vivian's desk – Christ, there were floppy disks in here! I emptied the whole drawer into a trash bag. I was moving fast now. In the bedroom I emptied his underwear drawer onto the floor, then his sock drawer. Something hard clattered on the wooden planks and an envelope fluttered on top of the pile of socks. I opened the envelope. DNA results. It seemed to be the results of the work Cleo's investigator had done, with matches on the crime scene and Juliet's foetus: Samsara, Josh, Mr Bentwell, all as expected. But another name too, a match for Juliet's head wound swab. Cleo had not sent me that result. I looked for what had fallen on the floor. I felt through the pile of socks until I felt something solid. Inside the sock was a chrome USB drive. No label. What the hell? I knew there was a reason that this USB was hidden in a sock in the back of an old man's sock drawer, and that reason was probably a reason I didn't want to discover, but what sort of a journalist would I be if I didn't look? I pulled my laptop from my satchel, opened it and inserted the drive. It was a video file. Something told me as my finger hovered over the mousepad that there would be no going back. But I would always dive deep for the truth, and I would always keep going until I hit the bottom, or ran out of breath. I hit play and watched the CCTV footage of Juliet's death. I saw William, Mr Bentwell, Samsara attacking Juliet. But there were 45 minutes of video footage left. I let it run and after a few more minutes, as I was making a cup of tea by the sink, I caught movement on the screen. I'd recognise that figure anywhere. I stood dead still and watched my life fall apart before my eyes.

89

JULIET

How I remember it

R achel was the last person I expected to turn on me. Samsara had hated me. And I didn't blame her. I said some terrible things. *And* I was sleeping with her father. That *was* unforgivable in retrospect, from the vantage point of eternity. But she didn't want to kill me. Sure, she hit me that night, knocked me right out cold, in fact, but we were best friends, always fighting and making up. It's something we would have laughed about later, if it wasn't for the spider who crept along the alley after us. I wish there was a way I could have told Samsara that she wasn't the one responsible for my death.

I had always thought of Rachel as harmless, pathetic even, a little bit in love with me. She didn't know her place. She thought she could be one of us. She didn't even know when she was overstepping. Well, turns out I didn't know when I had overstepped either. I never meant to push Rachel to her limit, I had no idea that I had. I never gave her much thought at all. I certainly had no idea about the fact that Samsara's dad had been abusing her and that he'd almost derailed her whole life ... She had plenty of reasons to hate us; I just happened to be unlucky enough to be in the path of her rage on that particular night.

The first thing I remember was regaining consciousness and seeing a concerned Rachel leaning over me. 'Juliet, I saw everything,' she said. 'I saw what Samsara did ...'

I remember being irritated by her, like she had taken a liberty in talking to me like this. As if I would turn to her over Samsara.

'God, it was just a stupid argument,' I said. 'It's fine. Get your hands off me.'

I suppose I could have been more gracious. She recoiled as if I had slapped her and her face turned hard. Then she said, 'I know about the baby, about you and Mr Bentwell. I overheard you in the demesne at the party. You know, we have a lot more in common than you think ... I think you and I are in the same predicament.'

My head was pounding. And if I'm honest I was disgusted that he had gotten us both pregnant. I told her we had absolutely nothing in common and that she was a freak, spying on people. I shouldn't have told her that she was just another statistic, just another young stupid girl fulfilling her destiny to be a single mother before she turned twenty. 'Your life is over, Rachel. Mine is just beginning. I'm going to get rid of this baby. I'm going to go to college and I'm going to get married and have my own children and live a beautiful life. Who knows? Maybe one day our paths will cross again; maybe you'll be my cleaner.'

I shouldn't have said it. I shouldn't have laughed either. I tried to stand up but my head was still spinning. 'Help me up, for god's sake,' I said.

She pulled up the hood of her sweater and pushed her hands into the pocket at the front of her hoodie. I remember looking at her then and noticing that her entire face had changed. She wasn't concerned any more, not sympathetic or worried, just filled with blank hatred. And suddenly I was scared.

I scrabbled around for my phone. 'Where's my phone ... shit, Dave has it ... Will you just help me up, Rachel!? I'm so dizzy.'

She moved closer until she was towering over me. When she spoke again, her voice sounded different.

'You don't care about anyone but yourself, do you ...? You make everyone feel worthless, expecting people to look like you, behave like you, treat you like a princess ... every time I come into contact with you people, you burn my life like a corrosive acid. You're rotten. You people have taken everything I have ever cared for away from me and I'm so sick of it ...'

My head was pounding and I just wanted her to stop. 'What are you talking about? I've never taken anything from you. Just get over it, move on. Please just shut up whining about it.'

I found some strength to push myself to my knees but she pulled her hands out of her pockets at that point and I realised she was holding a rock.

'No. You shut up, Juliet,' she said, and she hit me clean on the side of my temple with one swift blow. I watched her panicked footsteps flashing down the alley and a few moments later, Dave, sweet Dave, was on his knees, distraught and calling for help. But I was already watching him from a new angle, somewhere up above, so far up that I could also see Rachel, still running, all the way to the subway on 59th and Lex, where she took the train to Woodlawn, where she dropped the stone she had used to bash my head in and ran on to her apartment. I watched her climb into bed and lie there as if she hadn't just killed a girl. I couldn't tell for sure, as I was getting further and further away by then, but from up here, it looked like she was smiling.

EPILOGUE

The City Never Sleeps

The city had seen it all before. There was nothing new in this town. Every day, the sun rose and the sun set on crimes new and old, solved and unsolved. After that night, Rachel never stopped running. She ran through law school and internships, excelled at everything she did, she ran so fast that the line between her and her new persona Cleo blurred until eventually it ceased to exist at all, the force of physics erased by sheer force of will.

Cleo would never stop running, away from what happened that night, but also towards what she loved so much, and what was most important to her and always had been – money, status, success. And in the end she got everything she had ever wanted, as if she had ordered it express from an online catalogue – the penthouse, the pool, the job, the *life*. She ran until she became all of the things she had hated about them – privileged, wealthy, powerful, ruthless, spoiled, entitled, but most of all, utterly and lethally plausible. Respectability and plausibility were the two biggest blind spots when it came to the forces of justice. The semblance of plausibility and respectability were why the police had believed the Bentwells over Dave twenty years ago, it was why they believed Cleo when she directed them to look into Samsara's DNA, after she had broken into Marley's 23andMe account to delete the match with a woman called Rachel Little. It was why they believed Cleo when she identified Bentwell as the anonymous person in the CCTV on Marley's floor the night she was killed. Why would the police even think of looking into Cleo's DNA? They trusted respectability and plausibility. They trusted power. They trusted that Cleo was what she appeared to be, an upstanding officer of the court. They trusted that Cleo was telling the truth. You see, Cleo had long ago learned that the truth was flexible, that you could bend it without breaking it, until it became the thing that you wanted it to be. But she was discovering from the newfound emptiness of her glass tower that, unlike the truth, some people's principles did not bend.

Over on Ninth Avenue, Eddie's understanding of the truth had always remained the same. She could accept Cleo's actions were those of a desperate, abused and confused young girl. Hurt people hurt people, wasn't that what they said? But Eddie could not lie beside Cleo in bed, night after night, could not pretend in the same way that Cleo could. And she realised when it came to Cleo, she would never really be able to see the truth clearly. It was time to move on. From Cleo, from the Juliet story, from the ghost of her mother and her childhood. She sat at her new purpose-built dining nook, inserted the chrome USB stick into her laptop and clicked 'ERASE DRIVE'. She threw the useless drive in the bin. A female carpenter was putting the finishing touches to her new custom-built kitchen, an ivory shade that bounced light around the apartment. 'I think we're almost done here,' she said. 'Myself and the girls are going to grab a beer at Connelly's if you'd like to join us?'

Eddie smiled and accepted the invitation. She was finally allowing neglected areas like 'home' and 'friends' to re-emerge in her life. She clicked 'send' on her magazine cover story: *The Juliet Mystery – solved* and logged off for the weekend.

Across town, the *Post's* sub-editor printed off the next day's front page: *Bentwell Found Guilty on Sex Rap. Charged In Murder Case.*

The city shrugged. It had seen it all before. And like a tide returning to the sea, yesterday was washed away, darkness turned to light, and a new day began.

Acknowledgements

Thank you Marianne Gunn-O'Connor, Cal Kenny, Donna Hillyer, Zoe Carroll, Kirsteen Astor, Elaine Egan, Joanna Smyth, and all at Sphere and Hachette Ireland.

Thanks also to Orlagh Collins, Alan Moloney, and Bruna Papandrea.

Thank you to the booksellers, librarians and festival organisers who work so tirelessly to get my books into readers' hands. And thanks to you, the reader, for such loyalty and kindness.

Thank you to my friends and family, and to Jacinta.

And finally thank you to David, Henry, Arthur, Edith and Frieda. I couldn't do any of this without you.

RAISING READERS
Books Build Bright Futures

Dear Reader,

We'd love your attention for one more page to tell you about the crisis in children's reading, and what we can all do.

Studies have shown that reading for fun is the **single biggest predictor of a child's future life chances** – more than family circumstance, parents' educational background or income. It improves academic results, mental health, wealth, communication skills, ambition and happiness.[1]

The number of children reading for fun is in rapid decline. Young people have a lot of competition for their time. In 2024, 1 in 10 children and young people in the UK aged 5 to 18 did not own a single book at home.[2]

Hachette works extensively with schools, libraries and literacy charities, but here are some ways we can all raise more readers:

- Reading to children for just 10 minutes a day makes a difference
- Don't give up if children aren't regular readers – there will be books for them!
- Visit bookshops and libraries to get recommendations
- Encourage them to listen to audiobooks
- Support school libraries
- Give books as gifts

There's a lot more information about how to encourage children to read on our website: **www.RaisingReaders.co.uk**

Thank you for reading.

[1] OECD, '21st-Century Readers: Developing Literacy Skills in a Digital World', 2021, https://www.oecd.org/en/publications/21st-century-readers_a83d84cb-en.html

[2] National Literacy Trust, 'Book Ownership in 2024', November 2024, https://literacytrust.org.uk/research-services/research-reports/book-ownership-in-2024